THE CRITICS HAIL A SIZZLING NEW TALENT!

Bad Guys

"[A] taut, powerful piece of writing."
—*The New York Times Book Review*

"Fully dimensional characters, wicked wit and heady pace...Incredible suspense at the height of the author's faultlessly delivered adventure...Irresistible."
—*Publishers Weekly*

"[Izzi's] a writer to be read and to be on the lookout for...His books, short, punchy and filled with broken noses, cauliflower ears and guys who talk like dis, hum along from beginning to violent end....Dis is good stuff!"
—*San Diego Tribune*

"TOUGH AND STURDILY CONSTRUC-TED...*Bad Guys* proves that Izzi...is no one-novel phenomenon."
—*Chicago Sun-Times*

"A hard-hitting, gritty story of crime and punishment told in a sparse and compelling style...A fascinating, slow-building dance of death...Izzi has a great ear for convincing speech....Realistic."
—*Muncie E...*

"As in his critically acclaimed first novel, *The Take*, Eugene Izzi surrounds his hero with the oddest group of allies and opponents ever to hit the streets. His characterizations are rich and full of streetwise grit.... *Bad Guys* is an entertaining read that has you rooting for the good guys all the way!"
—Memphis *Commercial Appeal*

"IF YOU ENJOY ELMORE LEONARD AND ED McBAIN, YOU'LL PROBABLY ENJOY EUGENE IZZI.... Full of bad guys, but it's also irreverently funny, poignantly sad, and colorfully entertaining."
—Florida *Showcase*

"A well-told shoot-'em-up...Eugene Izzi's first book, *The Take*, steamed around the seamy mob scene at breakneck speed, and *Bad Guys* increases the pace."
—*Wichita Eagle-Beacon*

Praise for *The Take*

"If [his next novels] approach the quality of *The Take*, Izzi will become a national figure in crime literature, right up there with Elmore Leonard and Ed McBain and George V. Higgins."
—*Chicago Sun-Times*

"The best novel of vice and violence since the heyday of James M. Cain!"
—Robert Bloch, author of *Psycho*

BAD GUYS

EUGENE IZZI

ST. MARTIN'S PRESS/NEW YORK

This novel is a work of fiction. All of the events, characters, names, and places depicted in this novel are entirely fictitious or are used fictitiously. No representation that any statement made in this novel is true or that any incident depicted in this novel actually occurred is intended or should be inferred by the reader.

BAD GUYS

Copyright © 1988 by Eugene Izzi.

All rights reserved. No part of this book may be used or reproduced in any manner whatsoever without written permission except in the case of brief quotations embodied in critical articles or reviews. For information address St. Martin's Press, 175 Fifth Avenue, New York, N.Y. 10010.

Library of Congress Catalog Card Number: 88-1868

ISBN: 0-312-91493-8 Can. ISBN: 0-312-91494-6

Printed in the United States of America

St. Martin's Press hardcover edition published 1988
First St. Martin's Press mass market edition/July 1989

10 9 8 7 6 5 4 3 2 1

Dedication

This book is gratefully and lovingly dedicated to the cherished memories of Bill and the Doc, who started it all and made life worth living. . . .

Acknowledgments

Once again, I would like to express heartfelt thanks to a tremendous and brilliant author's representative, Mr. Philip G. Spitzer, who has kept me from having to find a real job. And to his California colleague, Mr. Jerome Siegal.

And, at St. Martin's Press, much thanks to: patient and kind senior editor Jared Kieling; his assistant and my buddy, Jesse Cohen; and senior (and super) publicist Maryanne Mazzola.

1 Jimbo was in a place he didn't want to be, listening to things he didn't want to hear, but the guy doing the talking had bailed him out of jail a couple of hours ago, and Jimbo owed him the courtesy of listening.

Jimbo was tired, though, and really not in the mood to be hearing Mikey Barboza. A little of Mikey went a long way at the best of times, and this was not one of them. But Jimbo, with one assault and battery charge already filed against him in the last twelve hours, decided to calm down and try to tune Mikey out before he lost his head, maybe belted him one.

Which was hard. They were sitting at the bar in the place Mikey owned, one of his legitimate businesses, the kind of place a mob fence owns to keep the I.R.S. off his back, and Mikey Barboza was reading the paper and commenting—loudly—telling everybody in the place what he thought, his voice rising considerably when he had something to say about black people. The problem was, the bar was filled with black people.

Mikey's Place was on VanBuren, less than a block away from the main post office, and the shift workers came by, cashed their checks and drank in relative safety while they shot pool and watched the X-rated video movies the bartender ran all day, even when the juke was playing.

Every time Mikey made a racist crack, Jimbo would wince and duck his head into his collar a little. He looked around. Jimbo never knew that the post office hired so many black people.

If he had his own car he would leave. Get up now, and the hell with Barboza, a big-time mob fence who was sitting there next to him getting off on this power trip, showing blacks who was boss.

Jimbo had spent the night in the lockup in the county jail at Twenty-sixth and California, his first time there, and until this morning he had thought that the stories he'd heard about the place were bogus, fairy tales embellished to make the teller seem like a tough guy. Now he knew the stories were true. Jeez, every time he'd tried to get some sleep, some fucker would try to take his shoes or unzip his jacket or something. He'd roll up and slap at the guy, his own head starting to swim from the beer he'd drunk before the arrest. The guy would wander away and then Jimbo would try to rest again and five minutes later, some other fucker would make a move.

By now he was tired, smelly and feeling mean, and Mikey wasn't doing much to help matters. In fact, all Mikey had done right so far today was bail Jimbo out. And not ask him about the arrest. Jimbo appreciated that.

Mikey was on a roll now. "*Look* at that," he said to Jimbo, his voice rising, his chubby finger stabbing at the newspaper story.

Trying to be agreeable—the man *had* bailed him out, after all—Jimbo looked at the article. Page three, something about high-class hookers carrying beepers so they would never miss a call.

2

"So what?" Jimbo said. "Jesus, for years now, dope dealers, gunrunners, all kinds of crooks been carrying beepers." He spoke softly. Barboza was alienating enough people in the bar without him offending any pushers or gunnies who happened to be passing through.

Barboza roared. "Not *that*, goof. Everyone knows that. *That*." Mikey pointed to the heavy-type headline, at the word *high-class*. "Calling a hooker high-class is the same as calling shit perfume, or candy, for chrissakes. Anything I hate, it's a reporter trying to make shit perfume. Let *me* get busted, even on a driving charge, and they got me written up: A-long-time-area-hoodlum-with-strong-syndicate-ties. Hookers, they get called high-class."

Mikey was scoring now, rolling. He said, "A hooker goes down for money, how can that ever be mistaken for high-class? It's like calling a child molester a sex therapist." He grunted and sipped his Scotch. Almost spit half of it out when he saw the next page of the paper.

"And look at this!" Barboza said, "Bears' quarterback makes new video. Goddamn, I'm sick of this, niggers dancing around the ceilings for a few bucks, like they don't make enough already." The bartender was coming over to them, his face set, about to go toe to toe with all six feet three inches and two hundred and forty pounds of his boss. Jimbo wondered how he'd play it.

"Mr. Barboza, sir?" the guy said, and Jimbo thought, wrong.

Barboza looked up, unhappy at the interruption. "What."

"Some of the patrons, they're getting upset . . . at the words."

Barboza looked around him—gee, I'm not alone?—and Jimbo was almost embarrassed for him. The guy acted like he didn't know who he was surrounded by.

3

"Hey," Barboza said, "fuck 'em. They don't like it, let them go to their own neighborhoods, drink booze at three bucks a pop." The bartender almost crawled away, and Jimbo watched some of the workers finish their drinks and leave; some of them muttered under their breaths but kept it to that because they knew who Mikey Barboza was; a few just moved to booths where they wouldn't be able to hear him.

Jimbo pushed off the stool, dreading the thought of the long train ride to the South Side, but enough was enough. "See you around, Mikey."

"Where are you going?" Mikey sounded shocked, like he was surprised at Jimbo's insubordination.

"I got to go line something up. There's this asshole I owe bond money to."

"You serious?" Barboza said. Jimbo didn't answer him. Barboza said, "You turning chickenshit, or what?"

Jimbo turned to leave. He'd had enough of sitting in a shabby bar in Chicago's West Loop, listening to the tough talk. Even if the guy *had* bailed him out of the County.

"Well hell, wait up," Barboza said. "I'll give you a ride home." Jimbo turned and watched Barboza slide his bulk off the three-legged red leather padded bar stool and heard him order another drink—for the house and on the house. Jimbo thought that was a pretty nice gesture, until later when he figured out that it was just another little move to get him back on Mikey's side.

Barboza drove a brand-new Mercury Cougar, maroon with black velvet interior. The Cougar for work, with a new Caddy in the garage at home for night riding. He had the seat all the way back, and still his head hit the padded roof.

Jimbo was three inches shorter and maybe forty or fifty pounds lighter, but he was younger and in reasonably good shape and he knew that if it came down to it, he could whip Barboza one-on-one. If the fight lasted more than thirty seconds, Jimbo was a shoo-in.

Mikey was rattling on again, bad-mouthing blacks and hookers and sports heroes and just like that he changed gears—one of the tricks he used to keep you off balance. In the middle of a sentence he'd just stop, and switch.

"You shouldn't have done that, back in the bar. Getting ready to leave like that." He took his eyes off the road for just a second to give Jimbo a hard, full glare. Let Jimbo know that the great Mikey Barboza was upset with him. "The past few months, what, three now, I been treating you like a son, paying you more than the rest of the thieves, shit, waiting for the right time to move you up, get you to meet some important people. You won't cut it with them, walking out in the middle of a conversation, Perino."

Jimbo said, "Listen, I been hearing this moving up business for months now, and I figure it's just talk, Mikey. And you pay me better because I bring you the best stuff, not the garbage your cowboys run through you. Jesus, TVs and stuff they robbed from some old widow. And let's face it, you didn't want me for the Beglund score, Mikey, I'd still be sitting in the can." They were passing the shuttered U.S. Steel South Works plant on Eighty-seventh Street now, and Jimbo turned his head to look at it, remembering when the place had been booming, thousands of guys working. Guys like his dad. And his uncles.

He pulled himself back to the here and now with an effort. Daydreaming wasn't in character, and Barboza was sharp. If the guy saw Jimbo getting down as they passed the plant, he'd start wondering, and Jimbo couldn't have anybody wondering about him now. Not when he nearly had Barboza by the balls.

"Hey," Barboza said, "as long as we're on this honesty kick, let me tell you, I'd done something for you sooner, you wasn't such a wiseass. See, I got the business with you and the other thieves, the bar, a dry cleaners, a couple laundromats and a piece of a couple restaurants. You want to know how I got all that?" He paused for effect, and it let Jimbo think a minute.

Barboza had said, "sooner," which meant that he was lining Jimbo up with something now. Which was what Jimbo had been working toward for the past three months. Meeting the bosses. All right, try some humility. He looked at Barboza, sitting behind the wheel as usual, Sinatra hitting his stride on the tape deck, sounding like he was singing in the backseat.

"How did you get that, Mikey?" Jimbo said, and Barboza ate it up.

"By showing respect." As if the word itself carried weight, Barboza saying it like a preacher says God. "You cry about I'm not doing anything for you. I'll tell you something, you talk to other guys I know the way you talk to me—Paterro or someone—kid, they'll whack you. Maybe me, too, just for introducing you. I intro you to them, you gotta show respect or they'll kill you, then go to the phone book, have someone whack everybody in it with the same last name as you, just for effect.

"And for your information, Jimbo, I don't want you on the Beglund thing." Barboza sounded hurt, as if the mere suggestion had cut him deeply. "I got bigger plans for you." He left it dangling there.

6

Jimbo said, "Like what?" and that made Barboza smile, probably thinking he was really running Jimbo now, owned him. Jimbo had to concentrate, show the respect, because Barboza seemed finally, finally to be walking into his hands.

Barboza said, "Like for instance, introducing you to some of these guys we were just talking about." And there it was, six months of hard work coming to a head, counting the setup time.

"But Jimbo, before I do that for you, you gotta do something for me."

The string that had to be attached. Everything in Barboza's world had strings. You got nothing for free. Jimbo decided to bite, see where the line led. Maybe it would be long enough to string Barboza up by his gonads.

"What's that Mikey?"

"There's a guy, getting out of the joint today. A whacko motherfucker. You stick with me, I'll show you who he is, and you, Jimbo, I want you to kill him for me."

Without hesitation Jimbo said, "You got it, Mikey."

Jimbo entered his apartment—a little one-bedroom flat on what was called the East Side but which was really the far South Side, less than a mile from Barboza's hedged estate—elated now, feeling no fatigue, the hangover gone. He went directly to the AT&T answering machine, hit Rewind, and started listening to his messages. He was smiling. The first message: from a girl he was seeing, the sister of the guy he'd started out drinking with last night. She'd heard he'd been arrested and wanted to make sure he was okay. The second message: Smokey, the bartender in the joint he'd been drinking in when the trouble started. The third message was from his mother. And she was the whole reason he even had the machine turned on at all.

"James," the elderly female voice said, "where have you been? Please call me when you get a chance. I'll be waiting by the phone at two if you're free." That was it. The beep sounded and Jimbo rewound the tape, erasing any other calls. None of them mattered now. He checked the Rolex on his wrist. Just past noon. He'd have to hurry.

2

Jimbo took a quick shower, cold, to wake himself up. He brushed his teeth and shaved, then put on a pair of jeans, a shirt, and a reversible jacket, one side black, the other white. He put an old dago billed cap on his head and grabbed his sunglasses. He tied his gym shoes and was gone, out to the street, jogging down the block to the tavern he'd been outside of when he'd been arrested. He thanked God when he spotted his car in the lot. He'd been afraid that the cops had gone hard on him, had it towed after they grabbed him. He got in his car and by one o'clock he was downtown.

He spent the hour shaking any possible tails. He parked the car in a garage, walked to State Street and bought a ticket to a movie. Jimbo entered the dark theater and immediately made for the emergency exit, pushed the bar and ran into the alley, stuck to the alley for a couple of blocks and came out on South State Street. He ducked into a restaurant he'd been in before and went into the lounge, ordered a beer, sipped it casually as he looked around him. Trying to spot anyone coming in out of breath. He paid for the beer and went into the men's room, locked the door behind him. Jimbo removed the jacket and reversed it, took off the hat and sunglasses and stuck them into his pockets. He opened the large window and crawled out into the alley. He shoved his hands into his pockets, hunched his shoulders, his collar up covering his chin, moving differently. He'd followed plenty of men in his time and knew that most of them had a walk as distinctive as their voice. He could tell someone by their walk if they were dressed up as Frankenstein's monster. Pretty sure now that he was moving without a tail, he walked east to Michigan, mingled with the foot traffic, popped into fast-food places and out side or back exits, covering his tracks. He made it to Water Tower Place with minutes to spare.

Jimbo took the glass elevator to the highest level the public had access to, Level Seven. From there he turned left and walked to the private elevators, which took the monied upper class to the high-priced condos on the upper floors. He leaned against the wall and checked his watch. Exactly at two, the doors whooshed open and Jimbo stepped into the elevator, backing in, looking around at the people walking on Level Seven. He didn't see anyone he knew. He pressed the button marked Penthouse, watched the doors close silently and only then turned to the man standing next to the control panel. Jimbo grinned at Detective Commander Franko Lettierri and said, "Say there, Mom."

Before Lettierri could speak Jimbo held his hand up. "Look, Commander, it was one in a million, believe me. I'm sitting there drinking with this goof, Christ, the guy introduces me to his own sister and says to me, 'Might as well keep the fucking all in the family,' and turns me loose on her. We're a block from my apartment, just playing around, having a couple. This Cuban comes up to me; right away, I make him from Miami. He's in this wiseguy bar probably setting up a dope deal, and he's staring at me." As they hit the twentieth floor, the commander reached out and punched the Emergency button: The cubicle glided slowly to a stop. Jimbo watched him, seeing the sorry look in the man's eyes, and knew he might well be in jeopardy of getting pulled off the case. Desperately, he continued.

"Like I said, one in a million. Maybe one in a billion, the odds of running into a guy from ten years back in a bar two thousand miles from where you last saw him. He's eyeing me, standing there looking like he's Geraldo Rivera and I'm a crack pusher, and he goes, 'Where I be knowing you from, bro?' and I tell him, 'Hey beaner, you don't know me from Christ, so fuck off,' and he pulls this blade, looks like a samarai sword; he clicks it open and I nail him, start pounding on him, and the bartender gets into it and pushes us outside into the alley. I'm planning on putting this guy away for six months, maybe give him some amnesia, when up rolls the squad, lights flashing. The dude takes off, probably had to crawl, so it's me the blues grab and to make a long story short, here I am." He tried to grin. The commander's face hadn't cracked an inch since Jimbo had entered the elevator.

"Are you through?" the commander said, way too calmly.

"No," Jimbo said, saving the best for last. "I call Barboza to go my bond and he comes, picks me up, on the way home tells me he's got me pegged for bigger things." Jimbo was warming up to it now; there was no way the commander would call him in when he heard this. "He wants to intro me to some of the big boys, and you know there aren't but two or three bigger than him. But first I got to whack some maniac out for him, show them I'm sincere.

"Commander." Jimbo was trying not to beg but his voice was betraying him. "This is it. Six months of ball-breaking police work, with three of them undercover, coming to a head. Man, not knowing from day to day whether they wised up to me, and finally we're gonna get them. I'm gonna meet Paterro, Campo even, all the way to the top. We'll bust them Commander . . ." Jimbo's voice trailed off. He'd said too much already. He was wheedling. Jesus.

"You through, now?" the commander said, and Jimbo bit his tongue. He nodded his head, staring at Lettierri, no longer trusting the tone of the commander's voice.

"I'm calling you in, Marino," Lettierri said. In spite of himself, Jimbo squeezed his eyes shut and pounded his thighs with clenched fists, once.

Lettierri was unmoved. "Hey, Jimbo, we got Barboza by the ass and you know it. He did a couple of bits years back, when he was a kid. He goes down under RICO now, corrupt influence, racketeering; he'll get life without parole. Guy like that, throw twenty years in his face, he'll roll. You've done your job." He patted Jimbo's arm, a father comforting the son who'd missed the winning shot in a basketball game with a second left to play.

"That was good work. No sense taking chances. We got Barboza. With the tapes and your testimony, we own him. Without you, though, he walks, and if they find out you're undercover, we might not have you." Lettierri hit the button and the elevator's power surged on, the cubicle heading down almost as fast as Jimbo's spirits.

"What is it, Commander? The real reason. No cop has ever been killed by the mob in this town. They wise up, they'll feed me garbage, try and run me, but they won't kill me. That's bullshit. And you and I both know it. Why are you calling me in?"

"GiGi Parnell got released from prison this morning."

For a split second Jimbo felt an unreasonable panic, as if he was atop a very high place, unprotected and looking down; his groin constricted and he felt nausea, then he got it under control. He reached past Lettierri and hit the Emergency button.

12

"Commander, listen, we pick Parnell up, revoke his parole, something, anything; all we need is a couple more weeks, we got the Outfit. Hell, Parnell, he's been in the joint bumping dickheads with killers; the joint probably ruined him." He said this hopefully, doubting the words as they came out of his mouth. He was thinking that if he'd been this bad an actor with Barboza, they'd have found him in the trunk of a car months ago.

Lettierri said, "Where you living?" Angrily. "In the United States, a guy does his time, he comes home. Parnell did ten years of a seven-to-ten bit. There *is* no parole. He did hard, straight time. He's got rights now." Lettierri said this with disgust, but he wasn't bending for Jimbo, either. "We can't arrest him. For what? Because you want to keep your scam running longer? Try telling that to the judge and the ACLU. They'll love that one. You know Parnell; he was Barboza's top thief ten years ago, before you busted him. With his mother dead, he'll transfer all that loyalty to Barboza. We can't have you and Parnell running into each other in Barboza's office, Jimbo. That guy, there's no telling what he'll do."

Jimbo had a far-off look on his face. "It's GiGi he wants me to kill." The more he thought about it, the clearer it seemed. "He told me I had to whack out a guy for him, getting out of the joint today. It was Parnell he was talking about."

"Is that right? Good. Maybe they'll kill each other, save the state a lot of money. Trials, prisons, that stuff costs more than we do." He thumbed the button and once again the elevator began to descend.

Lettierri said, "Tomorrow, nine o'clock, be at the U.S. Attorney's office for debriefing. Bring your lunch. You know how those guys are. We'll nab Barboza as soon as we pop his guys over at the Beglund score. Maybe some of them will roll, too. We get Barboza, file a hundred charges on him, see what happens. If nothing else, you had a good time, the last three months."

The elevator doors opened on Level Seven of Water Tower Place and Jimbo felt as if he was looking out at another world; gaily dressed people strolling the aisle, the gangbangers from the nearby projects cursing as often as they could, showing their colors and their pride and their manhood.

Lettierri said, "You want some guys, the next couple of days?" Meaning protection, telling Jimbo kindly that he didn't believe Jimbo could handle GiGi Parnell.

Jimbo said, "Don't even think about it. I'll cover my back myself. Jesus, I'm a *cop*."

As he walked from the elevator, he heard Lettierri say, "Then start acting like one. . . ," but he ignored it.

He was feeling empty, hurting. Abused by his boss and the world in general. He looked at the people passing by and wondered whether any of them cared one way or the other that he had risked his life daily for the past three months. Probably not. Half of them didn't believe there was a gangster problem in Chicago, and the other half saw the Outfit as kindly old men, Marlon Brando, like that, doing what they had to do to take care of their families. Those are the ones who would be shocked to see some mob stud going into a guy's house and dragging his wife and daughter out, putting them on the street hooking to pay the guy's gambling bill or dope bill or juice bill or whatever. That didn't happen in Chicago anymore. Bull*shit*, it didn't.

He took the escalators down to the ground floor, still feeling the vertigo that came over him when he heard about GiGi Parnell's release, not wanting to chance the ride in the glass elevator. He was trying to look on the bright side now, for a change.

He could get back in shape, for one thing. Playing the roll, being a crook, he'd been eating and drinking too much, staying up all night and sleeping most of the day. He had often wondered during the past three months why these mob guys didn't all have heart attacks by the time they were forty, the way they lived. He could work out again, running instead of just the light workout he'd been doing daily trying to keep in some kind of shape and to kill the hangovers.

He stepped out into the early September sunshine, into the thronging crowds of Michigan Avenue. Trying to look on the bright side. There were plenty of good reasons to end the undercover operation now. His work was finished. He should be happy.

So why did he feel like he'd just been shafted?

The apartment he was living in was a dive, in a neighborhood once thriving and vibrant, two blocks from the lake. Now it was in decay as the mills closed and the sharks bought the houses for the price of unpaid taxes. The homes wound up gutted, renovated, the single-family dwellings cut into four apartment units—each unit housing more people than used to live in the place when it was family owned.

Jimbo was on the second-floor rear, the apartment furnished with a Naugahyde La-Z-Boy and a refrigerator he kept beer in.

The only things he'd be taking with him that he hadn't brought in three months ago were the answering machine and the Precor 612 rowing machine that he used to keep in shape. The answering machine would come in handy when the reporters heard about the undercover work—Christ, he'd been through it once before in Miami when he'd broken the White Heat Bandit case—and they would ferret him out and start calling day and night, looking for their stories.

Every day upon awaking, Jimbo would row for a half hour, and the only sight he would see was the shadow shifting across the wall as the sun rose. Then he'd do a hundred sit-ups, a hundred push-ups. It would be good to whack a bag for a while. And to run. He sure wouldn't miss the apartment.

Jimbo ignored the messages on the machine, just unplugged the thing. There was no point now talking with anyone who might be calling him. He decided to skip the workout today because, technically, he hadn't gotten out of bed. He hadn't even been *in* bed. He took two beers out of the fridge and put them in an ice bucket on the edge of the tub, then ran hot water while he packed his clothes. He took them and the answering machine and the rower outside and put them all in the trunk of the car. He took a long, leisurely bath, sipping the beer from time to time, enjoying the iciness inside with his outer body submerged in hot water.

He was thinking how good it would feel to be one of the good guys again. No more night chills, wondering if they were on to you. No more bottle-a-day habit with Pepto-Bismol. No more duplicity. But he felt an odd sadness. Because it had been fun.

Jimbo Marino got out of the tub and dried himself, drank the last beer in the fridge, turned off the lights and unplugged everything. He stood, dressed, on the threshold of the small apartment, looking around one last time. Then he walked out the door and slammed it behind him.

If GiGi Parnell had been released, then Jimbo had better warn his ex-wife before she read it in the papers or somebody told her. He owed her that much.

Then the thought came to him: If GiGi was back, where was the first place he'd go?

Jimbo got into his car and began driving to the place he was certain GiGi would be. Just to check him out. Get a look at him after ten years.

See if the sight of GiGi still scared him.

3 Gigliamo Parnell had waited ten years for this day, his sentence including time served in jail awaiting trial and sentencing. When he became a short-timer, he heard all the stories and he listened to all the guys in the White Aryan Brotherhood—his gang—going on about what they'd do when they got out. The first day free. They'd talk about getting laid or drunk or putting scores together. All of it, to GiGi, being bullshit. What GiGi did, first thing, as soon as he stepped off the bus at the Randolph Street station, was get a bus schedule. Then some change. Then he got on the Seventy-ninth Street bus and took it to the corner of Yates, got off and walked three blocks west to St. Mary's cemetery.

When he reached the gravesite, it was midafternoon, with shadows deepening across the grassy landscape. He stood there looking down at the marker. He tried to remember a prayer, but it had been too many years. At the grave of the only woman he had ever really loved, and he couldn't remember a prayer. Well, he'd served ten years because of that love, and he figured that was better than empty words taught in Sunday school.

It never occurred to GiGi to get on his knees; he was wearing a suit he'd paid four hundred dollars for eleven years back that would probably cost a grand today, even if

18

it was a size too small. He'd beefed up in the joint. He'd worked out every day with the guys in the Brotherhood and picked up a lot about karate from Buck Shadows, the Indian teacher. No, he wouldn't get on his knees, but he still had things to say.

GiGi cleared his throat. "Mom, the warden said if I came to the funeral I'd a had to wear cuffs, and two screws would a had to stay with me the whole time. I'm out of the joint now, Mom, and I only wish you could have lived to see me get out. But you didn't. Just know that I'll never forget you and all you did for me."

The shadows were crossing his mom's grave now and GiGi stood there trying to cry, but he couldn't. That was strange, because, in the joint, thinking about this, after saying good-bye, he always saw himself crying, breaking down. The tears weren't coming, though. He said, "It's starting to get dark now and I don't want to get into any brawls with the jigs the first night out, in this shitty neighborhood. I done enough of that in the joint." GiGi imagining his mom down there under the ground, in a box. Trying to picture it. Trying to bring forth tears. Still, nothing. "I'm gonna go now, Mom," GiGi Parnell said, then softly, "Good-bye." He looked up at the sky, wondering whether she had heard him. He turned to leave.

And spotted the great big guy way across the grounds, silhouetted, standing just inside the gate. If GiGi had to guess, he'd say the guy worked here, because GiGi had never worked a day in his life and the only way he could figure a guy for a working stiff was by the way working stiffs dressed in the movies, and this guy was wearing one of those funny hats like the longshoremen wear on the docks on TV. The guy was probably waiting for him to leave. GiGi stared at him, resentful that the man was intruding on his first—and last—private moment with his dead mother, and the guy did a funny thing. He pulled on the brim of the laborer's cap, like the cowboys do in the movies when they want to say hello without opening their mouths. Then the guy turned and walked away.

GiGi took one last look at his mother's grave, trying again to conjure up something to feel. But nothing happened inside of him. He said, "See you around, Mom," and left.

The first time Jimbo had set eyes upon GiGi Parnell, he'd said to himself: Tommy Udo. The man looked exactly like young Richard Widmark had in the movie *Kiss of Death,* with Victor Mature, the one where Widmark pushed the old lady down the stairs in her wheelchair with an electric cord wrapped around her. Jimbo had been standing in the post office in Miami, surprised when he spotted the man whose picture they'd been shown just that morning at roll call, and he thought that the White Heat Bandit looked exactly the type to push a cripple down a flight of stairs and laugh because she bounced. That had been ten years and a lot of miles ago, and his busting GiGi had made him nearly a national celebrity.

Driving to his ex-wife's, remembering, Jimbo decided that he'd been an idiot to stop at the cemetery. Man, even from a block away, the man looked powerful; no longer looking like a wiry little kid who'd felt like a bag of snakes when Jimbo'd grabbed him. GiGi looked like a *big* bag of snakes now.

But the son of a bitch, he still looked like Tommy Udo.

Bitsy's Bits was the name of the boutique, on trendy Clark Street, about a mile from Jimbo's real home. He parked at the curb, enjoying the sights of the North Side after being south awhile. There were yuppies jogging and roller-skating down the sidewalk, little radios hooked to their ears. Women rushing it, in mink. Walking ugly little wrinkled dogs. A couple of guys with their arms around each other walked into the building next to Bitsy's, a hand-painted sign in the window telling Jimbo that it was the North Side Gay Alanon club. He laughed outright when a short-haired fellow on a fifteen-speed bicycle braked to a stop a couple of doors away and reached into his basket—his hand coming out with a portable cellular telephone.

Jimbo walked into the boutique and there was not a soul in sight. "Bitsy?" He felt funny calling out the name—what, fourteen years after he'd first said it. It still sounded weird, calling someone Bitsy. He walked toward the back, where a beaded curtain gave access to Bitsy's living quarters. Jimbo stepped through the beads and was in a small hallway; five feet away it turned left and you were in Bitsy's apartment. "Bits?" Jimbo began to step toward the bend in the hall, hoping that Bitsy wasn't entertaining. She liked to entertain. He caught movement, low, and spotted the Doberman racing around the curve, and he froze. The dog's lips were curled back, showing long white fangs. Saliva dripped from her mouth. She stuck her nose into Jimbo's crotch, growling low and deep. Jimbo stood there like a cigar store Indian, trying not to breathe, thinking, *shit.*

And there she came, good old Bitsy, sashaying around the bend in the hall without a care in the world, her shoulder-length blond hair sprayed stiffly in place, smiling when she spotted him standing there in terror.

"James!" Bitsy said, acting as if there wasn't a killer Dobie snapping at his balls. No, just two old friends running into each other on the street, her face lighting up with recognition and phony happiness.

Jimbo moved his eyes downward, then back at Bitsy, rapidly. He was frozen there in the hallway, standing awkwardly with most of his weight on his left foot. Bitsy looked puzzled for a second, then pretended to see the dog for the first time.

"Sparky!" she commanded, "you silly thing, leave James alone!"

Jimbo had to give it to the dog; it did turn its head to look at its mistress before sticking it right back there. He swore he could feel the dog's hot breath right through his jeans. He said, through clenched teeth, "Goddamnit, Bitsy?" He was about ready to take a chance, grab for the sucker and try to coldcock it before it ripped his throat out.

Bitsy stomped her foot. "Sparky!" she said, coming at the dog and slapping her haunches. The dog looked at her, then walked down the hall into the apartment.

Jimbo tried to regain his composure before speaking. He was afraid if he didn't, he might forget why he'd come here and maybe whack Bitsy one. Bitsy saw his anger and responded normally for her: with petulance.

"Well, it isn't my fault," she said, giving him the pout he remembered so well. The way Bitsy would always look at him when she wasn't getting her way, and all of the attention. He noticed that her accent had gotten stronger since he'd seen her last. There was always a bit of Scarlett O'Hara in her.

When they were married, he believed that Bitsy could probably bury him and have his replacement with her at the funeral. She gave him some of that attitude now, as if the dog hadn't nearly had Jimbo's balls for lunch, looking at him with that same phony surprised look she'd first given him.

"James," she said, and it came out Jayaymes. "My, this is a pleasant surprise!" As if Jimbo was a neighbor dropping by for a cup of sugar. Rhett Butler stopping in between blockade runs. She frowned now, looking at the dyed hair under his hat, his altered eyebrows.

"James, you didn't just come over from next door, did you?" Bitsy smiling, a little joke at the expense of her gay neighbors.

Jimbo said, "Bitsy," on safe ground now, an icebreaker for him, "what does *alanon* stand for?"

"Alcoholics Anonymous."

"That's an AA meeting place?" Jimbo was shocked.

"Don't make fun, James. Why, those boys know how to spend money."

Enough. "Bitsy, do you think I could come in?"

Sparky was back, roaming around at his feet now, sniffing, and every time Bitsy looked away, Jimbo would slap lightly at her muzzle, hoping to drive her off. It wasn't working.

They'd exhausted small talk quickly, Jimbo getting more irritable every time she opened her mouth, wondering how he'd ever been stupid enough to drop out of school and run down to Florida with this pretty little airhead. Finally he collected the nerve to tell her, knowing exactly how he would have to play it. "Bitsy? How's your father doing?"

Bitsy looked puzzled. Jimbo's feelings for her father were no secret. "Fine, James. Why do you ask?"

"I was thinking. Maybe you could go home for a little while, see him."

"James, really! I just can't up and leave here. I've got a business to run all by myself." She gave him a look, letting him know that her plight was all his fault.

Jimbo said, "I can see, you're pulling them in." He was

not about to be manipulated into giving her anything. Her father owned half of South Miami, and she was crying about having to stay around to run an empty boutique.

But he had to get rid of her. He gritted his teeth. "I'll take care of things," he said, not meaning it. Bitsy's eyes filled with tears of gratitude, shining brightly in the kitchen of her apartment. Jimbo just hoped she wouldn't break down.

She said, "Are things that bad, James?" Trying for serious.

Jimbo took a deep breath. "GiGi Parnell got out of prison today."

Bitsy's hand went to her throat and the game playing stopped. There was terror in her eyes for a second, before she caught it and the mask came back up. She bit her lower lip and gave a dramatic toss of her head, but her heavily sprayed hair did not move.

Bitsy returned from locking the outer door and found Jimbo on the phone, speaking in low tones. Her hero. The star running back at the University of Kansas where she'd met him and gotten him to fall in love with her. The big strong city boy who never had a chance. All she'd had to do was say, "Ah think ah'm preg-a-nant, James," and he'd dropped out of school and gone home with her to Miami. After meeting her father, they'd eloped, but nothing seemed to go the way she planned after that.

Her daddy was an ex-lieutenant governor of the state, and he had squirreled away a fortune during his eight years. He had more than enough influence and power to take care of his baby girl and her new husband. But Jimbo would have none of it. He wouldn't even allow her daddy to pull any strings when he took the test for the Dade

County sheriff's police. He made less money as a rookie than her father used to send her every week when she was in school, and he was too damned independent to let daddy help them after they got married. Of course daddy sent an envelope every month for her, but she had never told James about it. He would have made her send it back and they would have starved to death.

And then he got into that terrible fistfight in the alley with the Chicago fugitive, the White Heat Bandit, battling him in a to-the-death struggle all alone, the fight ending when a squad car turned in and even then the officers had needed another five minutes to subdue that animal, Parnell. Bitsy's first thought upon seeing her husband on the television news had been, My hero! When he came home from the hospital, she threw herself at him in a fit of sexual excitement she'd never before known. But as the weeks went by, he refused to tell her about it, forcing her to make up lies for her friends in order to stay in the spotlight. Even daddy had been impressed.

Then Chicago's mayor went on the late-night news, trying to get political mileage out of the arrest, stating for the reporters that the native-Chicagoan policeman who had single-handedly captured the White Heat Bandit could come home anytime and there'd be a job for him on the force. The city needed a few good men like him, and that had been all that James had needed to secede from the South. He'd shown up at city hall; and what could a mayor do?

But then the letters had started coming from GiGi Parnell, terrible letters, and James would do something and they'd stop for a while, but they always came again. Still James never shared anything with her, always keeping his business to himself. Even about how he finally stopped the letters from coming altogether. Why, she'd had no choice but to divorce him!

Daddy had set her up with a disco, which had folded, and an aerobics center, which had died, too. And now the boutique, in which there hadn't been one customer all damn day long.

And here comes James back into her life, his beautiful head of black hair cut short and dyed almost white.

She knew better than to ask him anything. She'd read the article in the paper when he'd resigned, the paper making a thing out of it because he was the cop who'd captured Parnell, and she thought right away that he was probably into something illegal; her daddy had always said that James was a natural-born crook. And there was no better judge of character alive than her daddy. But daddy didn't want her coming home; he was living with his fifth wife who was younger than Bitsy was; the two of them would be embarrassed by having her around. But daddy couldn't refuse to take her in now. Could he? With her life in danger? No, he'd take her back into his palace with the security guards and dogs and the high fences, and she'd winter there, get out of this place before the cold settled in. Safe from the White Heat Bandit. Until James could take care of him again.

But right now she was two thousand miles away from all that protection and care. In the kitchen of her apartment with James on the phone still, now hanging up and turning to look at her—if there was one thing Bitsy knew how to do, it was bring out the protective instinct in the male animal. She smiled at him hesitantly, giving him a bit of fear, yet showing him what a brave little trouper she was.

"James?" she said, hesitant still, biting her lower lip. The frontier wife before the Indian attack, helping to circle the wagons. "I'm frightened." She allowed a tear to roll down her cheek but brushed at it quickly, showing him she was ashamed of her cowardice, and as usual, he came out of the chair and stood before her, cupping her chin in his big hand, giving her that brave it's-going-to-be-all-right look that always made her believe that it really and truly would. She melted against him, allowing her body to tremble some, and, as always happened when she went to war with the opposite sex, she won. She felt the bulge down there in his pants and buried her head in his shoulder.

Jimbo went to the phone and made a couple of more calls, learning that the next nonstop to Miami International was at midnight. Six hours to kill. He hung up and turned around and there she was with her blouse open, new, larger silicone breasts staring out at him, and he lost his urge. He just couldn't make love to a woman who'd had her breasts enlarged. Even if he closed his eyes and pretended that it wasn't Bitsy beneath him. Christ, knowing her, there was no telling what she might have these days, either. There was a way out, though, without hurting her feelings.

He followed her into the bedroom, Bitsy turning the motor on now, and as she reached for him to pull him down onto the bed, he whispered in alarm, *"What was that?"* She stiffened. Jimbo immediately felt ashamed of himself because her eyes filled with terror again, the real kind.

"Oh dear God," Bitsy said, and Jimbo thought, that's the same thing she says when she comes. He felt a little less ashamed.

"Will that dog bite?"

Bitsy whispered, "She's attack trained. But only if you say the word *Pasha*."

Jimbo said, "Pasha?"

Bitsy said, "What did you hear?"

"I'd better check it out."

He sat in the kitchen with his head in his hands and wondered where he ever got the nerve to call Bitsy a manipulator. She was a piker compared to him.

Sparky came and sniffed at his leg. Then Bitsy came out of the bedroom hesitantly, dressed again, frightened. "What was it?" she asked, and Jimbo shook his head.

"Why the word, Bitsy?"

"What word?"

"P-a-s-h-a."

"You need to come up with a word no one ever uses, so I came up with—"

"NO!" Jimbo screamed, and the dog came at him a few feet, growling, her head going from Bitsy to Jimbo, back and forth.

"Bitsy," Jimbo said, "why don't you go pack?"

He sat and waited for her, wanting a cigarette desperately, but he hadn't smoked in a couple of years and wasn't about to begin over some con with a hard-on for him. GiGi probably didn't even remember his name. Hell, the character hadn't threatened Bitsy through the mail now in over four years. Maybe he had changed. Had got rehabilitated. Maybe Jimbo was just being paranoid.

There it was, that word. Every person who knew him well sooner or later told him he was paranoid; just because with the exceptions of Lettierri, his friend Gizmo, and Judge Chris Haney, there was no one he trusted. Well, he was cautious. And it kept him alive.

Bitsy came out of the bedroom carrying a small overnight case.

"That's it?" he asked her.

Bitsy said, "There're a few small things by the bed, if you'd be kind enough."

Jimbo got up, walked into the bedroom and started moving the baggage that was stacked there. He bent to the task, hurrying to get her out of harm's way.

4 GiGi Parnell had nothing really important to do until morning. Then he had to tend to the house and his mother's will, and straighten out Barboza about the money Barboza owed him. Barboza did not worry him, mob or no. If Barboza gave him any trouble now about the money, why, GiGi would just tie Barboza's old lady up and start cutting off her fingers.

He was irritated with this man. Last couple weeks, the guy hadn't even taken GiGi's collect calls from the joint, giving him some line about the hundred he sent every month had used up GiGi's dough. Which was bullshit. GiGi knew a guy inside who had worked for Barboza, and the guy had told GiGi that Barboza had paid the other crew members twenty grand apiece for that terrible night ten years back. And that guy, he was owed nothing, and he still got his hundred a month, the same as Gigi. The hundred was only a goodwill gesture, to keep the guys on the inside quiet, not talking to the Man. GiGi would straighten Barboza out.

Right now GiGi had other problems. Inside, he'd heard countless times about guys who got out and were busted again before they even got their dicks wet. That wasn't going to happen to him. Which was the reason he was strolling Rush Street—my God, how things had changed—looking around for a good bar to go into and have a couple pops. With the three hundred in his pocket, he figured he could get through the night no matter how much things had changed.

GiGi walked on, his chin on his chest, giving the world the Badeye. Kept you out of a lot of trouble with the boo-boos who were impressed with things like this. In the joint, a good Badeye was worth a lot.

The sign on the glass said MUGSYS, and he liked the looks of it, so he dropped the Badeye and went in, feeling strange, smelling smells and seeing sights he hadn't encountered in ten years. Beer and peanuts and perfume and counter polish. Seeing *women,* man, outnumbering the men two to one as he strutted up to the bar. It was a long one with a curve down at the end, a smoked-glass mirror that took ten years off the women sitting in front of it. Two drinks, maybe *fifteen* years. There were a few booths in the back near the johns and a stand-up phone booth with the glass around it behind them, a cigarette machine and jukebox.

The bartender was polishing glasses, rapping to one of the chicks, a babe with black ringlets falling over her forehead. Slim neck and dark, dark eyes. GiGi had to call the guy twice to get him down to where he was, the asshole coming as if GiGi was putting him out, wearing a white short-sleeve shirt with a red bow tie. The bartender was young and going bald already.

GiGi ordered a Dewar's neat and paid with a crisp twenty. He waited until the bartender brought him his change before picking the glass up and raising it. GiGi said, "First one in ten years, buddy-boy," and gulped the whiskey. Jesus Christ, GiGi felt the stuff hit his gut and spread to his toes, warming him, filling him with good cheer. He slapped the glass back onto the bar and looked at the bartender. The jerk stood there looking back at him, arrogantly.

The bartender said, "You want another?" and GiGi was at a loss for words. The least the guy could have done, he could have asked why it had been so long. GiGi nodded and the bartender picked up GiGi's glass and walked slowly to where the White Label was standing. GiGi had the urge to whack him one, just once, upside the head, show him some manners.

Thinking dark thoughts, he noticed the babe the bartender had been hitting on walking confidently his way. Her slit skirt was cut almost to her can. She had on a silk shirt, with some kind of funny-looking running shoes on her feet. Big woman, maybe five-seven, a couple of inches shorter than GiGi. Fine rack on her chest, and her legs looked shapely enough.

She said, "Don't let me have come over here and learn that you've been in AA ten years, okay?"

GiGi smiled. "The hell's AA?" he said.

They were sitting in the booth next to the jukebox now, GiGi sipping at the Dewar's after the first blast, staring into black large eyes and falling in love. But losing her somehow.

She'd been more than interested at first, leaning over so he could light her smoke without ever taking her eyes from him, giving him a shot of her bra as she leaned. She'd wanted to know, mostly, about cons' sex lives.

He'd told her all she'd heard was true and then some, AIDS now getting to be a panicky situation on the inside, it bothered the niggers about as much as a head cold. He told her about the young fish coming in and the niggers raping them one at a time, maybe ten in a row, and then turning the kid out, making him tie his shirt in a knot on his chest and wear makeup. They'd sell his fish ass for a pack of smokes and brutalize him until he either went into protective custody or killed himself one.

But the more he talked, the less interested she seemed. Every time he said nigger she flinched like he'd slapped her or something, so he changed it to spade or boo-boo but even that didn't seem to be doing any good.

GiGi decided this was a good time to make a couple of phone calls. On the phone, maybe he'd think of something to say to this girl. Without a word, he got up and walked to the booth, digging in his pocket for some change. He closed the door behind him and dialed the local number he'd been calling collect for two years.

A male voice answered and GiGi said, "Brian."

"Geege?" the voice surprised and happy. "Is that you?"

GiGi said, "Broham," happily, "how's it going?"

"A lot better, knowing my home boy's out, shit."

GiGi looked over and saw the babe was gone, her smokes and her drink, too, so she wasn't just in the can. He turned back to the booth, trying to get back the good feeling he had gotten when he'd first heard Brian Solt's voice.

He said, "Broham, I need a favor."

Brian said, "Shit, you name it, brother. You need a place to stay, come on by; I'd put the old lady out for you."

"Naw, that's cool, but I think I'm going home." There was a short silence as GiGi thought about walking into the house that was now his without his mom there. Uncle Lester would be there as always, but not his mom. To

Brian, he said, "I need a pistol, say, a forty-four; I want to get a guy's attention and the thirty-eight I usually use might not be big enough."

"That's all? Shit, I ain't got to even leave the house for that, babe. How about some blow?"

GiGi said, "You playing with that shit, Brian?" a threat there in his voice; God, how he hated guys who snorted.

"No, no, selling a little babe, not using."

"And a car."

"I got the Caddy, you can have," Brian said, to make up for the remark about dope.

"A little too flashy for what I got to do."

"How about the old lady's Chevy? It's a couple of years old, but it runs good."

"That's fine."

"When you want it, broham?"

GiGi looked at the empty booth, thinking he wasn't going to get his dick wet. He said, "I'll be there in a little while," and hung up.

The babe was at the bar again, with a couple more chicks sitting around her, laughing it up. GiGi wondered if they were making fun of him. He took his drink and walked to the bar, sat down next to her on the stool, the fake leather making a squeaky sound. The babe said something real low, false fear and fun in her voice. She was making fun of him.

GiGi lit a Camel—someone inside had once told him that when he put on the Badeye while he was smoking, he looked evil—and got into his Badeye, the smoke curling up around his eyes and forehead. In the mirror he could see himself. Bad.

Good.

He turned to the girl, tapped her on the shoulder, roughly. GiGi said, "Hey, don't they teach you city bitches manners?" The girl turned toward him, fighting fear, then gave him a loathful look. GiGi could tell she was going to say something cute to impress her girlfriends.

She said, "What are you trying for? James Dean?"

He said, "What?"

She began to turn back to her friends and GiGi grabbed her shoulder roughly, turned her to him and mashed the cigarette into her face, going for the eye but missing, hitting her nose dead center because she turned her head, screeching, at the last second, but he twisted it, the girl screaming in pain and terror now, his fingers sliding past her nose and—there, he made it, into her left eye.

The bartender came running down quickly, stopping dead when he saw GiGi standing there, the girl's hair held in his left hand, the cigarette hanging out of her eye. She'd leaped, trying to get away, and he'd kicked back the stool, grabbed her and held on. His face still held the Badeye and in the heat of action it grew into something more than evil, worse.

"You want a piece a me, huh? Hey goof, I'm talking to you!" The bartender put his hands out, looking about to cry, and GiGi dropped the girl's head, let her slide down the bar to the floor, sobbing. He said to the bartender, "You let cunts like this in here, they'll wreck your business." Then looked around the bar, waiting, hoping, keyed up and ready, the wimps all turning their heads away when their eyes met his. "Not your problem, right?" GiGi said, disgust in his voice, then said, "Shit," telling them all what he thought of them.

GiGi Parnell turned without a backward glance—they'd already rolled over and shown him their asses; they didn't have the balls to try anything now—and put on the jailyard stroll to the door, the cock of the roost, thinking that he'd trade a piece of ass anytime to get the feeling that had a hold of him right now.

5 It was hard getting away, but at last GiGi walked out of Brian Solt's house with the .44 magnum Smith under his suitcoat and the key to Brian's old lady's car in his hand. The car was a two-year-old Chevy and the woman had acted like it was a new Lincoln, telling him to be careful ten times. He got in and experienced the pleasure of sitting behind the wheel of a ton and a half of rolling steel on rubber for the first time in ages. GiGi took his time, trying to check things out and relax. He had a call to make in a little while, but it was only eight; he had about an hour to kill, think of things to say.

He drove, checking out all the new stuff, McDonald's everywhere you looked, Pizza Huts, 7-Elevens on almost every block, it seemed. Gas stations with little bulletproof glass windows to pay at. When he'd gone in, gas had cost more than it did now. Goddamn towelheads. Didn't know how to act.

GiGi figured that the worst thing he saw was all the boo-boos walking hand in hand with white girls. That ate him alive for a while, then he figured to hell with them, if they wanted black cock so bad, they deserved it. He thanked God he had no sisters or worse, daughters. He'd have to kill somebody if his daughter brought home a jig. Christ, what was the world coming to? Thinking about the zebra problem, GiGi rolled into one of the little armored-car gas stations, filled the car, and bought a pack of smokes. He got back into the car and pulled over to the little drive-up telephone, made his second call of the night, punching the number, from memory.

"Yeah?" Mikey Barboza said to him.

"Mikey, how's it going?"

"GiGi?" Barboza sounded shocked, uneasy. "Where you at?"

"I want my money, Mikey."

And that quick, Barboza was all friendly, as if he hadn't refused to accept the charges on GiGi's calls for the past two weeks, the prick. He said to GiGi, in a shaky voice, "Sure, hey, buddy, that little misunderstanding we had? Forget about it. Okay?"

"*You* had the misunderstanding, Mikey, not me. I figured, all along, you owed me twenty."

"Sure, sure thing, Geege. I can have it for you, a couple of days. Give me a couple days to get it together."

"Tomorrow, Mikey."

"Gigi, come on."

"Tomorrow."

"Okay, Christ, Geege. Tomorrow, call me, the same time."

Barboza seemed to want GiGi off the phone. Maybe he had someone with him and didn't want the guy to see him sweating, the pig.

GiGi said, "You got anything for me, any action? I need more than the twenty, make up for lost time."

"Sure, hey, GiGi, I got a thing, make you the same as what I owe you, one night's work."

"Any of the same crew from the old days?"

"A couple, but the other three, they're with me since you went away. Stand-up guys, though, you'll enjoy working with them."

Hurrying now, wanting to get Barboza's mind off what he'd just told GiGi without even knowing it, GiGi said, "Mikey, not this soon. Hell, I ain't even got my dick wet yet." He liked the way the words sounded together. "After tomorrow, though, after we square up, I want my old spot back, yeah?"

GiGi heard Barboza agreeing to anything GiGi asked for, and that knowledge made him sure that Barboza was not about to pay him. Not in money. He might try and pay him off in lead. So it was no surprise when Barboza kept rushing it, telling GiGi no problem, anything he wanted, he'd have the dough tomorrow and good-bye—

GiGi said, "Wait a minute. You got a line on the cop who arrested me? I read in the paper, he quit the force; they called up all the lies from ten years back. A couple reporters asked permission to interview me." Pause, then, deadly, "I want him."

Barboza said, "GiGi, tell me you're bullshitting me."

GiGi didn't like the tone of Mikey's voice, like GiGi was nuts or something and Barboza had to straighten him out. He said, "Tomorrow, Mikey," threateningly, and hung up.

GiGi drove slowly away from the gas station, thinking. About what Barboza had given up without knowing it. About how tonight's score could get GiGi the same amount of money he had coming, which meant twenty grand. Also that there were five guys in on it. Barboza always paid on delivery, out of his warehouse office in the South Side industrial park. He would get there hours before the heist he'd lined up. In case something went wrong, the guys would know where to reach him—if somebody got sick or didn't show. And later, if somebody got busted.

As GiGi had.

But Barboza hadn't been there for him back then. Nor in the ten years since. GiGi checked his watch. 8:50. He guessed that Barboza would probably be leaving his house just about now, so he stepped on it. He had to get to the warehouse first.

Mikey Barboza hung up the phone and forced himself to calm down. Christ, where was Perino. Give a guy an answering machine and he doesn't even plug it in. He dialed Jimbo's number again, his finger shaking, missing a number. He had to hang up and start over again. He listened to twenty rings, then slammed the phone down.

He had to get Jimbo, and now. Had to get him to cover his ass, take out this whacko Parnell before Parnell got to him, or, worse yet, to Paterro. If Tommy Campo ever found out that Barboza had not paid a loyal crew member . . .

"Clarice?" he shouted, his mouth turning down at the ends when he heard his wife pounding down the hallway, rushing. He made a bet with himself that she'd be twisting that damned rosary in her hands when she came in. Clarice knocked once, then entered, the hairy ape of a woman; if she hadn't been the daughter of one of the top mobsters in the country, he wouldn't have looked at her twice all those years ago. Marrying her had been what really put him in, though, and if he dumped her now, Don Laccavvia would reach his Sicilian arm all the way from New York to squeeze Mikey's balls for him. The hairs over her eyes were a single line. Barboza had told her more than once to shave the damn eyebrows and pluck the little hairs on her cheeks, but Clarice thought vanity was sinful.

Mikey Barboza won his bet on a technicality. She was wringing her hands for lack of the fucking beads. Looking worried. Good. That was the way Mikey liked her. He had to put up with her, but there was no rule about having to be nice. He said, "I got to go out for a while. If Jimbo

Perino calls, you tell him I got to talk to him, now. You understand?" He gave her the famous Barboza stare, the look that had stricken fear into mob underlings for years.

She was nodding her head, knowing that if she opened her mouth, he'd blow up no matter what she said.

He told her, "Go on, go say one of your novenas." She winced at his words, and Barboza knew that she would indeed be praying for his soul. "Just make goddamn sure you listen for that phone."

When he'd been trying before to think of positive things about being yanked off the case, he'd completely forgotten the most important one: being able to run with Gizmo again.

Gizmo. The Giz. Roland Jefferson, Jr. Maybe the best friend Jimbo had. A short, rotund little fifty-year-old black guy who could run a bug into the buttons of your shirt or into a roll of toilet paper in your bathroom. This never ceased to amaze Jimbo, seeing that Gizmo was deaf.

He left the car running at the curb with Bitsy there in the passenger seat, looking miffed. She and Gizmo did not get along. Gizmo opened the door and stepped out on the porch as Jimbo approached, wearing his regular outfit, green work pants, with suspenders, a lumberjack shirt, warming the entire neighborhood with that patented Gizmo grin.

The first thing Gizmo said to him after three months apart was, "You look like Rutger Hauer," his eyes on Jimbo's hair, then adding, "I see you are back with the little woman." He motioned for Jimbo to follow him inside, turning his head away so he couldn't lip-read Jimbo's reply. Jimbo figured that was the only advantage to being deaf, the ability to tune out anyone, anytime.

Jimbo walked over to the kitchen table Gizmo used for a

desk, the Tandy computer with new modems sticking out of it smack dab in the middle, surrounded by the things that had given Roland his name: gizmos. Gizmo locked the door behind them and turned, looked at Jimbo, who said, "I'm working the Morlane case? Where the doc and his entire family got whacked? Christ, three days without rest and I get home, she's nowhere to be seen. Married two years and she'd never be home. I fall into bed with my clothes on, next thing I know somebody grabs my arm, starts shaking it. I leap out of bed, grabbing for my piece, scared to death, there's Bitsy. She says, 'Honey-bunch? You seen the *TV Guide*?'" And Gizmo laughed. His laugh sounded like his speech, a monotone without inflection. It reminded Jimbo of a comedian he'd seen on TV making fun of the handicapped, going, huh-huh-huh. Maybe one of the smartest men Jimbo had ever met, and people who should have known better thought he was retarded because he was deaf.

Jimbo turned to look at the computer monitor while Gizmo calmed down. He noticed that his message had already been erased. Gizmo did not take chances. When you called Gizmo, his custom phone modem converted your voice into characters and displayed the text of your conversation on the screen. When you were quiet for three seconds, a red light flashed and Gizmo would type in his end of the conversation, and a computerized voice would speak to you through the telephone. Eerie, but effective.

"You're lucky, I just had your car tuned last week," Gizmo said. Jimbo guessed that Giz probably tuned it every week just in case Jimbo came back and needed it. He was curious to see his house. Giz had probably hung plants all over and quilted the walls.

"Let's leave the city car out there in the garage; my luggage is in it. Turn it in tomorrow. After I get my stuff. I just want to take Bits to the airport and sleep." He had to be at the Federal Building at nine. He would not be getting a lot of sleep. He said, "You have enough dough to take care of things?" and Gizmo turned, headed for the drawer where he'd kept the checkbook, Jimbo calling after him, "I'll get the money tomorrow," then remembering that Gizmo could not hear him. He walked to Gizmo hurriedly, tapped his arm. Gizmo turned and read Jimbo's lips as he said, "I'll get it tomorrow when I come for the clothes." Gizmo nodded.

They went to the garage and brought Jimbo's LTD Crown Victoria around front, and Gizmo gave Jimbo a hand transferring Bitsy's luggage. He waved them off and headed back to the house, not a word exchanged between Gizmo and Bitsy. Jimbo felt awkward; ten Bitsys couldn't make one Gizmo. He hoped the old man's feelings weren't hurt.

She waited until they were on the airport road, 394 North, the Illinois Tollway, before putting in her two cents. "Smelly old thing," Bitsy said, wrinkling her nose. Sitting primly and properly way over against the door. An unwilling participant in the entire matter. Jimbo had to fight the urge to reach over and slap her. "And don't be defending him over me any longer, James. Your cop friends are half the reason we broke up."

Jimbo thought that she was the other half, but didn't say it aloud. "Gizmo's not a cop," he said, just getting his own point across, angry with himself because even after all this time he was trying to get the last word in.

"Gizmo's not a cop." Bitsy mimicked him, feeling her oats, safe now and not having to be nice to him anymore. Jimbo thanked God he hadn't fallen into bed with her. He'd hate himself now if he had. Under her breath, but loud enough for Jimbo to hear, she said, "Smelly old nigra queer."

Jimbo steamed, but knew better than to start an argument now. Gizmo was too good to defend. But he did say, "Watch it."

"Well, he is."

"One more word, Bitsy, one more goddamn word out of your mouth and I swear to Christ I'll turn this car around and take you right back to the fucking boutique." Jimbo drove quickly, looking at the night traffic and the orange glowing reflective glass set in the dividing lines of the Tollway. If he timed it right, at the airport, he'd be able to get in the last word with Bitsy for the first time in twelve years.

GiGi was parked across from the warehouse, checking it out, just eyeballing it, wondering what to do. Best thing to do in a case like this was play it by ear.

He went around back and broke a window, jackknifed his superbly conditioned body over the sill, landed on his side and rolled until he hit the edge of something hard. The desk. So, Barboza still had the same office.

And he hadn't changed a thing. It felt as if he had stepped into a time machine and gone back ten years. Everything in the same place it had been the last time he'd been here. Even the clock and the telephone on the desk.

GiGi sat down at Barboza's desk and put his feet up, laid the huge .44 on the desktop.

Barboza would have to die. That's all there was to it. Made mob man or not, he had to go.

GiGi was under no illusions about the mob in Chicago. They were ruthless, dispassionate killers who struck back ten times for a single hurt. And Barboza was one of their top money-makers. GiGi had been on a crew, working as an independent contractor, but once he'd gotten locked in

44

with Barboza, he was death to any other fence. The ones who paid top dollar. It was mob fence or nothing after he made the jump, so the least he'd expected from the mob was loyalty. Which they hadn't shown.

The only thing in his favor now was the fact that no mobster worth his stiletto would ever call another mobster and ask for help. That would show weakness. Calling a mob hitter in to deal with a renegade thief would lose Barboza respect, and respect was all he lived for, so it was out of the question. Campo and Paterro, the top dogs, would probably not even know about a small-time thief like GiGi Parnell. These men were so far above the daily workings of the family that his name would not ring bells to them. So what Barboza would have to do would be to call in one of his contract crew, an outsider wanting to curry favor with the man, and get him to kill GiGi.

GiGi would have to get to him first. Like right now.

The mob would more than likely wipe out a couple of pushers as a show of strength, but they would have no reason to come looking for GiGi. His entire strategy rested on the fact that they wouldn't.

GiGi allowed his fingers to lovingly stroke the .44 barrel, up and down, softly and gently. Waiting. By the red digital-readout display on his watch, it was 10:15 when Barboza entered the office.

"Hey!" Barboza screamed the word as he flipped the light on and saw GiGi. GiGi smiled. Barboza spotted the gun and his face went quicky blank. GiGi had to admire him, the guy walks into his office and sees a man with a gun and right away the wheels start turning. Trying to figure a way out.

"How's it going, Mikey?" GiGi spoke softly, casually, as if he cared one way or the other.

"What's with the gun, GiGi?"

"Mikey, I come for my money."

Barboza tried to smile but didn't quite make it; the lop-sided grin he came up with was almost sad. No longer the player, but the one who'd been played upon. The game was over, and still he was trying to fool around with the rules. GiGi had to hand it to the guy.

Barboza said, "Tomorrow, I told you. *Tomorrow*, GiGi."

GiGi shook his head. "Now, Mikey."

GiGi hefted the gun, turned it over in his hand, the barrel pointing directly at Barboza's stomach. Let him see death up close and real for a change. See how much of a player he really was.

"You should have taken my calls, Mikey." He had him there; there was no way to wheedle out of that.

Barboza didn't say anything for a while and he didn't have to; his face was expressing his thoughts quite well now, anguish and pain twisting it; terror. That was the best part for GiGi, seeing the terror in Barboza's eyes and on his face. He hoped the guy would crap himself.

Barboza said, "All right. Jesus, I was wrong. I fucked up. But I sent the hundred every month." Barboza had hope in his voice, as if the piddling hundred meant anything. "And here it is, the first day out, I agreed already to pay you. Even, Christ, GiGi, even if I had taken your calls, you still wouldn't have gotten the money till you got out."

"You could have sent it to my mom."

Barboza stared at him and there was another fear there in his eyes this time, the terror GiGi had seen in the eyes of screws inside who'd been trapped on the block during the riots in '81, the screws locked in with crazy men who stuck broom handles in their butts. GiGi didn't like the look, the-sane-man-trapped-with-the-crazy-man look Barboza was giving him.

But man, he was enjoying the feeling of power.

"Pay up, we forget the whole thing, eh, Mikey?"

Barboza wasn't good enough to hide it. Relief and surprise flooded his face, the guy looked like a woman who'd just dropped a baby, the pain still there but no longer unbearable.

"We could make it all like it was before, Mikey. I wouldn't have to worry about anyone coming after me."

GiGi was playing with him and Barboza too dumb to realize it. He was nodding his head up and down, sweat pouring down his face, staining through his armpits and making half-moons on his suitcoat.

Barboza said, "Come after you? Who the fuck is gonna come after *you*? *I'm* the one fucked up, GiGi. I give you my word, GiGi, we straighten this out now, no one will come after you."

"You're gonna do me a favor, right, Mikey? Keep the dogs away?" Then it was too much for him at last, and besides, Barboza had run out of words. "Open the safe, Mikey."

Barboza nodded his head like a disobedient child trying to placate an angry teacher. GiGi pushed himself back in the chair when Barboza came toward him, kept going back as Barboza pulled the desk away from the ratty carpet and unzipped the hidden lining under there, exposing the round face of the safe—a Mosler. GiGi knew guys could open it in fifteen minutes, but none of them was free at the moment. GiGi watched as Barboza's trembling fingers turned the combination, the guy whimpering a little now, sweating in torrents, making little mewling noises that sounded like prayers. GiGi was enjoying himself. He sat back in the chair, relaxed and moved his wrist to bring the gun around to point at about the middle of Mikey's back. As soon as the safe door hit the carpet, GiGi fired.

And the chair went back a good two feet and his hand wound up pointing at the ceiling—Christ, what a kick. He would have laughed if he hadn't seen Mikey Barboza scurrying from the room. He fired again, one-handed, going way into the doorjamb, and this time the recoil almost broke his grip. Then he was out of the chair and running into the hallway, but there was no sign of Mikey Barboza. Christ, he had fired from point-blank range with the world's most powerful handgun and missed.

GiGi ran back to the safe and stared down at more cash than he had seen in his life—and he had been out on some healthy scores. He put the pistol on the carpet next to the safe and began to scoop out the banded piles of hundred-dollar bills, shoving them into his suitcoat pockets and when they were full, the inner pockets, and there was still plenty left over for his pants pockets, front and rear. He ran out of the office the front way, looking for Barboza. No sign. Still, he backed over to his car, his eyes scanning the street, just in case. He got into the Chevy and forced himself to stay calm as he dug through the money in his right pants pocket for the key. He got the car started, put it in drive and drove left-handed, stuffing loose bills back into his pocket with his right.

All right. So far so good. He had to stay calm, that was the first thing he had to remember. He'd been in ass-tighteners before. This was nothing, some two-bit mobster scared out of his wits not knowing where to go or what to do. Where would he go? The first place? Shit, where else, where all the mob guys felt safe. At home.

GiGi parked the car a block away and a block over and ran the distance to Barboza's house, leaping the hedges and rolling on the grass until he found the protective cover of an ancient oak. He lay there breathing hard, the .44 in both hands this time, eyes scanning the grounds for guards, for Barboza's car, seeing neither. All right. Maybe Barboza was already in the house somehow, loading up the arsenal GiGi knew was in his den. Calling guys—no, Barboza would die before he let anyone he knew see him all sweaty in his piss-stained pants. GiGi told himself this, listening to his heartbeat slowing in his ears, his breath slowing down some, too. Then he heard the sound of a car.

Barboza's Cougar turned into the drive and circled to the front of the house. GiGi tracked it with the front sight, waiting. Barboza got out of the car and—before he could take a step, GiGi squeezed off a round and goddamnit, it was *high,* and Barboza was racing up the steps, shouting something, and GiGi emptied the gun at him but didn't hit a thing except bricks until it was too late. Barboza was in the house.

GiGi got out of there quick. He raced back to where he'd parked the Chevy, drove with the lights off just in case anyone around had heard the shots and was looking through a window. They wouldn't get these license plates. He couldn't do Brian that way.

GiGi cursed himself. He fired six times tonight at a guy with a weapon that, had one bullet caught him in the ankle, would have killed the guy from shock, and he hadn't hit anything but house and office furniture.

But there was nothing to be done about it now. They would be after him, or they wouldn't. Or Barboza would keep it to himself, and come looking. GiGi hoped that was the case, because Barboza and a couple of self-styled tough guys who never spent a day inside, well, that was an even fight.

Still and all, it wouldn't be smart to head home right yet.

Stay in a downtown hotel for the night, or a couple of nights. Make a few calls, see where he stood.

GiGi took the car back to Brian's wife and traded the .44 for a .38 Colt, his weapon of choice. He and Brian had a little private chat in the bedroom and they wound up stashing the bulk of the money in the extra bedroom, where the English sheepdog slept. They put it under the animal's blanket. Brian had trained the dog and it was loyal only to him. If his old lady went near the mattress, the dog would take her arm off at her shoulder. He took Brian's car this time, the Coupe de Ville, flush, in the money, about five grand still in his pockets. Enough to last awhile. Brian's old lady didn't like GiGi taking the car, and she stood there watching him leave, giving Brian a ball-breaking look that told GiGi his old cellmate wouldn't be getting laid for a while.

GiGi walked into the North Side gin mill like he owned it, which was his style going into any strange place, be it a tavern or a cellblock. He rolled his shoulders, his toes pointed out; he stepped lightly, looking neither left nor right. His arms swung in the player's strut. He went to the bar and ordered a Dewar's neat, water back. Paid for it with a crisp new hundred. He told the bartender to bring him back fifty change and to keep the rest for himself. That got his attention, and the guy wouldn't be walking away like the one at Mugsys.

GiGi lifted the Dewar's to the sky, sighting through the amber liquid philosophically. Like he should have done the first time. He said, "First one in ten years, buddy-boy," and gulped the drink, smacked the glass back down onto the bartop. The bartender was staring at him with interest.

"Ten years?" the bartender said, really sounding like he cared. "Where the hell you been, pal?"

Around the bar there were murmurs, babes eyeing him; people had heard his remark and they'd been watching since he'd told the bartender to keep the fifty.

GiGi smiled. He knew how to learn from his mistakes.

Jimbo didn't wait around for the plane to board. He didn't even want to carry in her baggage. All he wanted was to get her safely away from GiGi Parnell. A skycap took her luggage and Jimbo didn't bother to say good-bye, just walked around after slamming the trunk and got back into the car. Before he could turn the key in the ignition, Bitsy was there, on the driver's side, hitting the window with her knuckle. Jimbo powered it down.

"What?"

Bitsy didn't seem to know what role to play. She tried biting her lip for a second, then she tossed the keys onto his lap roughly. He knew where she'd been aiming. "You need the keys to take care of Sparky and the shop." There was a flatness in her voice, vaguely reminiscent of the sound of Gizmo's computer. Maybe at last he was seeing the real Bitsy.

"Will that frigging dog bite me if I walk in without you?"

"No." An almost evil look twisted her face, distorting it, taking away what beauty there used to be. "She'll bark and growl and sniff, but she won't attack unless you say Pasha."

She turned and walked away without another word. Jimbo followed her with his eyes, shocked by what had just happened. God, was she that plastic, that phony? That shallow? He got his answer watching old Bitsy turn on the charm for the black skycap, the southern-belle lilt back in her voice.

Jimbo decided that he should have left her alone at the boutique. She seemed to be more than a match for GiGi Parnell.

*   *   *

He entered the boutique after making plenty of noise opening the door. He did not trust a word Bitsy had said and wanted the dog to see him and smell him before he stepped two feet into the place. Sparky the Doberman was there, ready, lips back and long teeth bared, snarling, and Jimbo slowly stepped into the shop, hands at his sides. All three of his handguns had been in the glove compartment and he wore one now, ready to go for the gun if he had to. She growled and sniffed and he pushed her away gently and she did not attack. He had to search the place for a minute before he came up with a bowl and a large economy-size bag of food, and her leash. A choke chain with a short leather lead. Good length for Bitsy, but he would have to bend way down to walk the mutt.

And then it hit him. Christ, he was surprised that it hadn't entered his mind before. He could stay here, alone with the dog in a place where no one expected him to be. Stay here and be safe.

Then thought, safe from what? From GiGi goddamn Parnell? And who the fuck was he, that he had to hide out from that son of a bitch? If anything, Parnell should be hiding from him.

Jimbo dragged a snarling Sparky into the Crown Vicky, his mind made up that he would shoot the thing if she used his car for a bathroom.

He drove home to the two-story on Orleans Street, thinking. Lettierri had been a jerk, offering protection. Well-meaning, naturally, he hadn't meant it as an insult, but Jimbo couldn't accept the fact that his boss thought he might need help covering his rear for twenty-four hours. Jimbo had to feel a little resentment at that, it was just the way he was. But in the city of Chicago last year there had been 744 murders, 3,708 sexual assaults, 30,678 robberies,

33,409 serious assaults, 56,077 burglaries, 121,455 thefts, 48,400 auto thefts—Grand Theft Auto, not punks joyriding and later leaving the car unattended and unharmed—cars that had just disappeared. In a city that had a reported 294,469 felonies two years ago, the operative word here being *reported*, there were probably twice as many of every type of crime except murder that weren't reported, and his boss wanted to waste man-hours and man power guarding a veteran undercover sergeant?

There it was, ahead of him. Home. He hadn't been near it in three months and now felt as if he was returning from a war. Mama and Papa long gone now, but the place still standing, bought and paid for by the sweat of Jimbo's father's brow, working long hard hours in unbearable heat in the mill, in the furnace, for the family. The mill gone now, too, but the house, the house was still there.

Jimbo dragged Sparky up the porch stairs and locked her in the house, then went back for her things and his other two weapons. He locked the car and set the alarm, and went back into the house.

As he flipped the light on, he saw the phone machine hooked up and his baggage on the floor, resting next to the rowing machine. Goddamn Gizmo. That son of a gun.

Jimbo did not unpack. He was too tired. He did, however, change the message on the answering machine before getting the dog a bowl of water. After which he just stripped off his clothes while walking to his bedroom. He fell asleep the moment his head hit the pillow, the one with the 9mm Beretta pistol under it.

6 The telephone jangling next to his ear shocked him awake. Through the blinds in his downstairs window, he could see bright sunlight and he stretched, not bothering with the phone. The machine would pick it up after the fourth ring. What he did not know was that Gizmo had set it on full screening, so he could hear his voice answering the caller and a second after the beep, there it was, the sound of Bitsy's voice bringing him full awake.

Sparky was wrapped in the sheets at the end of the bed and a pungent foul odor assaulted his sense of smell. He swung his feet over the edge of the bed, narrowly missing a brown lump of dog feces on the carpet. Bitsy was whining about something, so he picked up the bedroom extension and said hello. Angrily.

"Oh, you're there now." Bitsy acting as if the sound of her voice had commanded him to pick up. Then, "James, I open at eight."

"What?"

"The boutique. I called there and you didn't answer, so I tried your house."

"Your dog shit on my rug."

Bitsy giggled. "She's just defining her territory, marking it. Now are you going to go open the place or shall I come back on the next plane?"

Jimbo said, "You come home on the next plane, Bits. Do that. Just let me speak to your father." He gritted his teeth, getting ready to speak to the colonel. After about a ten-minute wait, he got the privilege.

"Hello, son!" The colonel's hearty voice was full of man-to-man cheer. The first time Jimbo had met him, he'd told the colonel, "I'm not your goddamn son," and they'd never got along since.

"Sir," Jimbo said, keeping it formal, "do you remember GiGi Parnell?"

"Son, my little girl told me all about it, and I want you to know that I—"

Jimbo cut him off. "If Bitsy is allowed to come back here, there's a chance this punk will murder her. He's been threatening her since I arrested him. You keep her there, Colonel, because I can't protect her here."

The colonel said, "Don't you worry, son, I know how to take care of my women," and he hung up. Jimbo put the phone down, disgusted. At himself though. He'd lost control and the bastard, being who he was, had no choice but to imply that he was a better man than Jimbo.

He got off the bed, eyeing the dog, went down the hall to the bathroom. He came back with a huge roll of toilet paper and breathed through his mouth as he picked up the mess. He flushed it away and went to the kitchen, under the sink for the scrub bucket and the rags, adding the Pine-Sol as an afterthought. He wondered whether the stuff would harm the carpet, and vowed to get rid of the dog if it did. He filled the bucket with hot soapy water and took it into the bedroom, got down on his hands and knees and scrubbed the carpet roughly, over and over again, spilling Pine-Sol directly on the spot and then scrubbing it some more. He was sweating when he finished. The goddamn dog was still rolled up in the sheets, watching him. He looked at her.

He said, "Asshole."

Sparky yawned.

Jimbo searched the house and got all the old newspapers and magazines he could find. He dropped them around the basement floor, trying to cover all of it, not making it by half. The basement was divided up into three sections, and he should leave her in this one because the other two could be closed off from it. He went back upstairs and got a large pot, filled it with water, then filled her bowl with the dry dog food. When he rustled the bag she came running and he walked backward down the basement steps, coaxing her in a little baby voice, then dropped both pot and bowl on the papers and retreated hastily. He looked back as he reached the top. The dog was eating, with her eyebrows raised and her head in the bowl and her eyes on him there on the top step. From the spot he was standing, she looked betrayed. That *had* to be his imagination.

He closed the door after him and thought of what Bitsy had said. She opened the place at eight. Jesus, what time was it? Eight-seventeen and he had to be at the Federal Building at nine.

Afterward, Jimbo felt that it went pretty much the way he'd figured it, after he straightened them out on a couple of things.

State Attorney Richard Corneale sat in, so Jimbo wouldn't have to go through the same thing twice, and there was U.S. Attorney John R. Drumwald, the head man, running the show, helped along by two toadies he called his aides. Jimbo sat in a comfortable leather chair, the center of attention, a recorder in front of him on a table and a blue-haired stenographer a few feet away. They were taking no chances. It was a gigantic room, certainly the largest Jimbo had ever seen outside of a warehouse.

The place had to have a twenty-foot ceiling, easy, and the paneling went all the way to the top. A gigantic desk was against the wall, near the window so Drumwald could put his feet up and look out at the skyline. There was nothing else for him to do, by the looks of the desk: Except for a telephone, the thing was bare. Corneale sat in what looked like a padded funeral parlor chair, and the main man and his aides walked around, back and forth, shooting questions at Jimbo that were duly recorded by both the machine and the old woman. From time to time the three of them would walk off and have conferences, speaking in urgent whispers that almost but not quite reached him.

The first problem he had was the men didn't want to hear any of the good stuff. He kept trying to give them insights into the criminal mind, and all they were worried about was the legality of his work. He wished Chris Haney was doing the questioning. Chris would ask him, "Did you commit any felonies at any time in the course of your investigation?" and Jimbo would raise an eyebrow, shrug a little, tell Chris, "Well, just a few, get their trust, you know." And then smile, waiting to see how Chris would play it.

But he couldn't do it with these guys. They would give him funny looks and tell him to answer the questions in short, articulate phrases. Without embellishment. And so he did, wanting to give them hell but only speaking up one time, when Drumwald stroked his mustache and asked him if he had at any time during his investigation had sexual intercourse with any mob prostitutes.

Jimbo said, "Depends on what you mean by fucking."

Corneale stifled a laugh, but Drumwald stomped over to the recorder and stopped it, then told the steno to strike the remark. He turned a red and angry face upon Jimbo.

"Do you understand the gravity of your investigation, Detective Marino?"

"You're goddamn right I understand the gravity of the situation. It was my fucking ass out there taking all the risks."

Drumwald said, "This is an order, Marino, so listen carefully. You will not answer any more questions with wiseass remarks, and you will not again use profanity in this room. Do you understand me, Marino?"

Jimbo said, "It's Detective Sergeant Marino, sir." Then said, "And I want to tell you something. My sex life is none of your business. I'm here for debriefing. You want to get tough, I'll take a stroll over to city hall with Mr. Corneale, give him everything, and you can go before the grand jury unprepared." He sat back, angry, looking at the three men in their three-piece Brooks Brothers suits, turning white in the face. The men gathered for another breathless conference and Jimbo looked at Corneale, who did a surprising thing. He winked.

At last, Drumwald came back, pacing up and down in front of Jimbo's chair. "Detective Sergeant Marino, every question we ask you is designed to protect you as well as us. Defense lawyers, especially the defense lawyers Barboza can afford, will stop at nothing to malign you. We have to know everything. Do you understand?"

Jimbo said, "Yes, sir."

Drumwald relaxed a little. Buddies already. He said, "After all, we're all on the same side here."

It was on the tip of Jimbo's tongue to tell Drumwald the hell we are. But U.S. Attorneys had a habit of going on to become governors.

"Yes, sir."

Drumwald flipped the recorder back on and said, "Detective Sergeant Marino, during the course of your investigation, did you have sexual intercourse at any time with mob prostitutes?" and Jimbo said, "No, sir," feeling as if he had just had sexual intercourse with himself.

He answered their questions all morning long, giving precise accounts of crimes and describing the legality of Gizmo's bugging devices that had been put in place on the basis of warrants signed by Judge Chris Haney. He answered their questions and left out all the good parts. All the fascinating insights.

Like Barboza out drinking, taking shit from his chippy whores and the hookers, covered with diamonds that Barboza had paid for, sitting at tables. Then going home and treating his wife worse than an animal.

Or listening to Tony Bennett sing "I Left My Heart in San Francisco" twenty times a night, literally. The mobsters giving their girlfriends money to feed the juke. Telling them to play the same thing over and over again. Always Sinatra or Bennett, sometimes Louis Prima or Keely Smith.

Or the night Barboza had been trying to keep one of his chippies happy and made Jimbo dance with her. Jimbo had taken her back to the table later and had asked Barboza why he hadn't gone out on the floor, and Barboza had stolen a line straight from Frank Costello and told him, "Tough guys don't dance." Jimbo had laughed, the guy had been so sincere. Then told Barboza that James Cagney and George Raft could cut a pretty good rug. Ray Danton. Barboza had looked at him strangely and said, "Ray, *who*?"

As he gave his testimony easily, by rote, he thought about these things and couldn't wait to tell the atmospheric parts to somebody, Chris, Gizmo, maybe Lettierri if he'd lighten up and go out and have a few drinks like they used to. Before Lettierri's ass had got so tight.

They took no breaks until noon; then suddenly the three lawyers were stretching and smiling at each other, a good morning's work done. With the recorder off and the steno lady out the door on her way to eat, Drumwald had said the thing that had caused the second dispute of the day.

He said, "Of course, Marino, we'll have marshals guarding you."

But this time, Jimbo won the argument.

They told him to be back at two on the dot, and Jimbo admired them, getting two-hour lunch breaks daily. Jesus, when he was on the street, he was lucky to eat a hot dog in his car while surveilling some bad guy. He got into the LTD and drove directly to Morrie Mages Sports, went in, got what he needed and paid with his VISA. He locked the packages in his trunk, then had an Italian beef sandwich at Tomanuchi's, with a Coke and fries.

He'd got used to living like one of them, sleeping until he felt like waking up, staying out all night, resting most of the day. Now, after six hours sleep, he felt dead on his feet. He went into a Walgreen's and bought a pack of No-Doz. He'd rather load up on caffeine from coffee, but he'd already done enough to anger the powers that be and he didn't want to be running off to the bathroom all afternoon. He parked the car and entered the Federal Building, bought a paper from the blind lady who ran the concession stand, wondering how the hell she knew what denomination bill you handed her. Without hesitation, she handed him back his seventy-five cents. Uncanny. He took the elevator back up to the U.S. Attorney's office and dry-swallowed three of the pills. He sat in the chair and opened the paper. He searched through it for mention of the arrests made last night at the Beglund construction site. Nothing. Obviously it had happened too late to make this edition.

At ten till two, Corneale came in, smiling, rubbing his hands together and winking at Jimbo once. Jimbo nodded, polite but reserved. State's Attorneys had a habit of becoming mayors. And mayors ran police departments.

"I like your style," Corneale said.

Jimbo said, "Thank you." What Corneale meant was, before lunch Jimbo had won an argument with the most powerful and influential politician in the district. Few men ever did, and certainly no cop ever had.

"About time," Corneale said, "somebody put that pompous dork in his place."

Jimbo leaned forward in his chair, his face inches from Corneale's. "Mr. Corneale—"

And the guy surprised him again. "Call me Richie."

"Richie, listen, you think this room might be bugged?"

Corneale looked at Jimbo strangely. "What, aren't you being a little *par*anoid?"

The afternoon session was brief and political. At first all the man wanted to talk about was the validity of the warrants, Jimbo telling him once again that Judge Chris Haney had personally listened to every request and had then gone ahead and signed the order. Then they went over the way Jimbo had been introduced.

What happened was, a mobster named Vinnie Franchetti had gotten religion on his deathbed. Introduced Jimbo to Barboza as a thief, "Like a son to me," the outgoing mobster had whispered. Drumwald nodded his head and accepted it. That would stand up; the mobster Franchetti was dead. No one could question him about the tapes they had of the event. Only he and Lettierri knew how it had really happened, and neither of them was telling.

They'd gone to Franchetti with evidence that would have convicted Vinnie's only son and put the kid away for fifteen years. Asked the guy if he wanted his kid rotting in jail while his old lady and the grandkids went on welfare. The only son, who was supposed to take care of the family business and make sure that Vinnie's widow lived out her remaining years in comfort. Vinnie had repented after countless arguments, the man wanting to go to his grave hard, as he had lived, but Jimbo and Lettierri had gotten to him at last and the intro had been made scant weeks before the man went to his reward.

Jimbo couldn't say anything about that here. He could tell Chris, maybe, and Gizmo. These guys would not see the beauty of it. They were shortsighted.

Then Drumwald, with the tape running and the stenographer pecking, asked Jimbo if he had any reason to believe that the investigation was set up as a political ploy by the mayor.

Jimbo almost fell out of his chair. He saw call-me-Richie Corneale rock with the question, his chin falling to his chest. It was too much, even knowing of the bitter hatred between the mayor and Drumwald.

Jimbo told him that in his opinion the investigation had been set up only to get some scumbag mobsters off the street. He put scorn into his voice, resentful that he was being used as a political tool to further some jerk's ambition.

Drumwald said, "That's all, Detective Marino."

Jimbo looked at his watch—2:23. Twenty-three minutes for an afternoon session? Something, suddenly, seemed very wrong.

He drove to central police headquarters at Eleventh and State, wondering why the hell they'd taken a two-hour lunch only to work again for less than a half-hour. Something smelled bad, but he didn't have time to think about it. Officially, he wouldn't be working until he testified before the grand jury almost a week from now, on Monday. But he had to go to the office, get the lowdown on the bust last night. His crowning glory.

Jimbo walked through the glass doors like the conquering hero returning. He felt even better than he had last night returning to his home. Probably because this place was filled with cops who would give their right arm for an assignment like Jimbo had just had, and the house, well, the house was just . . . empty. He took the elevator to the seventh floor, marched past the MCU office where he had once worked—Major Crime Unit being the elite of the force, second only to the Organized Crime Task Force. Jimbo's outfit. Past the dreaded Office of Professional Standards, the Chicago answer to Internal Affairs, the ambitious headhunters who wanted to be commissioners someday and climbed their way up over the fallen bodies of their brothers. The last door on the right furthest down the hall was the one. The glass half-door painted: OCTF. Classy. They did not have to advertise. Everyone knew who they were. Jimbo entered the room—the smallest in the building—and let the atmosphere wash over him, the feeling of being a cop on his home territory. He felt safe here, felt that nothing could touch him within these walls. He felt, most of all, power.

There were seven men in the unit, not counting Franko Lettierri. Their seven mismatched desks, in a room built to hold maybe three, had been pushed together, with a tiny aisle leading to the washroom and the commander's office. A Mr. Coffee machine sat on a wooden desk next to the computer. Two of the teams were out on the street. One two-man team was here now, Jimbo the lone wolf having no partner. And disliked for that freedom. By his own people, who were in turn disliked by everyone else. The elite of the force, the OCTF was, and they had to wait three days for a requisition form to order pencils. Man, these hot shots were *hated*. The OCTF did not do your normal everyday police work. The seven men did not keep regular hours, did not sign in, did not write ten-page reports in triplicate detailing their every action, accounting for every second on the job or every cent spent. The OCTF had one job only: to break the back of the mob in Chicago.

The rub being that half of the politicians in Chicago were on the take and linked to the mob. Everyone knew that the mobsters worked overtime trying to get someone in council chambers to disband the renegade elite unit, push a bill through, whatever. But the politicians, even the dishonest ones, stayed away from it like the plague, knowing that the first alderman who made a push against the task force would be hounded out of office by the press, because it would be proof enough to their readers that the politician was in the mob's pocket.

But only if the OCTF produced, which it did with a vengeance. And Jimbo's little undercover act here would ensure the task force at least two years of continued efforts, that's how good the deal was. And how dangerous. This was a headline-maker, no doubt about it. Jimbo was not looking forward to the future. He hated the press.

Francis Mahon was typing away at the computer terminal, set on the desk next to the coffee machine, just to the right of the bathroom. He was the elder statesman of the crew, a twenty-six-year veteran detective who knew every gangster and mob soldier who had come up since the days of Sam Giancanna. His partner, Valentin Klenck, sat at his desk looking at Jimbo with humorless angry dark eyes. He looked at Jimbo as if he'd never been away, while Francis raised his arms and made sweeping gestures. Francis shouted, "Quiet, everybody, he's motivating!" and gave

Jimbo a broad wink and a warm welcoming smile. Before turning back to his keyboard, he said, "Great work, kid."

Jimbo thanked Mahon's broad back, smiling at the large head of pure white hair worn short, shaved like in the old days when you could tell a cop by the way he dressed and cut his hair and walked. He wondered for maybe the thousandth time how an extrovert like Francis could work day in and day out with a humorless son of a bitch like Val Klenck, whom Jimbo had never seen smile, let alone laugh. He'd have to ask him sometime, maybe over a beer. Or maybe right there in the room with Klenck listening. Jimbo had no use at all for Klenck. He was grateful that Francis had made a joke about his being back. The official line had been that he had retired after an altercation with a superior. That was a story everyone who knew him could believe. Being cautious, Jimbo had made good and damn sure that no one on the force except Lettierri had known about his operation. There were too many cops taking money from too many crooks for him to feel safe otherwise.

"Boss in?" he asked, and Klenck nodded grudgingly, probably mad at having to expend the effort.

Jimbo walked to the commander's door and knocked, once, then went in.

Lettierri was every inch and every pound as big as Barboza. Maybe even heavier. He reminded Jimbo of a retired heavyweight fighter gone to fat. He was smoking, and the little office was filled with blue haze. A small brown air cleaner was having an electronic stroke over on one corner of his desk. The rest of the desk was filled with papers, papers everywhere, in disarray but in perfect order for Lettierri, who more than once had been shouting at Jimbo and reached out and pulled a sheet of something or other off the messy pile without even looking at it. He had a deep voice, a commanding voice. He was used to being in charge and brooked no bullshit from anyone in his command. Jimbo could never tell whether he was about to be chewed out or praised, because the man always looked sour. But he could tell Lettierri was not happy.

"What happened with Barboza?" Jimbo asked.

"We got problems."

"What problems?"

"Worse than Barboza."

Jimbo's head was reeling. This made no sense. What could be worse than three months of work down the drain? Then he knew what could be worse. Something political could be worse. He said, "Who'd he get to?"

Lettierri checked his watch, as if he had an urgent appointment. He looked at Jimbo and Jimbo saw something there on Lettierri's face he had never seen before. Lettierri was looking at him with pity.

"Barboza got away. We were over at FB & S staking the place out when—"

"Wait a minute, Commander, slow down. What's FB & S?"

"Ferd Beglund and Sons. The construction site you set up for us. Christ, you'd think you'd remember. Listen, this guy Beglund is no slouch. He says to us, after we tell him the score, he says, 'Well, sir, if I'm gonna get robbed, why don't you just go on home and let me and the boys handle it?' I tell him, 'Look, Mr. Beglund, you don't understand, we've been working on this case for months; we can lock up a lot of thieves, here.' He tells me, 'Yeah, but if *you* get them, they'll get *out* pretty damn quick, no offense intended.' Implying that if he and his boys grab the guys, something worse will happen.

"The score goes down, our guys are in Porta-Potties waiting with weapons drawn, we round them up when they're driving the equipment away so they can't cry they were only hanging around. We got them dead to rights, Jimbo. Naturally, nobody wants to say anything; they all want a lawyer, but that's okay because we are going to go get Barboza, who will naturally, we know, take a hard look at life in prison and roll over on his bosses.

"Only it doesn't work that way.

"We go to Barboza's warehouse, where there have been men posted for over an hour, and at his house, same thing. Lights on in the warehouse, the genius stakeout guys figure he's inside. We go in, ready, nobody. The safe's open, empty; there's nothing in the office."

Jimbo said, "So Barboza figured it out, maybe when he couldn't find me. We still have the tapes, all the evidence that he conspired. Come on, Commander. The guy conspired to cross state lines with the equipment; that's federal, not to mention maybe two dozen state charges we can file ourselves. He takes off with the money, big deal. We APB his ass, run him to ground. The feds can follow a guy like Barboza with their eyes closed. Check the hotels, the bars. He'll show up."

"I don't believe he ran."

Jimbo said nothing, waiting.

Lettierri said, "There were chunks of dry wall missing from the far wall, I mean a couple chunks the size of your fist. The far window was broken, smashed in. You could still smell the cordite in the room."

"Parnell."

"Either he killed Barboza and carried the body away, which we doubt, Barboza's too damn big, or else he grabbed the money, kidnapped Barboza."

"Which makes it federal, I'm telling you."

"The feds won't even listen to that. Who's Parnell to them? No one. They never heard of the guy until I put it together for them. Then they go, 'Oh, yeah, from years ago. Pretty weak kidnapping case you got there, Franko.'

"Jimbo, what you got to understand, we have no evidence linking Parnell to Barboza, except my word. Barboza's name was never even mentioned at Parnell's trial. Anything I say is strictly hearsay; Parnell's name is on no tape in connection with a crime. What we have is GiGi calling Barboza once a week from the joint, asking him how it's going. Big deal. Feds won't even think about getting involved."

Jimbo was thinking of all the repercussions. Without Barboza, there *was* no case. The entire thing was designed to get Barboza, flip him, get him to turn on Campo and Paterro. Wreck the mob. Without Barboza, what did they have? They had Jimbo and Barboza, a disappeared witness, talking on the phone about crimes. They had Barboza calling guys and telling them to meet him at certain places, and then Barboza would go and meet these people, take them somewhere public and safe and they would talk their business there. The entire case rested on getting Barboza in custody and turning him. Without Barboza, there was nothing. Campo never spoke on the phone to anyone, ever, not even family. And Paterro, the number-two man, Campo's right hand, carried goddamn voltage readers with him to check any phone he was on, had his own personal phones and those of the places he frequented swept constantly. It all rested on Barboza, and Barboza was missing.

Jimbo, mind racing, said, "Hey, Commander, how about this? Barboza knows Parnell's after him, takes the money and scoots. Waiting for me to show up and whack Parnell for him."

"We got a phone call on the tap; Parnell called Barboza right before nine last night. Telling him he wants his twenty. Now *you* know it's twenty grand and *I* know it's twenty grand, but the jury, they can get a reasonable doubt planted by a good lawyer that it's twenty grand. Can be made to believe it's twenty bucks. Or twenty rides on a Ferris wheel, anything. Barboza mentions the score that night and damn if GiGi didn't pass. That would have made our lives a lot easier; he'd have come along on the Beglund score." Lettierri paused to light another cigarette and Jimbo was on the verge of asking him for one but did not. He would not start smoking again even over this.

Lettierri said, "Now, listen. The last thing GiGi says to him is, he asks Barboza if he got a line on you. His exact words were, 'I want him.'"

Fear again, deep down but still there. Jimbo could fool anyone at any time with one of his acts, his games, but he could not fool himself. The thought that GiGi was thinking of him and wanted him caused him to be afraid and he knew it, all right.

As he'd known it all along. He'd never doubted that GiGi would want to settle things. The problem was that now it was out in the open and there was no doubt about it—it was no longer in the back of his mind, something known intellectually but maybe not believed. It was like someone who walked around for years thinking that sooner or later there would be a nuclear war suddenly hearing the air-raid sirens. It was for real and it scared the shit out of him.

Jimbo said, "I can take care of myself."

Lettierri, damn him, was lighting another cigarette from the stub of his last, the smoke puffing out between his lips and circling the room. It was stifling hot in there already and the smoke made Jimbo claustrophobic. He suddenly noticed that he'd been standing the entire time, his hands now balled into fists held tight against his thighs. He sank down into the chair directly across from the desk and slumped there. Lettierri was staring at him.

Lettierri said, "I'm not through yet, Jimbo. That was the *good* news."

Jimbo was afraid to even think about what could be worse. Suddenly the entire day was shot. He'd come into the office expecting to hear that Barboza was singing songs, expected to kid around with Lettierri awhile, call him mom a few times, maybe get him to cut out early and the two of them have a few drinks and be pals for a while. Maybe he could tell Lettierri all the things that the big shots hadn't had time to listen to that morning. Instead, he was sitting here finding out that GiGi Parnell was coming after him and the case was blown wide open and that this was the goddamn good news.

He waited.

"At precisely twelve-fifteen this afternoon," Lettierri said, "United States Attorney Drumwald had a press conference in his office. Announcing the completion of a joint federal-city investigation into organized crime in Chicago."

Jimbo slumped still further in his chair, defeated. If Parnell hadn't killed Barboza, then the mob would now. Especially if Jimbo's name had been mentioned.

Lettierri came around the desk and popped a cassette into his setup, a little twelve-inch Sony color monitor on a stand in the far corner with the VCR under it. He turned the TV on and as the thing snapped into bright life, Jimbo turned in his chair and watched his undercover career go straight down the tubes. Maybe his life, too.

There was Drumwald, flanked by his two little ass-kissers, smiling into the camera, surrounded by reporters who jumped in his face every time he paused to take a breath, shouting questions. One woman, more aggressive than the others, asked him why the mayor was not at the press conference with him. There was no station logo on her microphone and it took Jimbo a second to understand that it was just a mike attached to a cassette recorder hanging from her shoulder. That explained the other reporters' annoyed reaction to her. She was freelance, unattached, without a contract. Maybe even from the dreaded print media, crashing what had obviously been set up as an opportunity.

Drumwald tried to brush her off but she held her ground, asking the questions the others were afraid to ask. Politicians, Jimbo knew, had a lot of power with the media, the public's beliefs notwithstanding. At last he assured her that it was indeed a joint investigation, or how else could his office have used Chicago detectives on the case? The man completely brushing off the question about the mayor's nonattendance at the conference.

"*What* Chicago detectives?" the girl asked, in a way that said she did not believe him. An old trick to get him to respond. Which naturally Drumwald did.

Jimbo could see the wheels spinning up there, turning, Drumwald wondering if there was any reason—legally—to keep Jimbo out of it. He knew the precise instant that the man figured that there wasn't. It was like a light bulb going on over the guy's head.

"The undercover operative in this case was a Chicago police sergeant named James Marino." He paused for breath as the collected reporters gasped, some of them old-timers who remembered who Jimbo was, others just shocked that this man had given out the name of a key witness against the mob well before the man's testimony was to be heard by the grand jury.

Drumwald rubbed it in. He said, "Some of you veteran reporters," gazing through his questioner as if a woman had no business in a room with men who made history, "might remember him from the White Heat Bandit case."

Drumwald smiled directly into the camera, figuring he'd snookered the woman, instead of being cornered and put out of his misery like the dumb rat son of a bitch that he was.

"The cassette came directly from the mayor's office." Lettierri was opening a window now, his own smoke beginning to get to him. "And man, Jimbo, let me tell you, she is *pissed*."

Jimbo said, "I bet."

"Well, it was her case from the beginning. A way to make headlines and sweep right back into office at reelection, on the tide. This was supposed to make Greylord look small-time by comparison. Crime in the streets is supposed to be the number-one issue. Her opponents have been yelling for four years that a black woman won't crack down on crime. As if she likes to see it, the city on fire again."

"Hey, screw the election, Commander. What about *me*?"

"*You?*" Lettierri said, "*You* have about"—he checked his watch again—"fifteen minutes to get to city hall with me. Judge Haney will meet us there. I managed to keep Gizmo out of it."

"Thank God for that. I can see him saying to the mayor, 'What's going on, pretty mama?'"

"She wants all the principals there for her own press conference. Try and get some of the wind back in her sails."

Jimbo said, "Do I have to do this?"

For the first time, Lettierri smiled. "You could always resign."

"Or commit suicide."

Lettierri's smile broadened. He said, "Blow the whole

case out of the water, that. Unless you could do it in a way to make it look like the mob killed you. Then maybe we could make something positive out of this mess."

In the car Jimbo tried to keep it light, asking Lettierri what he should call the mayor, Mrs. Your Honor, or what. Lettierri told him not to worry about it; the mayor probably wouldn't let him get a word in.

Lettierri said that they would now have no choice but to assign men to Jimbo, and Jimbo told him to stop the fucking car, right now, he was through. They argued until Lettierri ordered him to accept it and Jimbo responded in a way that ended the conversation right then and there. Lettierri drove angrily, hand on the horn, his face a set mask. He looked ready to kill.

Jimbo said, "I hate this political shit, you know it?" and did not get a response. He said, "Do I have to do this?" Nothing. He said, "I get it. You're mad at me because I didn't say good-bye to you yesterday morning at Water Tower Place."

This time Lettierri grunted. Still staring out at the traffic, looking like a stone idol carved by mushroom-eating tribesmen. He said, "Hey, Mr. Macho, why don't you just shut the fuck up."

This did work to shut Jimbo up, because he was remembering that with all that had happened in the office, he'd forgotten to ask whether they had found anything at Barboza's house. He decided it would wait. If it had been important, Lettierri would have told him already.

The legendary fifth floor of city hall intimidated Jimbo, particularly when they walked past the pressroom and reporters surged to the door to get a look at him. Lettierri paused at the door to the mayor's office and they both had to show their ID to the huge uniformed patrol officer-body-guard before they were allowed access to the inner chambers. Inside was a spacious waiting room, with an attractive middle-aged black woman sitting behind a desk. She smiled warmly at them. "Hello, the mayor's been waiting for you. The judge is already inside." She sounded to Jimbo as if the two of them were doing the mayor a favor by dropping in, rather than the whole thing being a command performance. She led them to the door leading to the inner sanctum, opened it and waved them in, Lettierri entering first as protocol demanded.

She was a tall woman, filling her dress, wearing white in stark contrast to her black face and shiny styled hair. A woman to whom vanity was just a word but who had nevertheless dressed with an eye for the cameras. She was sitting behind a cluttered desk, talking with a couple of men, one white, the other black, both of them wearing suits and calling her by her first name. Jimbo got an immediate sense of her power and charisma because when she saw them she stopped talking and pinned him with a look, evaluating, sizing him up. The mayor showed him, in that look, the strength and will he had only heard about before. Tommy Campo was supposed to have that kind of aura. As did Al Capone. John Kennedy. He'd never seen a woman with it, though, until now. She was a force to be reckoned with. Even Lettierri was walking softly, like he was in church.

She finished looking him over and seemed to thaw suddenly. A good smiler, the mayor. She came around the desk, her hand going out. "Franko, good to see you again," with just a trace of South Side drawl in her voice, which surprised Jimbo. When he saw her on television, she spoke with the precise enunciation of a carefully schooled radio announcer.

Then she was taking his hand, giving it a man's handshake. "Jimbo Marino. This is a pleasure." She said, "I heard you're quite a character." The mayor tipped him a fast wink, obviously spotting his confusion. She said, "Richie Corneale told me how you straightened out those federal clods. They wanted to surround you with marshals, make it look like you were struggling for survival. Get all the glory for themselves, maybe plant a few seeds in the minds of potential jurors." In spite of his troubles, Jimbo smiled at her. He'd made a friend in the right political camp, apparently. That was rare for a man in his position, especially one with his temperament.

Speaking to the mayor, but for Lettierri's ears, he said, "I can take care of myself, Mayor." And she eyed him again, no longer just the political animal sizing up her warrior, but looking at him as a woman looks at a man. Jimbo felt his cheeks flush at her frank stare.

She said, "I'm sure you can."

He was saved from having to think up a response by the sound of a toilet flushing. In this hallowed room, the familiar noise seemed almost otherworldly. A paneled door opened before the water stopped swirling and Judge Chris Haney entered the room, wiping his hands with a paper towel. Jimbo could tell that it was scented; he could smell it all the way across the room. Jimbo's buddy Chris, a big tall sucker who'd spent two tours as a Marine captain in Vietnam, going to sleep each night with two flak jackets on —one on his chest, and one wrapped around his head because his own troops had a habit of throwing grenades into the officers' hooches at night to show their displeasure with the way things were going. So Chris would not be too very impressed with the trappings of a mayor, or by protocol. The mayor turned away from Jimbo and smiled at Chris. She cleared her throat.

"We never had any plans to put you before the public, Jimbo, until that ass Drumwald pulled the plug out this afternoon." As an afterthought, she added, "God, I hate election years." She studied Jimbo again, putting the weight of the city on his shoulders. He was getting a feel for her, of the strength in her mind and spirit. He liked this woman.

She said, "Now, here's what I want you guys to do . . ." She was speaking to all of them, but her eyes never left Jimbo's face.

As they walked down to the pressroom, Jimbo hung back, waiting to fall into step with Chris. When they were side by side, he whispered, "Do I have to go through with this?"

The twinkle Jimbo had seen so many times came into Chris's eyes. He shrugged his shoulders, the suitcoat he was wearing kind of rising up and settling down. It looked like an Alp in an earthquake. Chris said in his loud voice, "You could always resign."

Later, the three of them were in the lounge of the Bismarck Hotel, waiting for the news to come on. Lettierri had lightened up as soon as he had had a couple of Brandy Alexanders in him, and if Jimbo could get what had happened out of his mind, it might seem like old times, three buddies who believed in the law having a good time. The problem was, Jimbo couldn't.

He looked at Lettierri, whose eyes were already going a little glassy; man, the guy just couldn't hold his liquor. He was listening raptly to a story Chris was telling.

There had been a black kid robbing a currency exchange, and the only problem, as far as the rights of the defendant were concerned, was in the way the plainclothesman had arrested him. Chris told the story with a lot of body language and impeccable timing. He had Lettierri on the edge of his seat, the smile growing broader as he got into the story. Chris would stop to bum a cigarette from Lettierri, or to order another round, pretending to ignore Lettierri's impatience.

Jimbo could not get into it. He sat with both hands wrapped around the bottle of Miller in front of him. He hadn't even tasted the first two. He was on his sixth now and feeling clearheaded, trying to listen to Chris, but his eyes kept going back to the TV set on a platform at the far end of the bar. He was waiting for the news broadcast. Dreading it.

The story ended when Chris told about the little blue-haired old lady telling the court, reluctantly, that the arresting cop had not said, "Police, drop the weapon," as the officer had testified, but rather, "Freeze motherfucker or you're one dead nigger!" The defendant had wanted Chris to throw the case out because he had been unjustly defamed.

Jimbo thought that he'd probably get away with it. Stranger things had happened. Punks got to carry guns and throw their weight around, beating up old folks, and when you busted them, boy, you had better not even think about laying a hand on them, even if they had their peckers up an eighty-year-old woman's backside. You'd be violating their rights.

The world was full of psychos hiding behind the Constitution and the legal system, behind the laws, hiding out and pulling out chapter and verse, citing actual cases and precedents when you busted them. Animals like GiGi Parnell did whatever they wanted and never even had to go to ground. They'd kill someone and bury the weapon and throw their hands up when you brought them in for questioning, saying, "Who me?" with their eyes rolled up, then get a lawyer to sue for abuse of process. You'd talk to the lawyer like a man, tell him you had his client dead to rights, and the lawyer would look at you and say, "Prove it." Jimbo wondered how come more lawyers weren't held up by their own clients after proving to them how easy it was to walk away.

Chris dragged Jimbo away from his dark thoughts. "Hey, movie star, why so morose? Hell, you're going to be famous." Chris saw the dregs of humanity every day, saw injustice, and had to go along with it a lot of the time. Chris saw pictures and listened to chilling testimony related to every evil act that could be hatched in the human mind, and he could go home to his wife and kids and sit down to dinner like everyone else. While Jimbo sat there in the bar at the Bismarck thinking about what he'd do if he ever had the chance to get GiGi alone in a room without witnesses.

Lettierri said, "I think he's scared GiGi Parnell's gonna see him on the television and come whip his ass for him." Lettierri was slurring his words, his manner telling them that he knew how far away from the truth his statement was.

But Jimbo knew that it was closer to the reality of his thoughts than he'd ever admit.

Chris got all solemn for a moment, then said, "Jimbo, if this guy aces you, I swear, I'll pull every string I have dangling to get him in my courtroom and I swear to you—" He started giggling now, and Lettierri was laughing too, Jimbo the only one being a party pooper, not even looking at Chris, who got control of himself and finished. "—I'll get him in my court and give him a hundred and ha-ha-ha, a hundred and heh-heh—" Lettierri finished it for him. "And ninety-nine years." And the two of them were off, laughing to beat the band, Chris hitting the bar in a little drumroll with his fingers, Lettierri giggling drunkenly. Chris managed to get out, "Without parole!" and that really set them off, the two of them making a spectacle of themselves in perhaps the most influential bar in the city.

Jimbo poured down the beer and watched the TV set.

When Chris went to the men's room, Jimbo asked Lettierri, "What happened at Barboza's house?"

Lettierri looked confused for a moment, and Jimbo hoped to God that he'd leave first so Jimbo could call the Mobile Crime Squad and have them arrest him for drunk driving. Teach him a lesson about getting uppity with his friends.

"Last night you mean?"

Jimbo nodded.

Lettierri said, "Just about the same as at the warehouse. GiGi was there, too, or someone else was. That's one of the reasons I threw out the murder theory. The front of the house was shot up. I figure GiGi tried for him at the house and missed, went to the warehouse to wait. Barboza comes in and GiGi holds him up, takes the money, only it ain't enough, so GiGi—"

"What about the house?" Jimbo said.

Lettierri looked about to say something mean, then maybe figured out he was too drunk to defend himself against a man who was staring at him as intently as Jimbo was at the moment. He said, "The old lady, she shows us around; we got a warrant for the guy, so we need her like we need a hole in the head; she's walking around behind us, telling us he ain't home, wringing her fat little hands, carrying a rosary around with her." He lit a cigarette and looked at Jimbo, smiling again. He said, "You ever seen that woman? Jeez, ugly?"

"What *happened*?"

"Christ, lighten up, will you, Jimbo? You won't let me

help you, you won't let the department help you, and now you can't even lighten up and have a few laughs. What're you gonna do? Leave here and go jump on the mayor? I seen the way she was looking at you."

"Goddamnit, Franko."

Lettierri sighed. "She tells us she hasn't seen him since he left on business that morning. We know this is bullshit because we got the phone wired and the office, too. Thanks to Gizmo. We know her husband left the house at eight fifty-four that very night. But we don't tell her we know. He might still call, say something we can use. I ask her, I says to her, 'Mrs. Barboza, what about the brick chunks scattered all around the porch, there, looks like someone took a couple of shots at the front of the house with a cannon." He took a deep drag on the cigarette, butted it, downed his drink and called the bartender over. Lettierri ordered a round for all of them, got another pack of cigarettes and removed the wrapping. Without thinking about it, Jimbo thumbed one out.

"This fat dago broad, excuse me, Jimbo, but I'm Italian, too, there just ain't no other way to describe that woman, she looks me dead in the eye and tells me, 'We're having some remodeling work done.'"

"So what'd you do?"

"Do? The fuck you think I did? I cut my losses and went home to bed."

Jimbo felt dizzy from the cigarette, a Camel, shit, first time in years and he had to start on the strongest brand. Chris Haney was working his way back to the bar, stopping at tables to say hello to politicians who were unwinding after office hours and getting down to the real business of running the city. He came over to the bar and shook another cigarette from Lettierri's pack. "I quit, you know." He was grinning, ignoring the smoking butt in Jimbo's hand.

Chris said, "You ever been in the mayor's shithouse? Jesus, scented soap, scented paper, one of those little things hanging down into the toilet water, scented like they have in urinals." He and Lettierri were enjoying themselves, waiting for the newscast so they could see themselves on television. Jimbo would gladly pass.

Chris said, "Jimbo. Franko. And your little buddy, Gizmo. Maybe I should start calling myself Christo. We could be the O brothers."

Lettierri said, "It's been done. Chico, Harpo and Groucho." And they were off again, laughing and drawing stares from the growing crowd.

Jimbo had never paid any attention to it before, but Chris Haney dwarfed him. He noticed it now as they watched the news, saw the two of them, Chris and Lettierri, up there really dwarfing him, and Chris was a couple of inches taller than Lettierri. Jimbo guessed that he himself looked about as tall as the mayor. Great big guys up there and the star of the show without his elevator shoes, looking like a cop trying to look like Frank Serpico for the cameras. Jimbo listened and watched as the mayor praised him, the judge interpreted legal questions, Lettierri fielded all the straight questions and his undercover career flew away on wings. From now on he would be chained to a desk next to Francis Mahon, a guy who knew everything there was to know and was relegated to a passive role in the war on crime in Chicago. He felt like crying. He ordered another round.

Three rounds later, Lettierri staggered out to the street, and Jimbo decided not to drop the dime on him. The commander had told Jimbo what he wanted to know. He and

Chris repaired to a booth, Jimbo ordering a pack of Camels to take with them.

Chris with his martini and Jimbo with his beer, looking at each other. At last Jimbo said, "She didn't know, did she?"

Chris said, "She was aware that there was an undercover operation happening, but no, she didn't know your name. We followed your wishes on that one." Jimbo was afraid to ask what they hadn't followed his wishes on.

He wouldn't have worked undercover if anyone other than his three closest friends had known about it, and he had made that clear. Even now he would feel betrayed and demolished if they had told anyone else. Chris would not even tell his wife; this Jimbo knew. And Lettierri would turn in his badge before jeopardizing one of his men's lives. Lettierri could be a real pain in the ass sometimes, but he was solid where it counted. And Gizmo, well. Gizmo would commit suicide before risking Jimbo in any way. Jimbo was the only family Gizmo had. Not a lot of people took the time to learn how to sign so they could communicate with a deaf man.

No, he didn't want to know. Barboza was gone, on the run or dead. The operation was a bust. It would grab headlines and some low-level hoods would go away for a couple of years, but the mob would flourish as it always had, and if someone had done something to derail this operation, Jimbo did not want to know about it anymore.

"You think I'd tell her?" Chris said, referring to the mayor. He said, "Christ, you're fucking paranoid." But his eyes were twinkling.

Jimbo was drunk or close to it. Feeling no pain, that was for sure. The cigarettes were robbing his oxygen, making him feel more light-headed perhaps than he already was. Anyway, drunk enough to say, "Chris, I think I'm going to kill GiGi Parnell."

Judge Chris Haney stirred his martini, probably wondering how much of what Jimbo had just said was drunken nonsense. He looked Jimbo square in the eye, no twinkle in his own now, serious, death about to be discussed, perhaps murder.

"Why, Jimbo."

Jimbo took a deep breath, appreciating Chris. Anyone else, they'd have argued or started talking shit, tell him he was drunk and to go home and sleep it off. Chris had said, "Why, Jimbo" and he would tell him. He would tell him because it was important for Chris to know. For someone to know. And right here in the bar with the booze flowing was as good a place as any to bare his soul.

He said, "Chris, every cop in the city has put away some fool, talks trash, sends cards from the joint, makes threats. What you do, you watch your back for a few days after the jerk gets out, you see him hanging around, you set him up, put him back inside.

"A lot of other guys, they go and do their time, never blame the cop or the judge, they know they fucked up. And some guys, they go into deep depression after the conviction, look at you in court like you betrayed them, hey, the judge is sending me away where the criminals are, man. They wind up in an interracial marriage inside and survive. Three kinds of guys, usually, the vindictive kind, the kind who don't blame you, and the guys who feel you betrayed them, hurt their feelings but there's nothing they can do about it. Then there's guys like GiGi Parnell."

Jimbo called the waitress aside and ordered a nightcap for them.

"Chris, I'm gonna tell you something. I was a rookie cop still on probation, about to go out and fight crime, writing tickets on the Seventy-ninth Street Causeway, and we get a little speech at roll call, this dangerous fugitive who crossed state lines to avoid prosecution is known to be in the Miami area, just the sarge going through the motions. He hands out flyers with GiGi Parnell's picture on it, a description. I forget all about it as soon as I'm out the door. Let the feds find their own fugitives. They get all the glory. Later, off duty, I'm in the post office getting a roll of stamps, for chrissakes, and there the guy is, wearing a silk shirt with pelicans all over it, bananas, red shorts, sandals, skinny little guy with blond hair looks about a hundred and a half, his hair white now from the sun. He's in the line right next to me. I go out, wait in front, real casual, a guy taking his time wondering what he's gonna do for the night; Parnell comes out and walks into the alley; he's parked in the tow-away zone, too hip to park on the street and walk a block like everyone else. I follow him, broad daylight in downtown Miami; I'm wearing white cutoffs and an undershirt, no piece, nothing. He turns around and looks at me, his hand on the door handle. 'Got a problem, there, shitheel?' he says to me, tough guy, looks like Richard Widmark forty years ago. I tell him I'm the heat and he's busted; the little guy about as big around as one of my thighs, Chris, he smiles at me. He fucking *smiles* at me. Then he attacks."

Jimbo's hands were shaking as he raised the bottle to his mouth. He lit another Camel and inhaled deeply, remembering.

"Chris, I never been in a fight in my life lasted more than thirty seconds. You bust a guy one, he goes down, maybe you kick him a couple of times to keep him from getting ideas, it's over." Jimbo sucked the butt down nearly to his fingers, stubbed it.

"We fought for fifteen minutes in that goddamn alley before a squad car shows up, and this guy, this skinny little *shit*, he fights the two guys from the squad for maybe another five minutes before they club his ass down. Meanwhile I'm lying in the alley, gasping for breath, my nose broken and two teeth missing, covered with bruises; knowing how Ali felt after the first brawl with Frazier. And wondering what would have happened if the squad guys hadn't shown, if someone somewhere hadn't been a good citizen and called the cops to tell them about a couple of guys beating on each other in an alley.

"Chris, they finally get the cuffs on this guy and I get to my feet; I'm standing at the mouth of the alley as they drive away, about to give my report to my own guys, and our eyes lock when the squad stops to check out traffic before turning onto the street. I look at GiGi Parnell and he looks at me and we know, Chris, right there the both of us know that this was just round one."

"And you think this is something personal between the two of you, now, right? That's why you refused protection so far?"

"I don't *think* Chris, I *know*. This won't end until GiGi Parnell and I are in a room somewhere alone with our clothes off and our fists up. He won't let it."

"And you would, right? I mean, let it end?"

Jimbo took a minute to answer, but he finally said, "No, I don't see why I should."

He entered the house, carrying his packages, staggering, sniffing, man, the place smelled like a zoo. Well, it was his own fault. This time he couldn't blame Sparky. He'd left the animal alone in the house for an entire day without giving her a chance to go out. He dropped his package on the living room table, staggered to the basement door, opened it. Sparky came out like a bolt of lightning, barking, howling, jumping up and down, pawing Jimbo roughly. He went to the kitchen door and let her out to play in the fenced backyard while he worked.

He got a Miller out of the fridge, opened it, and went out of the kitchen to the living room again. The red light on his recorder was flashing wildly. How did everybody get his number? Ignoring it, he picked up the phone and dialed Gizmo, hoping his friend was sitting at his computer so he wouldn't have to leave his own message. When the computer voice ordered him to speak, he said, "Giz? Jimbo. Pick up if you're watching," then waited the mandatory three seconds.

The computerized voice came over the line with: "How-you-doing-Robert-Redford." Jimbo smiled.

"I'm home, you feel like dropping by for a couple beers."

"You-live-in-a-white-neighborhood."

"So make sure you grin real big so I can see you."

"Your-mammy-could-find-me-in-the-dark," then a dial tone. Gizmo had hung up.

Smiling, Jimbo went to the kitchen and got the buckets out from under the sink. The detergent and the Pine Sol, too. He breathed through his mouth as he walked down the steps, his lips still twisted with the remnants of the grin. He always felt better after talking to Gizmo.

He had opened all the basement windows and was scrubbing the floor for the third time with Pine Sol and hot water when he heard Gizmo stomping down the basement steps.

"It smells like shit in here," Gizmo said.

Jimbo turned to him so Gizmo could read his lips and said, clearly, enunciating each word perfectly, "It is shit," then turned back to his scrubbing. Gizmo tromped up the steps and grabbed them both a beer, brought them downstairs. Jimbo heard him sniffing.

"You smoking again?" Gizmo had a habit when he wanted to ask a question of making his voice jump about three octaves on the last syllable of the sentence, and when he spoke it reminded Jimbo of his mother or a school-teacher reprimanding him. He smiled and finished scrubbing, dropped the rag back into the bucket and turned to Gizmo, accepting the beer gratefully.

"Just a few," he said, motioning for them to go upstairs. He was smiling to beat the band because he was about to get the drop on Gizmo.

Jimbo walked casually to the refrigerator and opened it, looked inside, waiting for Gizmo to walk out of the kitchen and into the living room. The second Gizmo was out of sight, he raced to the kitchen door and opened it, yelled for the dog and Sparky came racing in, all sleek muscle and teeth, bounding in faster than Jimbo ever thought any animal short of a cheetah could move. He smiled and followed the madly barking dog into the living room, saw Gizmo standing there with a sad, sad look on his face, rigid, looking like a black cigar store Indian.

Sparky was giving Gizmo the same treatment she'd given Jimbo the day before; growling, her muzzle stuck in Gizmo's crotch, sniffing madly. Gizmo said, "Asshole," through clenched teeth, his face looking sad and terrified while Jimbo collapsed with laughter, holding his belly, eyes streaming tears, laughing in great whoops and guffaws until Sparky squatted, her muzzle never leaving Gizmo's crotch. Her teeth bared and making deep snarling sounds in her throat, Sparky peed on the living room carpet and then it was Gizmo's turn to laugh. Sparky finished up as Jimbo reached her and swatted hard with the flat of his hand, hitting her square in the behind and she spun, snarling, backing away, looking from Jimbo to Gizmo.

"Bad dog!" Jimbo shouted while Gizmo relaxed, apparently relieved that the heat was off him. Jimbo walked to the table and ripped the packages open, pulled on the heavy-duty snowmobile outfit, snapping it closed while he cursed Sparky. He pulled the hood up over his head and grabbed the hockey mask, which had fallen to the floor, and snapped it into place, angry because he'd had to remove the hood to get it on. Next he roughly pushed his hands into a pair of hockey gloves.

Gizmo was sitting on the couch now, looking as if he'd just witnessed the sight of his best friend having gone round the bend, but he leaned back with an anticipatory smile on his face and watched; Jimbo could see him through the eye slits in the goalie mask. Jimbo advanced on Sparky, who was eyeing him quizzically, shaking her tiny nub of a tail, her hindquarters rocking back and forth from her frenzied movement, her tongue hanging from her mouth, looking as if she was dying of thirst.

Jimbo grabbed her by the throat with his left hand and slapped her hard across the muzzle with his right, then again, and she pulled back and snapped at him, her teeth tearing into the arm of the snowmobile suit. He swung the hand again, back and forth, pulling her forward with his left hand as he slapped her with his right, until they were in the little puddle of urine. Jimbo pushed her muzzle roughly into the puddle and hollered, "No!" at the top of his lungs until Sparky was quivering and cowering, defeated. Now came the hard part.

Jimbo squatted next to Sparky and held her muzzle so she could not look away, then with his left hand slowly reached up and removed the hockey mask. Sparky lunged and as Jimbo fell onto his back, she was licking his face and he hollered and sat up and she sat down, obedient now, looking at him. He pointed at the urine puddle. "No!" he shouted, and Sparky lowered her head, looking at him from her submissive position, eyes rolling to the tops of their sockets.

Jimbo began to take off the outfit, sweating inside it.

He'd thought, when Sparky'd lunged at him, that she was attacking, and his heart was just now getting back to normal. Gizmo was looking at him very strangely.

"What was that all about?" Gizmo said.

"Defining my territory," Jimbo said. "Marking it."

Gizmo said, "Jimbo, you are very, very strange."

Jimbo was scrubbing the spot on the floor when Gizmo said, "And speaking of strange, man, you go undercover, you go all the way. You dye your hair and eyebrows, take off the mustache, lose twenty-thirty pounds. Your own mother wouldn't recognize you. Except for one thing. You go up against the mob and use damn near the same name as your own. That's weird."

Jimbo put the cleaning gear away and came back into the room, staggering some. He was feeling good. "You've never seen *Nevada Smith,* with Steve McQueen, or you'd understand."

"What?"

"It's a movie. Steve McQueen goes after the guys who killed his family. Brian Keith tells him, always use a name almost exactly like your own. Someone yells at you, calling your real name, you turn; you can always say hey, it sounds just like mine. Someone would have got wise, Barboza or somebody, called me Marino instead of Perino, my undercover name, I had every right in the world to respond. Shit, you got any idea how many Perinos and Marinos there are out there? Both common names. For dagos."

"Everything you do, you do the way some jerk in the movies would do it."

"Hey, don't knock it. Movies are pretty realistic."

"Except that, in the movies, they kill you, you get up, walk away. In real life, they kill you, you stay dead."

"Life is either a risk or it's nothing."

"Like I said, Jimbo, you're a weird fucker."

Jimbo said, "You want strange, Gizmo?" Feeling no pain and a little fed up with everything. "I'll tell you something strange."

Gizmo said, "Do me a favor, okay, Jimbo? You talk all night, I'll listen, but lay off the beer. I'm having a real hard time reading you."

Jimbo felt a moment's shame; he'd embarrassed his friend by slurring his words drunkenly and assuming that Gizmo could hear him like anyone else. Making a distinct effort to enunciate, he said: "I'm a cop. Been one for a third of my life. So what does that stroke Drumwald say to me this morning, before lunch, strictly off the record? He says to me, he goes, 'We'll give you around-the-clock protection.'" He stared at Gizmo expectantly.

Gizmo shrugged and said, "Sounds good to me."

Jimbo shook his head angrily, just drunk enough to be philosophical. "I told you already, I'm a fucking cop!"

"Hey, I know what you do for a living."

Jimbo was feeling that he wasn't getting through to Gizmo. Maybe he hadn't explained himself fully. He leaned forward, staring hard into Gizmo's face, trying to make him feel what he was saying as well as read the words from his lips.

"You don't see anything wrong with a cop having bodyguards to protect him from the bad guys? Huh? In the car, after Lettierri lays the bomb on me about the press conference, he says to me, 'Well, Marino, with this kind of coverage, your face in the papers and the TV, we'll find some men to guard you around the clock.'" Jimbo sat back, ready to tell how he'd handled the insult, but Gizmo interrupted him.

"You know who you're playing with here, don't you, Jimbo?" Even with that toneless voice, there seemed to be wonder there, disbelief. "This is the fucking mob, Jimbo.

Not some rapist or even the White Heat Bandit. These are the guys who kill people just because they think there is a remote chance that the guy might be talking to the cops."

Now Jimbo was amazed. "There hasn't been a cop killed by the mob in this city since its inception."

"Since its what?" Gizmo hadn't read the last word properly.

"Since it was founded. And I'll tell you something else. The day they tell me I need a guard to do my job is the day I throw my fucking badge out the front door. I am a cop, one of the good guys, goddamnit. I work to keep scum like Barboza off the streets. Stoolies hide, not cops. At least not this cop.

"Lettierri says to me, if I give him a hard time about it he'll lock me up in protective custody, and I told him if I see one squad car, one tail, one cop protecting me instead of out there on the street doing his job, then I walk, I clam up, I'll refuse to testify."

"What did he say?"

"He clammed up and didn't say another word to me almost until after the conference. Until he gets a couple of drinks in him and into a joke-telling mood with Chris Haney, then we're buddies again.

"Going to get my car, Chris wants to know how dumb I can be, so I ask him how many guys he's sent away, and if he hires bodyguards every time one of them gets out of the slam. He didn't have anything to say to that."

"Say you're right. Jimbo, if the mob doesn't come after you, which they probably won't, you're right about them, they couldn't take the heat that would come down if a cop caught it and it could be linked to them, okay, but what about GiGi Parnell?"

It was a day for telling secrets. Jimbo had done it in the bar earlier with Chris, telling him about the fight in the alley, how it had been plain old blind luck. Now it was time to give Gizmo his share of Jimbo's private life.

"Let me tell you something." I was never afraid of anything in my life until that day in the alley with GiGi Parnell." He said it all in a rush, getting it out before rational thought and pride could stop him.

"That's something to be ashamed of, eh, being afraid?" Gizmo was eyeing him strangely, anger there and something else—Jimbo couldn't put his finger on it right away, and then he got it. Gizmo was embarrassed, ashamed of something that he was about to share.

"You know what I got to put up with, every day of my life? Sitting in my basement with the brass and all the dicks coming down there, needing this or that right away? You don't know about fear, about turning your back on someone and knowing good and damn well that as soon as you do they're cussing at you knowing you can't hear them. I turned around more than one time to see some cop saying something nasty about me and then had to pretend that I didn't read him. It's enough to make you paranoid, Jimbo.

"Or if the house starts on fire at night, Jimbo, how am I supposed to know? The hours I keep, a hearing dog is out of the question. Thing would starve to death before I come home one night.

"How about going out and not being about to hear a car horn honk or somebody yelling 'Look out'?

"And here's the big one, Jimbo. Listen carefully. When I was a kid, I was terrified to go out of the house, man, because every kid on the goddamn block would point and make fun of me, call me dummy and beat me up because I was short and scrawny.

"You want to tell me about fear, you want me to feel sorry for you because some psycho got you scared ten years ago, you come to the wrong guy. Shit, I envy you your one fear."

Jimbo said, "It's not the same thing."

"Hell it's not."

Jimbo turned his head a little so Gizmo could not read him and said, "It's not." He turned to Gizmo full front then and said, "Gizmo, it's the principle of the thing. I am a cop, not a junkie stoolie. I refuse to hide and be guarded because someone I busted got out of jail, and I don't care who the guy is. I can take care of myself."

"How about I alarm the house for you."

"I'm gonna dye my hair back the way it was before I go to bed. Grow my mustache back. Carry my piece with me everywhere I go. Even to the john. I'll be careful."

"And you'll have alarms on all the doors and windows, too."

"Okay, you can do me a favor, alarm the place for me. But that's as far as I'll go, Gizmo. That is it."

Gizmo said, "Jimbo, why don't you tell me the high points of the last few months in your life, because you are really starting to piss me off and I'd like another beer before I go on home."

Jimbo, glad that the serious stuff was out of the way, began to tell Gizmo all of the things that the U.S. Attorney did not want to hear. Jimbo knew he'd been right in the bar. If he thought about it enough, he could find rationalizations, bullshit his way out of the reality of things, find ways to make people think he was noble rather than just wanting to kill GiGi Parnell.

7 While Jimbo was telling Gizmo about the week off he had coming and what he'd been doing the past three months, GiGi Parnell was doing what he'd set out to do early the evening before. He was getting his dick wet. The little babe under him was in love, she'd told him that half a dozen times in the twenty hours since they'd been in the room, getting especially turned on when she'd learned that he was the White Heat Bandit. She'd been a teenager when the case was in the headlines, or claimed to be. GiGi put her closer to thirty-five than the twenty-seven she admitted to, but he never blamed a babe for lying about her age. His mom had always told him that was a woman's prerogative.

She'd wanted to hear the whole story, how a renegade thief had been caught because he'd been sending money home to his mother and they'd learned he was in Florida from the postmark on the letters he'd sent with the money orders. She thought it was romantic. She saw him as a rebel, a modern-day John Dillinger. She told him that he never would have been caught if he hadn't loved his mom, and he told her that going to prison was worth it. Through tears she'd told him how very sweet he was, and a few minutes after that she declared her love.

Now GiGi was driving into her, staring directly into her wide-open eyes, green ones alive with passion, her mouth whispering words into his ear that he'd never heard a woman use before. She wanted it bad, this babe.

But his mind was elsewhere. He'd gotten half-drunk and he'd eaten well, and he'd gotten his oil changed. Now it was time to think about business.

After he finished up here this time, he was going to take off and get his money from Brian, give him back his car and maybe throw him a couple grand for letting him borrow it. Hell, he could afford it. While the girl, Agnes, was sleeping earlier, he'd called the lawyer and been told that he was the sole beneficiary in his mom's will, which he already knew. What surprised him was the fact that his mom had left him, in addition to the paid-off house, $213,000. And here he'd always thought she was broke. When he'd heard the news he'd had to fight off resentment, because the first thing he'd thought was that he'd spent ten years in the penitentiary because he was sending her money from his little capers in Florida and she was always, his entire life, complaining about how broke she was. He had split everything fifty-fifty with his mom and now she'd left him almost a quarter of a million dollars, counting the house. He'd covered his shock and told the lawyer he'd pick up a check the next day and hung up the telephone while the lawyer was blustering about how you just didn't come in and pick up a check for— *Click.*

Which brought him to another thing. If he'd known he'd been left so well off by his mom, he wouldn't have robbed Mikey Barboza the night before and risked the wrath of the entire Chicago Mafia. Geez.

His mind wandered back to himself as he felt the now familiar stirrings down there and he focused on Agnes and watched her face turn red, saw her shut her eyes tight and toss her sweating head back and forth on the pillow, shouting obscenities, actually begging him to make her come.

Sweating himself, he obliged her and himself, staying astride and kissing her for a while, listening to her gush on and on about how much she loved him, GiGi eating it up, feeling good, forgetting all about the people who wanted to kill him. He was still young, and he was rich and he had a woman who loved him. If the mob wanted to mess with him now, when he was on top, well, that was a two-way street.

She came into the shower after him, while he was soaped down with his face lifted to the hot spray, and she scared him badly and he had to teach her a lesson. He pushed her roughly away while he was still jumping in shock and figuring out who it was, and he had her throat in his hands before her head bounced off the tiles. Soap was running into his eyes now, stinging them, but he ignored it, working through the pain, the way he'd learned to in the joint.

"Don't ever sneak up on me, again," GiGi told Agnes. *"Ever."*

A half-hour later they were in their separate cars. She followed him. GiGi had wanted to spend another night in the hotel, but Agnes said that was a waste of money; he had a house and she had a North Side apartment; why splurge on rooms at the Holiday Inn? He decided to spend maybe one more night away from the house, try and get a line on Barboza, see what was happening before walking into a trap or something. There was an even chance that he had nothing to worry about. If the mob was after him, they'd have found him. Hell, he had given his real name to the clerk at the Holiday Inn, without thinking about it. That meant Barboza was going it alone, which sounded right. The way he figured, it would have to be last night; Barboza having to settle his own beefs. Campo and the mob were too busy to interfere in petty squabbles. He'd get his money from Brian, find out where Agnes lived, and take her car and go take care of business with Mikey Barboza. Maybe paying the mob back out of the hundred grand he had hidden at Brian's house, less his twenty, of course, maybe that was a good idea.

He parked the Cadillac at the curb and waved to Agnes to wait, then bounded up the steps to Brian's house and rang the bell, shave and a haircut, two-bits. He was feeling jaunty, in control. Bad.

He knew something was wrong the second Brian opened the door, and a second later knew what it was. Brian was looking at him with a sheepish grin, like he'd been caught with his pants down, in the saddle or something. What it was, GiGi knew, was good old cellmate and fellow Aryan Brotherhood partner Brian Solt had copped some of the cash.

The trouble with Brian was, he couldn't keep his mind off pussy. Even in the joint, he'd always had a sissy ready to take care of him, all hours of the day. Brian would skip exercise or karate class to get his ashes hauled, pissing off some of the more militant members of the Brotherhood. Every time, GiGi had gone to bat for him, getting him out of scrapes with the militants, some of whom even went so far as to suggest Brian be thrown out of the nation. Which would have turned Brian into some stud's woman, instead of the other way around. And GiGi had saved him. Foolishly. His mom had always told him not to trust anyone who didn't have the same last name as he did, and she'd been right.

He didn't let on to Brian right away, though. He smiled back, shook the keys off his little finger and tossed them into the air, catching them behind his back, hearing that phony little bitch of a wife of Brian's clapping when he caught them. Not mad at him anymore, uh-uh. Sucking up now, now that they'd ripped him off. GiGi sauntered into the house as if he was strutting the tier, showing his strength, his power.

"Bro*ham*," he said. Then he smiled. "Sorry about taking the car so long, bro." He tipped a wink at Brian's old lady, rubbing it in a little bit, and said, "I was getting my dick wet." And the both of them, they acted as if Milton Berle was in the room, cracking up, sneaking looks at each other. GiGi said, "I got someone waiting; let's get the—uh—the business done." He gave them a wide smile, playing dumb.

Brian led him to the extra bedroom where the dog stayed and shooed her from the room, closed the door behind him. Then put his foot in his mouth, as far as GiGi was concerned. He said, "It's all there, Geege. Every penny of it."

GiGi said, "Well, why shouldn't it be?" He was smiling still, but letting a puzzled frown cloud his face.

Brian was sweating now, his face looking ready to crack from the strain of having to hold the smile in place. He hurriedly said, "No reason, no reason, Geege, just making conversation, you know?" And he backed out of the room, sliding out of the door and closing it shut behind him. Immediately GiGi raced across the room and lay down against the floorboards next to the closet, whistling, so Brian would think he was getting his money out of the doggie bed. He got his gun ready, held it in two hands, aimed at the doorway.

The door flew open, Brian's old lady pushing it open, releasing the knob and stepping back as Brian flew into the room, a gigantic pistol held in both hands, pointed where he thought GiGi would be and GiGi fired twice, catching Brian in the chest both times. GiGi leaped to his feet, catching Brian's old lady before she got out of the hallway, his hand on the back of her head, dragging her by the hair to the ground, dropping his gun and putting his right hand over her mouth.

"Where is it?"

Her terrified eyes begged him to release the grip he had on her face. He relaxed; he'd been squeezing pretty hard. There were bruises around her mouth from where he'd been holding her. "Where is it?" he said again, letting her mouth go, his left hand still holding her hair, now against the rug. Brian's wife's eyes shut tight and she bit her lip, knowing a scream would get her killed, and she said, "What—what are you talking about?"

GiGi Parnell said, "Wrong answer," and showed her his right hand, now holding the gun again. He slid it down her body slowly, feeling himself getting hard as the barrel crossed her largish breasts; down her belly, to her knees. He slid it up her dress and up her thigh, the steel making a whispery sound against the tight pantyhose. He stopped there and said, "Where is it?"

She said, "In my purse." She was staring at him now, most likely thinking GiGi would maybe screw her and let her go. Dumb babe Brian fell in love with probably came out of a cathouse he'd visited.

"How much?" GiGi said calmly, letting her guess she was safe now that she'd told the truth.

"Only two thousand, GiGi, that's all, I talked him into it, I made him do it, he told me he loved you like a brother . . ." and he let her rattle on a little bit, holding the pistol against her thighs, enjoying the act, the reverse psychology. The woman was trying to make him ashamed that he'd killed his old cellmate and let her go because he was feeling guilty. He listened to about ten seconds of it before he got mad.

"You stupid bitch," he said, "I was gonna *give* you *ten,*" and pulled the trigger.

* * *

Five minutes later GiGi was sitting in the passenger seat of Agnes's little blue Mustang, his arms behind his head, the money stuffed into all his pockets, smiling, thinking that Brian's pussy problem had been resolved once and for all.

Agnes was silent, driving slowly, eyeing him carefully when she thought he wasn't looking. He turned to stare at her straight on, challengingly. "What's wrong, love-bug?" he asked, feeling pretty good. Agnes hesitated. GiGi laughed. "Come on, what's bugging you?"

Agnes said, "Honey?" tentatively, frightened.

"What?" Playing with her now, knowing what was wrong but making her tell him, his answer ready.

"Were—" slowly, then she blurted out, "Were those gunshots I heard from the house?"

"*Gun*shots?!" GiGi laughed loudly, going for amused cute, as if Agnes was so dear to him that what she'd said wasn't stupid, just lovingly confused. "Why would anyone be shooting off *guns*?"

Agnes was smiling now, looking at him, then back to the road; at him, then the road, a sheepish look on her face, a silly-me smile on her lips. "Silly, huh?" Like: How can you love an airhead like me? GiGi smiled and reached out his left hand, lovingly rubbed the back of her neck.

He said, "I'm a lover, not a fighter."

"Boy, don't I know it."

At her apartment, he admired her as she undressed, a little bitty thing but stacked, man, a set out to there; tight, lively can without wrinkles or dimples, curving hips; long legs for such a tiny thing. Sort of wispy blondish hair, lots of it, though, falling to her shoulders. Green eyes staring at him hungrily.

100

GiGi was lying back on her queen-sized water bed, naked, his hands clasped behind his head, his fingers feeling the short blond hairs on his neck. Feel good to grow it out, get rid of the rigid discipline of the Brotherhood, Jeez, crew cuts even in winter. He liked the way her eyes never left him, how she reached around back and unclasped the bra and slid the straps down her arms ever so slowly, a slight smile on her lips. She knew how long it had been for him, and was showing him a good time. Making sure he got drained real good. He felt better about her than he had about anyone since he'd found out his mom had died. He hoped she'd forget about gunshots. He'd hate to lose her, too.

GiGi tightened his pectoral muscles one at a time, making them jump up, relax, then jump out again. He wiggled his toes, spread them; raised his knees.

Agnes walked over to him with an exaggerated sway of the hips, doing a little bump and grind. "My, my," she said, staring at the valley between his upraised knees, "what have we here?"

"Come sit awhile, love-bug."

She put one knee on either side of him, the water bed undulating madly, making her nice big breasts jiggle some, too. Agnes said, "Love to, honey." Then sat down on him.

Later, while Agnes slept, GiGi thought things over with his hands behind his head, staring at the ceiling. He was thinking about who he had left in the world. He hated Uncle Lester, but wouldn't put him out. Somebody had to take care of the place, pay the taxes, the bills, all that junk GiGi didn't want to bother with. Outside of that, there was nobody. Brian was dead, bless his soul. He'd given GiGi two more pistols, posthumously, along with a box of .38 shells GiGi had found in the closet in Brian's bedroom. No, there was no one. Nobody except this little bitty sex fiend lying next to him who said she loved him. Nobody except his mom had ever told him that before. Agnes had called in sick that morning, wanting to make sure he got his ashes hauled good and proper. You had to love a babe like that, not getting any younger working as a word processor, talking about maybe writing a book someday; accomplishing her lifelong dream. Well, you didn't sit back and write books after you busted your ass all day doing whatever it is word processors do. She deserved better. And here he was.

GiGi checked the red digital display on his watch. 10:18. He gently shook Agnes's shoulder, feeling the bed rock, not unpleasantly. He was in the process of solving not only her problems but one of his own, because if she agreed to go along with him, then later she read in the paper about the double killing at Brian's house, he wouldn't have to kill her when she put two and two together. He shook her again, harder. Agnes came awake and dreamily rolled over onto her back, reaching for him with an understanding smile.

"Not that," GiGi said, softly. "Wake up."

"What's the matter, hon?" It nearly broke GiGi's heart, her thinking he was splitting. Was *she* in for a surprise.

"You awake, love-bug?"

She nodded there in the dark, and GiGi could swear that there were tears rimming her big green eyes.

"I want to show you something." He got out of bed and padded naked to the adjoining bathroom, flipped on the light and turned back to Agnes. She was sitting against the headboard, holding the sheet against her breasts, her hair hanging around her face.

"You're leaving, aren't you?" Agnes said, and GiGi thought, there you are. He leaned over the bed, and tousled her hair.

"Leave *you*? Shit, you're the best thing happened to me in fifteen years." Thinking he should have said his whole *life*—it would have sounded better—then feeling an unfamiliar tug in his chest when he saw that she was staring at him adoringly. He said, "Come on," and went over to the straight-backed wooden chair he'd hung his suit on. It stood next to the closet, across the room from the bathroom. It was perfect, with the light coming dramatically across the room, out of the john. GiGi slipped the pistols from the outer jacket pockets and put them on the closet shelf as he heard Agnes coming up behind him.

"Sit down," he said, and she obeyed. GiGi got some bills out of the inner pockets of the jacket and worked the bands off with his thumb. He dropped a handful of them in her lap, laughing when Agnes gasped at the feel of money fluttering over her thighs. He worked faster now, emptying all the bills out of his jacket and pants, dumping them on her, then stepped back and stared at her, naked in a chair in her bedroom, with a hundred grand in hundreds in a pile from her knees to that great firm rack.

"I think you should quit your job," he said. "Take some time off, Agnes, maybe write your book."

"What?"

"Quit. Take care of me. I'll take care of you. Anything happens to me, then all that," he nodded at the money in her lap, "is yours."

Agnes said, "Honey you're *kidding* me." Her green eyes blazed with hope and maybe a little fear. "You're kidding me," she said again, almost a question. With each breath more bills would float off her lap onto the rug.

"I never kid about money," GiGi said in his prison voice. Then he softened. "Or about love."

Agnes was off the chair and kissing his face, his eyes, forehead, chin, pecking and murmuring, saying I love you and meaning it. At least it *sounded* like she meant it. Then she was running back to the money, grabbing big handfuls of it and tossing it onto the bed.

"Let's leave the light on and, you know, do it," she said.

GiGi was wondering how she could be so shy about saying the word when she would scream it at the top of her lungs when they *were* doing it. He was ready to oblige her, but had to ask something first.

"Love-bug?"

"Yeah, honey?" Agnes sounded impatient now, atop the money mattress with her legs beckoning.

"What did you hear back there, when I was taking that guy's car back to him?"

A sly look came across her face and she arched her hips on the bed, making it slosh madly.

"What guy?" Agnes said. "What car?" and GiGi guessed it was time to do it on a pile of hundreds.

8 He was drunk, Sparky asleep at his feet, using her as a hassock, his crossed ankles balanced on her muscular back, listening to his buddy talking in that flat, uninflected voice of his, the last syllable of a question jumping up peculiarly.

"This new neighbor of yours," Gizmo was saying, "gotta be the most gorgeous animal I ever saw in my life. Jogs bright and early every morning, with the little radio, comes running up to introduce herself, tells me later she called out from behind and almost thought I was arrogant when I didn't turn around. She comes in front of me, gets my attention, and I'm stunned. Never seen anything like her before. So I tell her to speak slowly so I can read her lips and she doesn't miss a second, never even gets the usual sympathetic look. She tells me her name's Mandi and I tell her mine, we chat awhile, she splits, I watch her wriggle away. This is a big woman, here, my man, maybe five-eleven. Long blond hair, down to the middle of her back. Big white smile. Next day, after work, here she comes again. Dressed to kill, driving a little gray Z-car. Bounces up the stairs and rings the bell, then hits herself in the head, knowing I can't hear the buzzer. I'm watching her from the upstairs bedroom window, where I set up a computer, and it's rigged so a green light flashes when the doorbell rings. I go let her in and pretty soon she's sitting in the same leather chair you're in now, her shoes kicked off, and I'm looking at a pair of crossed kissable ankles." Gizmo waited a couple of seconds while Jimbo laughed, then continued.

"She drills me for a while; I tell her I'm single, the wife died." Jimbo laughed again; Gizmo had never been married. "So she asked me what I'm doing, living in a four-bedroom two-level on Orleans Avenue all by myself, and I get her game. I says to her, 'Just used to it by now,' and she tells me she can get me a hundred thou for the house, tomorrow, and could I get used to maybe living somewhere else, and I get real interested, playing the dummy, like I don't know what a two-level in maybe the most fashionable part of Chicago is worth."

Sparky moaned in her sleep and her hind legs kicked a little.

Gizmo said, "She's a real estate agent, this girl, figuring me for an easy mark. I hem and haw around, trying to get her to come right out and ask what a black guy looks like a day laborer is doing living on this street full of yuppies, but she never brings it up. I'm like everyone else to her, all she sees in me is the color of money."

"How long did it take to get her in the sack?"

Gizmo smiled. "Three days."

"What am I supposed to tell her when she shows up?"

"Hell, that's your problem."

Gizmo finished his beer and left and Jimbo wondered why he had been slurring his words when he didn't feel drunk. He knew a guy once who swore he only drank at night alone in his bed, and Jimbo had asked him, "How did you know you were drunk if you didn't ever fall down?" but now he understood. Every so often you talked to yourself, and if you were slurring your words, you were drunk.

He rose slowly to his feet and walked over to the twenty-six-inch Sony stereo television, flipped it on. He straightened up and looked at the bookcase filled with hundreds of VHS tapes next to the TV, smiling. Even drunk, he could watch an old movie and appreciate the good parts.

He scanned the titles, his vision blurring, but not feeling tired yet. That was another thing he didn't understand about alcohol. If it was a depressant, then why did it always make you feel so wide awake even when you had been dead tired before you started drinking?

Jimbo loved old movies, loved them passionately, and when he was home, working regular hours, he would average five or six movies a week, watching them alone or with a girlfriend, this being one passion he couldn't share with Gizmo. Too many people talking with their backs turned. He didn't much care for new movies or new actors, preferring movies before the sixties, but he'd order anything that had Brian Keith in it or Bernie Casey or his heroes, Henry Silva and Jack Palance, who were the best bad guys he'd ever seen, even if they *had* hit it big doing color movies. Palance in *Shane,* God, one of his favorites.

Okay, Jack Palance it would be. Maybe *Portrait of a Hitman,* where old Jack played a killer with an artistic talent, wanting to get out, going into the death broker's living room, Rod Steiger sitting at a table stuffing his face, saying to Palance, "Some people jog, I listen to music," then going into one of the best examples of Method acting Jimbo had ever seen in his life.

Or maybe *Kiss of Death.*

He walked to the VCR and popped the tape in, grabbed a beer out of the fridge and hurried back to his chair. He put an ashtray on the arm of the chair and held the beer while he chain-smoked, watching Victor Mature and Richard Widmark do their rehearsed, precisely choreographed dance of death. After four cigarettes he'd had enough. He shut off the machine and put the tape away, turned the ringer off on the phone, looked at the square high-tech AT&T answering machine.

He hit Rewind, and when the tape was all the way back, Play. Three reporters in a row, Christ, talking for the entire thirty seconds, asking for interviews, one offering money for an exclusive. A frantic call from Bitsy, demanding that he open the boutique, telling him she'd be coming back with some of her daddy's bodyguards if he didn't. Not even asking if he was okay, if GiGi Parnell had maybe blown his head off yet.

More reporters, and he started fast forwarding the calls now, scanning through them, listening for the beep then giving the next caller a few seconds before going forward again. Reporters. Giz's computer voice asking him if he'd accept the Academy nomination, and if he'd serve if elected. Another call from Bitsy. Then more reporters.

He was supposed to lay low until the grand jury appearance on Monday. Today was Tuesday, Wednesday morning, really. Five days off. Maybe he could pass all five days without listening to another phone call. It would be a nice goal to set.

He let the dog out, waited at the door so she wouldn't start barking and wake up the whole neighborhood.

He sipped his beer, remembering his promise the day before about laying off the food and the booze. Tomorrow, he'd start. Hell, he hadn't done even a light workout today. He'd sweat it all out, tomorrow.

Jimbo let the dog in and padded up the stairs, going to the two-bedroom-and-bathroom second floor, prompted by something Gizmo had said. His curiosity was satisfied when he opened the door to the first bedroom, his old room when he had been a kid. The walls were freshly painted, the furniture polished and shining, all the cobwebs gone from the corners. Down the hall to the other bedroom, the same thing. He padded down the carpeted stairway, thinking the place hadn't looked this clean since his mother had died.

Goddamn Gizmo. What a pal.

GiGi Parnell was sitting in Agnes's living room, on a soft couch, figuring out a strategy. He thought of calling his Uncle Lester, but that could wait until morning. Hell, the old guy might have a stroke or something, the phone rang after midnight. He listened to Agnes snoring in the bedroom, sexually spent, happy. He wondered if maybe the mob had gotten a slow start and was out looking for him after all, in force. Maybe watching his house. His *house*. GiGi thought about the invasion of his privacy that would imply, and it made him mad.

There were three types of people in the world as far as GiGi was concerned. First there were the shitheels. Most of the people he had ever met had fallen into this category, even Brian and most of the other Brotherhood members in the joint. Fools waiting for the day they got out so they could go and do the same thing all over again that had gotten them locked up, thinking that they were smarter, wiser now that they'd done some time, that the cops had gotten dumber.

Then there were the pukes, where almost everybody else fit in. Just plain dumb or ignorant, going through life trying to get by, not hurting anyone but not doing anyone else a hell of a lot of good, either. Most politicians were pukes. As were all reporters, working stiffs, and the rest of the guys in the Brotherhood, the ones he liked. They were pukes. As was his Uncle Lester.

The last category in GiGi's mind was the only important one.

The people he put on a pedestal. He'd never admit to it,

but that was what he did. His mom, she was the first one. Way, way up there, she could do no wrong. And now Agnes, she was on a lower pedestal than his mom, but up there anyway, the third person he'd ever allowed in that hallowed category. The second person, who was somewhere in between the other two, was a con he'd met in the joint. An Indian guy who wasn't in the Brotherhood but who taught them all he knew about the martial arts, at least the ones who were serious and would train. His name was Buck Shadows, a Crow Indian who wouldn't join the Brotherhood because he wasn't white—even though they would have made an exception for him—and who couldn't join the black or Chicano gangs, either. All alone in a world that judged your worth by your affiliations.

But nobody ever, ever messed with Buck. Not the shitheels or the pukes. Not after watching him doing his T'ai-chi exercises in the yard after breakfast, moving like a ballerina, slowly, studied movements not even his best students could imitate. GiGi loved Buck, put him up on that pedestal, gave him his devotion and became his disciple.

What would Buck do if he had robbed the Mafia? After a few minutes GiGi figured it out and smiled, shaking his head, thinking, Jeez, Buck—as if Shadows had given him the idea and he was in his cell admiring the beauty of it. A way to save face and come out alive; get rid of all his problems at one time by lying and lying convincingly.

GiGi would put it to work first thing in the morning, or afternoon, whenever he woke up. Get it out of the way and get down to living the rest of his life in his own house with his mom's memories all around him. And Agnes.

He got up and went to the little portable color TV on the stand in the corner, flipped it on, then went to the bedroom door and closed it. He didn't know if Agnes was a light sleeper or not. At ease now, his strategy set, he settled back on the couch and put his feet up on the round glass coffee table, naked in the dark, feeling good.

He liked the babe who was doing the news, recorded at ten o'clock and being shown again now at two, before the station signed off for the night. GiGi wondered if they still played the national anthem before going off the air. This announcer, a black-haired gorgeous babe with flashing happy eyes and white teeth, looked into the camera and gravely told the viewing audience that "A potentially massive blow was dealt this afternoon to the Chicago Mafia after it was learned during a televised mayoral press conference that for the first time a successful undercover operation had been concluded against them." GiGi wondered who the hell wrote their scripts for them. Had to be a jig, trying to confuse the white people watching.

The screen flashed then to the press conference, and there was the mayor, ugly, lesbian-looking black bitch. At first he didn't make the connection after seeing the white-haired skinny guy standing there between two other guys. Then, when the white-haired guy began to speak, his name was flashed at the bottom of the screen and GiGi squinted and got a real good look, paying close attention for the first time.

GiGi said, "Jesus Christ." He stared at the screen.

"Jesus Christ, it's him."

It was Jimbo Marino, and GiGi hadn't even recognized him.

In the Chicago mob there was one top dog, indisputable and undisputed by anyone who wanted to live. His name was Tomasino Camponaro, but everyone knew him as Tommy Campo. Under him was his right-hand man, Angelo "Tombstone" Paterro. Paterro ran the daily business and gave the orders to the underbosses, or lieutenants. In

New York, and sometimes in books, they were called capos. Michael Barboza, who right now was very much on Angelo Paterro's mind, was an underboss, until just two days ago one of the best, a man everyone except Tommy Campo and Angelo Paterro believed would one day rise to take over after Campo died or retired. Campo did not believe in Barboza's ascension because he had no intention of dying or retiring, and Paterro did not see it happening either, because he hated Barboza passionately. This did not stop him from smiling at Barboza and shaking his hand and being decent to him because Barboza brought in vast sums of money for Campo's organization. Business before pleasure. But Paterro knew that he himself was next in line to the throne, even if Campo didn't. No way would he allow any fatass of a Portuguese to take over and give him orders, or worse yet, push him out.

Tommy Campo never spoke to anyone these days but Angelo, and Angelo passed the orders down to the underbosses, who passed them down to their soldiers, who got the job done using either their own crew members or freelance muscle if there was risk involved. This covered Tommy, who was protected by layer after layer of insulation. Although a year did not pass where one of his crew members or occasionally even an underboss went to prison, he himself could not be touched. An underboss would have to betray Angelo Paterro, which was unthinkable, and Angelo in turn would then have to betray Tommy Campo, which was impossible.

At least Tommy Campo thought it was impossible, sitting in his South Side mansion with his private police patrolling the grounds, taking the millions and throwing Angelo the bones. The crumbs off of which Angelo had been living well, most of his life. Angelo never even thought about what he'd do if anything went deeply wrong and it came down to life in prison or rolling over on Tommy Campo. Not until this night, when he'd been called into Tommy's office, received by the Sicilian like he was a visiting dignitary—important, but not very.

Campo told him Barboza had called, desperate, one of his crew turned out to be this *strunz* they were showing on the television news, and Tommy had hung up the phone, angry that this Portuguese idiot had dared call him at home on his private line and tried to talk business. He wanted Angelo to call Barboza back and find out what was going on.

Angelo called and listened to Barboza's lardbelly wife tell him that Mikey was out of town on business. He hung up without saying good-bye. He refused to be polite to people who lied to him. "Now what?" he asked the boss.

Tommy said, "Angelo, that was Barboza's crew got nailed the other night, over at the construction site. He don't tell you about this?"

Angelo shook his head and said, "Not a word."

"Why do you think this is?"

"Tommy, all I can figure, Barboza, he got a stoolie in his nest; he's either rolled over or he's scared we're gonna *think* he's rolled over and he froze up; he was scared to tell us right away."

Tommy Campo digested this. Angelo watched him, knowing that Tommy appreciated having a guy around who could think on his feet. It took Tommy awhile to figure things out, even when they were meaningfully arranged and handed to him on a silver platter.

Tommy Campo said, "What do you think?"

"Tommy, I think, either way, Barboza gotta have the right to come in, talk to you, explain his case. We can't just go around killing guys in his position."

"We did it with Roland DiNardo last year, and nobody said anything."

"That was different, Tommy. Roland was pushing drugs, and everyone knew it—except you and me. Besides, I had that kid, that thief, set Roland up. Nobody knew it came from us."

"But when Roland died in jail, waiting for trial, everyone saw we had a hand in that."

"Roland was one of the old crew, one of the maybe half a dozen guys left you started out with. He had talked to you all his life. He could have hurt you. He had to go. But remember, we had a jig do it, promised to pay his defense he did us this favor."

"I don't know, Angelo. I think Barboza has to go. We can't kill the cop. The heat would break us. But if grand jury indictments come down, this guy, not even Italian, he might roll."

"Maybe, but where you figure you'll be if you start whacking guys, get indicted? How long you think the other guys will stay loyal, they see you doing that? We call Barboza in, let him say his piece, assure him we're behind him, then before he can jump into the Witness Protection Program we give him a heart attack or something, a suicide, keep the other guys in line, figure he died from stress or something. Give him a stroke."

Tommy was smiling now, tapping the desktop lightly. "I like that. Get Barboza telling everyone with that big mouth of his that I'm a saint, I'm going to back him up, then we take care of him. But one thing, we're worried about loyalties; who you gonna get to do it? I don't like outsiders."

"Tommy, I don't trust outsiders, either." Angelo rose and straightened the crease in his trousers, shaking them. He knew this would bother Tommy, who thought himself above vanity yet lived in a fourteen-room house with five

114

bathrooms, just him and his wife and the private body-guards, now that the kids were gone. "Let me think about it," Angelo said.

"You think about it," Tommy told Angelo, softly. "But don't you do too much thinking, eh?"

Back home, Angelo "Tombstone" Paterro arranged bail and legal assistance for the crew Barboza had abandoned in the jug, doing it by rote, his mind turning over the problem of Mikey Barboza disappearing without a trace, not calling anyone or telling anyone about his problem with this undercover guy. He looked at himself in the wall mirror as he talked into the phone, liking what he saw there.

Fifty years old and trim, tennis and swimming took care of that. How many Italian men looked this good at fifty? Hair going, what was left turning white. Deep tan; deep lines too in the forehead and around the mouth, giving him a severe, angry look, making his smile seem spooky, breaking out of such a mean, tough face.

Through with the calls, Angelo hung up the phone and went to the wall safe behind the picture of his father hanging on the wall. He opened it, then walked clear across the room and locked the door to his den, although his wife never even thought about entering when he was in there with the door closed. He went back to the safe and looked around the room, making sure the heavy purple drapes were closed tight. Angelo took off his suit jacket and undid his tie, dropping two thousand dollars' worth of clothes on the floor when he added the monogrammed shirt with the gold cuff links still attached. He lifted his undershirt and there was the Sony minirecorder, taped in the hollow there between his pecs.

Angelo Paterro took the recorder off, gingerly pulling the tape away from the coarse white hairs on his chest. He removed the microcassette and got a pen out of the safe. He dated the tape and put it in the safe with the dozens of others stacked there.

He didn't tape every conversation he had with Tommy Campo, or he'd need the vault at Fort Knox to store the tapes. He only taped the ones where he knew that they would be discussing murder, or when he was called over to the house in the middle of the night, which could only mean bad news. He had all kinds of evidence against Tommy Campo, to be used when the time was right, in any way he saw fit. And there wouldn't be a goddamn thing Tommy could do about it.

GiGi was too wired to sleep. A couple of hours in the water bed next to Agnes and he was up, dressing. There was money piled all around the bed. He picked it up and stacked it neatly on the nightstand, trying not to waken Agnes.

If he lived through the first part of his plan, he'd have to buy some more clothes today. The suit was getting a little ripe. If he lived through the first part of his plan, hell, he could go out and fill every closet in his house with expensive clothes and not miss a penny spent.

GiGi went to the kitchen and made some coffee, then searched through the kitchen drawers looking for a pen and paper. He found them on the counter under the wall phone. He wrote Agnes a quick note, telling her not to worry, he'd be back.

His first stop was at the lawyer's, taking maybe fifteen minutes to convince the guy that he wasn't at all interested in tax-free municipals or IRAs or any other fucking investments, just gimme the money or get eternally disbarred.

He made the guy give him a blank sheet of paper, a stamped envelope and a pen. He endorsed the check, wrapped it in the blank sheet of paper, addressed the envelope to Agnes with her address. If he got himself killed, she would be able to write her book.

Out on the street again, he dropped the envelope in the first mailbox he passed, feeling funny—and then getting it. Christ, the last time he'd mailed a letter had been in Miami, getting it registered at the post office because it had cash in it, for his mom. Then that shitheel cop . . . Well, he'd be taking care of that little piece of business, soon, too. If he lived through phase one.

Shaking off the funny feeling, telling himself he had nothing to lose, GiGi headed for the Loop.

As the number-one boy on Mikey Barboza's criminal crew, he had been well aware of who and what Mikey was, and who he worked for. Although he considered the Mafia lightweights, he knew of their power, and respected it. He knew all about Angelo Paterro, knew that he was considered a free thinker, a fair man. Always on the lookout for a buck. A man GiGi could talk to. If he could get to him.

The sixth bar he walked into that morning was showing X-rated movies on the TV above the bar. A swarthy guy was tending bar, pouring shots of exotic liqueurs into rock glasses, topping them off with 7-Up or Coke, then dropping them in front of the players and pimps seated at the bar, looking like peacocks.

GiGi took out a hundred-dollar bill, ripped it in half. He told the bartender, "I'm looking for Angelo Paterro. I'll give you this half when you tell me where I can find him, and the other half if the skinny's straight."

The bartender was looking at the money in GiGi's hand. He walked to the register, locked it, took out the key and went back to GiGi. "You want to come into my office for a minute?"

GiGi had five and a half ripped—and eight hundred crisp—hundred-dollar bills in his pocket when he walked into the Ember's Restaurant on South Water Street that Wednesday morning, the remains of the hundred he'd given the bartender and the ripped evidence of five earlier attempts to find Paterro. He could trade the first five at any bank for clean fresh bills. The other half he'd give to Paterro if things went well, along with the name of the bar and a description of the doomed bartender who'd told GiGi where Paterro could be found. As a goodwill gesture.

The Ember's was a Greek joint, trying for class but not making it. Secluded booths offered privacy while you munched your goat heads or whatever. GiGi stood in the vestibule for a while, his nose detecting spicy smells, sickening smells, to him. He was used to smelling much blander things. Two thugs in suits were standing by the coat-check counter. He smiled. Their hands went inside their jackets.

"How's it going, fellas?" GiGi said confidently, seeing as how the three of them were in the same line of work. "I got to talk to Mr. Paterro." He kept it simple, but friendly, letting them know that they were pukes.

The first guy said, "Who the fuck are you?"

"Just tell him it's about Mikey Barboza and the under-cover cop on the television." He watched the guys eye each other for a second, confused. The second guy, obviously the less senior man, got the nod from the puke who'd spoken, and walked off to the rear booths.

He came back a couple of minutes later and nodded to GiGi, pointing his head toward the back of the restaurant, giving him the okay. GiGi wondered if he should give these two stiffs a hundred apiece for their trouble, then decided not to, because they'd frisked him quickly and found one of his guns.

Angelo Paterro visited his underbosses at a variety of restaurants and bars throughout the day, meeting with the ones he liked the most in restaurants, having his breakfast, lunch and supper with his underlings. His wife hadn't had to cook a weekday meal in ten years. She'd hardly *seen* him during the week in ten years. This morning he had a meet set for here at the Ember's, and he was angry because the underboss was late. He had no patience with people who didn't keep appointments, and if the guy wasn't dead or in jail, then from now on he'd be meeting Angelo in bars instead of breaking bread with him.

GiGi Parnell approached the back booth the same way he'd entered the restaurant, like he owned it. Show no fear, ever. Because guys like this, they thrived off people's fear.

He slid into the booth and stared at the tall thin old guy. He decided to get his attention right up front.

"Your boys out there are slipping," he said, pulling the second gun out of his waistband in back and popping it open, jacking the shells into his palm. Paterro was looking at him differently now, as if he was about to keel over with a stroke or something. That was better. GiGi put the bullets in his coat pocket, then put the gun back in his waistband. He said, "I'm GiGi Parnell."

And the old fart, he still had to play it tough, like he hadn't just nearly shit his pants when GiGi'd pulled the gun out. "That name supposed to mean something to me?"

I thought maybe it might, seeing's I'm the guy took about a hundred grand outta Barboza's safe the other night." And GiGi had to hand it to the guy, he got himself under control in a hurry.

"You what?"

"You don't know about it?"

"About what?"

Jesus, stupid shitheel guinea. He'd have to spell it out for him. GiGi reached into his pockets, smiling when the guy flinched just a little, and took out the wads of hundred-dollar bills. He dropped them on the table between them.

"I figure this is your money. I took it from Mikey Barboza Monday night."

The guy sat back in the booth and gave him the tough guy look again, too classy to try the Badeye, but close. "Tell me about it," Angelo Paterro said.

GiGi told him the lie he'd prepared, starting with the truth, how Mikey had beaten him out of twenty grand years ago, then getting into it, saying how Mikey had set up the meeting in the warehouse and had told GiGi the money was there in the open safe and how Barboza had shot at him when he'd bent down to look, and what was he supposed to do, not defend himself? Then telling Paterro that when he pulled his own piece, Mikey had run and GiGi figured the cops had to be on the way so—to protect the mob's money—he'd cleaned the safe and then brought the money to Tombstone.

"The guy tries to kill me over money he owes me, I ain't taking this to his house. There's eighty grand here; I took my twenty. I don't take what ain't mine."

Paterro was still eyeing him.

"I heard you were a man of respect," GiGi said, "fair-minded. I was done an injustice, and I settled it. I'm giving you your money, and offering my services to you if you want them."

"And you keep the twenty grand."

"That's my money, like I told you."

"Sure it is." The mobster sat back and lit a smoke, offering GiGi one. He took it and lit it, dragged the smoke deep into his lungs, keeping eye contact with Paterro. He had the hook in now, because deadly Angelo Paterro was smiling at him.

"And what services do you think you can offer me?"

GiGi gave it some thought. "How about I whack out Barboza and the cop?"

Angelo laughed. "Barboza would be enough. Without him there is no case. We don't kill cops. We can't. Christ."

GiGi went ahead and gave him the Badeye, wondering if it would work with a guy as hard as Angelo. "I'll give you Barboza to make up for taking the money. I should have come seen you or Mr. Cam—" Angelo held up a warning hand and GiGi said, "the other guy, before taking things into my own hands. For messing up, I owe you. I'll pay you back with Barboza.

"The cop, the stool pigeon, he will be my gift to you, show you what I can do."

"You're willing to whack out the cop, as a favor to me?"

"Show my loyalty. After that, you can decide if maybe you got something else I can do for you." A burst of inspiration; he was now a hitman.

Angelo was thinking, liking the idea of having a psycho cop-killer on his side, his own personal man, loyal to no one but him. Get him to whack out Barboza and the cop, get them all off the hook. Then kill him.

Angelo stacked all the hundred-dollar bills into two equal piles. He slid one toward GiGi. "Loyalty gets rewarded."

"You're shitting me."

"Kid, I never bullshit *any*one."

GiGi picked the bills up and stuffed them into his inside jacket pockets, grinning. Honesty is its own reward, just like his mom used to tell him.

Angelo said, "The ugly guy out front—" and GiGi said,

"Which one?" getting a laugh out of Angelo. "The one with the blue shirt on, you give him your . . ." Thinking about it, Angelo pulled out a pen and his notebook, pushed it across to GiGi and said, "Give me a number where I can reach you." GiGi scratched down the number at his mom's—no, *his* house, then pushed the notebook back and Angelo said, "Good meeting you, kid," reaching his hand across the table.

They shook, and GiGi the hitman said, "Call me GiGi, Mr. Paterro."

Angelo Paterro looked hard at GiGi and said, "Sure, kid."

And not wanting to push his luck, GiGi Parnell nodded and swaggered from the restaurant.

The ringing phone awakened Agnes and she hit out at the nightstand, trying to knock it off the little table, succeeding only in barking her knuckles on the wood. She said, "Shit," with feeling, and sat up in bed, seeing the little bedside clock, telling her it was after ten.

This GiGi Parnell White Heat Bandit guy was wearing her out.

She was angry at the phone dragging her from a dream she was having where she was famous, a somebody, no longer working at a computer terminal all day for her father. She barked a hello into the phone and her father's voice came back at her.

"Agie, Ag? You there?"

Agnes was tempted to hang up because she'd called in sick the day before, but hadn't even bothered to this morning.

"Pop?" She tried to sound like death, putting a lot into it, imagining herself sick. "Oh, Pop I didn't call."

"You okay, hon?"

"I think I better take some vacation time, Pop?" Good, don't pull the plug yet, see how serious this GiGi character was; what he wanted from her. She'd known enough guys in her time who fell in love for about three days.

"You see a doctor yet?"

"No. I been waiting for it to go away."

"Ag." Agnes scrunched up her face, knowing what was coming by the strict tone of her father's voice. "Ag, you fall in love again?" Just like him too, trying to make it sound dirty.

"Daddy!" Agnes said, with just enough indignation to let him know his slave labor was about to be emancipated.

"All right, just tell me, Ag, how much vacation you need this time?"

"I'll let you know." She sniffed and hung up. Bastard.

She lay in bed naked, thinking about this guy who'd offered her the way out. Was he serious? Could he possibly be? But God, ten years in *prison*. Maybe he did fall in love, first day out and he finds a woman who can suck him dry and start his engine all over again. Anything was possible.

But the gunshots last night—and she knew they *had* been gunshots. What about *that*? Did he hold someone up, take the money away from them? All that rich green money they'd done it on last night. He said he was serious about taking care of her.

Oh God could it be true?

Handsome, well-built and rich, in love with little Agnes Smycz. It didn't seem right to her, as if God were handing this to her on a platter and as soon as she started eating from it he'd pull it away or turn the meal into dog turds or something. Lay out the red carpet and let her get halfway down it before pulling it out from under her.

Better safe than sorry. GiGi seemed sincere, and he was a great lay. And he had money coming out of his ears, and a body that wouldn't quit. And God, he even tried to be gentle with her; she'd had to explain to him right out that she wouldn't break; that she liked it rough. Ten years in prison and he tried to be gentle.

But what about when she'd gotten into the shower with him? Banging her head against the tiles and telling her never ever to sneak up on him—was that a hangover from jail? Agnes wondered about the movies she'd seen about prison. Were they true? Did guys really try to do it with other guys in the shower? Yuck, she was getting sick thinking about it, seeing a big ape of a guy bending over another guy with the prison pants down at his ankles.

She'd give it some time, see how it went. If he was serious—and she could find out real quick by having him open a bank account in her name—then she'd quit daddy-dear-the-plantation-owner who hired family because he could pay them doodly and keep them dangling with the fourth most-often-told lie: "Someday all this will be yours."

Of course, GiGi had told her if anything happened to him, all that money would be hers, and he'd hidden two pistols in her bedroom closet last night. Maybe he wouldn't last long after all, maybe he'd get himself killed or arrested, and then if he really didn't love her, it wouldn't matter because it would create the ideal solution. Agnes with a ton of money and no one in the world she had to take any shit from. She decided to call her father back and tell him that she needed two weeks. That should be more than enough time to know something, one way or the other.

GiGi felt better than he had in ten years. Someone to love him, and a lot of money, and his own house, and now a good job in a growth industry, shit, all in two days, it was unbelievable. Came from living right. Not beating off too much in the pen, working out every day, learning mind over matter. Never putting it up anyone's butt or letting someone run him head, when it was all around him, guys begging him to be their daddy so he could keep the niggers away from them. Sweet young skinny car thieves and pukes like that, guys telling them that from now on they had to put Maybelline on their faces and call them honey-bunch and talk like women or they'd sell their young asses to the rough-trade studs for a pack of smokes.

GiGi never had any truck with that, not even when he'd wake up in the middle of the night with some punk in the bunk above him begging for it, so shit-scared all he would have had to do was whistle and they'd have come flying down and whistle on *him*, just to feel safe for a little while. And look how it was paying off for him. He was driving the Mustang now, going home for the first time in almost eleven years, counting the fugitive months in Florida. He wondered if Mikey Barboza had any guys on the crew who were loyal strictly to him. Maybe watching the house for Mikey, as a favor.

GiGi drove the Mustang into a 7-Eleven and got out of the car, bought a cup of coffee and had to break a hundred. Shit, grabbing the ripped ones, he'd forgotten to tell Angelo about the bartender who'd dimed on him. The girl behind the counter at the 7-Eleven told him they couldn't break anything over a twenty, but GiGi talked her into going in back, coming out with ninety-nine dollars and fifteen cents in her hand for him. A different time, he'd have filed that away in his memory for later. But not anymore.

GiGi went to the pay phone outside, smiling up at the sun, and dialed the number that hadn't changed as long as he could remember.

"Hello?" His uncle Lester. "Parnell residence." Sounded like a butler. GiGi liked the way it came over, even though the guy sounded to be about eighty on the phone. Maybe he could talk Uncle Lester into practicing an English accent.

"Uncle Lester, how's it going?"

Lester saying, "My God, Gigliamo, dear God in heaven it's good to hear your voice!"

Not having time to play games with Uncle Lester, GiGi said, "Yeah, me too, listen I'm gonna be coming home soon. You seen anything funny, any cars outside shouldn't be there?"

"Nope, can't say that I have . . ."

"You looked outside today, Lester?"

"Ain't done that, either, Gigliamo."

"You wanna take a look there, Unc?"

"Outside?"

GiGi sighed, said, "Uncle Les, do me a favor. Go look through the front room picture window, out into the street, see if you spot any cars out there don't belong there."

"You know, son, your mother told me you'd always take care of me, she ever mention—?"

"Goddamnit, Lester, *now.*"

The phone went *clack* on something hard and GiGi was thinking maybe he should kick Lester's ass for him real good, show him he didn't have squatters' rights in the house. The will didn't say anything about taking care of Lester. Even if his mom *had* asked him to. Then he heard the phone *clack* again and Lester's whispered voice came back over the wire.

"Damned if you ain't right, son. There's a dark green Plymouth parked across the street, two guys sitting in it."

"This is important, Les. Did this car have a long skinny antenna on the trunk, right in the middle?"

"You want I should take another look?" Meaning he hadn't noticed. Meaning he was trying to suck up so GiGi wouldn't send him off to the Salvation Army.

"No, no, stay away from the window, Les, and listen, you did real good."

Gratefully his uncle said, "You coming home, now, Gigliamo?"

"Uncle Lester?"

"Yes, son?"

"You wanna keep living in my house?"

"Why, I sure do son, your mother, she—"

"Lester, you call me Gigliamo or son again, and you're *gone,* you understand?" And GiGi hung up the phone.

He had to pull Agnes out of the damn bed. He tried to be nice about it, but she kept trying to get him to do it, so he had to tell her to get her ass up, now. He had her drive him to within a block of his house, the pistol and the money in the closet now, nothing on him, clean.

Back at the apartment Agnes had asked, "What happened to all the money?" and he'd told her he'd tell her all about it later, when he got back, but she had to listen to him real good now, this was important. Agnes was pouting because he'd cussed her, dressing but taking her time, talking over her shoulder at him.

"Cops are gonna pick me up at my house," GiGi told her. "If they bust me, I'll call you, you come down with the cash and bail me out."

Not pouting now. Her eyes widened with excitement and a little fear.

Agnes said, "What *for?*"

GiGi shrugged. "You know how it is, love-bug. They like to hassle a guy with a record." GiGi walked over to Agnes and rubbed her back as she bent down to tie her shoelaces. He liked the way she dressed, in plain jeans and a white blouse with a little lace at the throat. Gym shoes with the tongues hanging over the laces. Cute. He wanted to make up with her for being short a minute ago.

"You can handle this."

Agnes looked at him with surprise. "Are you kidding?"

GiGi kissed her before he got out of the car, with the change from the 7-Eleven in his pocket, ninety-nine dollars. He began to walk casually toward the corner. He turned it and ignored the unmarked squad sitting there so obviously that if it had teeth, it would be biting people. Going up his steps, he heard car doors slamming behind him. He stood on his stoop and winked at Lester, who was looking at him through the glass of the front door. GiGi reached for the knob.

"Gigliamo Parnell?" from behind him. He heard them shuffling, going wide to either side of him in case he came out shooting. He turned to them.

"Good morning, officers." They were two big beefy guys who probably hadn't been near a set of weights since high school. One white, the other Hispanic. Both looking at him warily with their hands around the back of their belts. Ready to draw on him.

The white cop said, "You want to come with us, please?"

"Am I under arrest?" GiGi said, moving his hand slowly to his chest, his fingers splayed wide, touching the area over his heart, acting shocked and amazed.

The Hispanic cop said, "Hey, you wiseass little shit, you coming with us or what?"

GiGi turned the Badeye on him, tightening his muscles so the seams in the suit coat strained. He said, "I asked you a question, nigger."

The white cop said quickly: "Forget about it, Rudi," to his partner, then to GiGi, through clenched teeth, "No sir, you're not under arrest. We'd just like to ask you some questions."

GiGi wanted to say, "About what?" piss them off a little, show them he had rights now—he was out of prison and had no parole—but he didn't. Instead he grinned hugely at them, showing his contempt, then swaggered down the stairs, dragging his feet on the concrete as he'd done since he was a kid. He looked at his watch and said, "Well, okay, for a little while. But I don't want to miss lunch, huh?"

The white cop grunted and the Hispanic guy said, "Hey, tough guy, with a little luck, you'll make supper time at the County."

GiGi said, "You got nothing on me."

The Hispanic cop said, "How's murder sound?"

GiGi said, "For supper? No thanks. Less I get to murder *you,* beanhead." He was smiling. That shut them up, all right.

9 It took Jimbo a little while to wake up, what with the hangover and all. He was lying in his bed trying to remember if he'd eaten anything at all yesterday; yeah, okay, a dago beef sandwich at lunch. That's why he felt so rotten. All that beer on an empty stomach.

He felt a dead weight on the end of the bed, dragging it down some. Opening his eyes, he saw Sparky curled up at his feet, eyeing him cautiously. Afraid she might be in trouble but too lazy to move; hell, he'd seen her now. She made a sighing sound and settled in more deeply on the bed, closed her eyes.

Jimbo sniffed warily. Nothing yet. God, he felt terrible. He staggered from the bedroom and out into the hallway, down to the bathroom, stepping slowly, watching where he was going, eyes looking for a surprise gift from the dog. So far so good. From the bathroom he staggered to the kitchen, noticing the little red light on the recorder flashing again.

Jimbo put coffee on to boil and opened the back door, called Sparky, let her out. As she passed him he said, "*Good* girl," and reached down to pat her head. Day two of the Doberman Invasion and she was already housebroken.

Jimbo walked up the stairs, into the first bedroom, his old room. Gizmo's old computer set up there on a wooden desk. He searched the closet for a pair of running shoes, then the dresser for some sweats. Time to get back in shape before he lost it. Hell, he was thirty-two. Not a spring chicken anymore. Everything was starting to slow down and spread out.

Dressed, inspiration striking him, Jimbo went through the kitchen to the basement door, down the steps, thinking, some cop. He'd left all the basement windows open the day before after washing the floor. But it smelled good now, clean, the air reminiscent of spring, smelling of warmth and flowers and grass. Summer was back and no killers had sought him in the night.

Jimbo looked around for a while, at last spotting the old clothesline all rolled up under his father's workbench. He got it out, and a pair of shears, and cut off a five-foot length. He looked around until he found a good brass ring, maybe an inch in diameter, inch and a quarter. He closed and locked all the windows, went back upstairs and found his keys, then locked the back door behind him.

He slipped the length of clothesline through the brass ring, put the loop around Sparky's neck, gave it a tug. Crude but effective. A decent choke chain. He wrapped a foot of the line around his wrist, got a good grip on it, headed out the alley to the lakefront, Sparky loping beside him slowly, tongue out, having the time of her life while Jimbo died.

Christ, it had been too long. He felt the weakness in his legs, his heart pounding, saying to him, "What the hell you think you're doing to me?" He ran at a very slow pace, maybe eight-minute miles. Just jogging, trying to get it back. Sparky obedient, not taking off after people or other dogs, checking them out as they ran past them, though; sometimes growling, sometimes barking. He'd shush her and she'd look ahead, regally, seeming almost embarrassed to be moving so slowly.

After a mile he no longer thought he was going to throw up, and after two his wind was getting a little better, the headache narrowing down to a dull thud rather than the gong-hammering it had been. Seeing the beach bunnies frolicking on the lakefront helped; bikinied dollies out for maybe the last real fling of summer. Tanned and lovely, checking him out as he passed, a couple of them making remarks.

Three miles, and he was at the underpass leading to the Lincoln Park Zoo. A slow turn around and heading back home, things working okay now, his casual workouts of the last three months maybe not keeping him in the shape he liked to be in but not doing him any harm, either. Lake Michigan was feeling its oats today; a bright blue with white-crested waves crashing against the breakwaters, rolling in majestically. Power and strength looking casual, easy. Sea gulls screeching above the water, every so often diving down for—what—an alewife? Christ, were there still fish in the lake?

He was breathing heavily but wasn't exhausted as he reached his house. Jimbo got Sparky a big aluminum pot of water and put it in the basement. Might as well let her get used to it down there. He drank a pint of orange juice right out of the carton. He was feeling human again, his self-esteem rising because he could still run without croaking.

He went to the far side of the basement, the room divided into three sections, the main basement with the sump-pump and the workbench and the power boxes, water lines. The second section was paneled off, the utility room with the washer and dryer and huge washtub; a small freezer his father once used to keep fish and venison meat fresh and edible. The third section was the smallest;

Jimbo's secret place. The world he used to live in after school, alone, working out and dreaming of the NFL.

There was a weight bench with an Olympic bar across it, three hundred pounds hanging off the ends, hundred and a half each side. A smaller curl bar with a hundred pounds locked on against one wall; barbells, lighter yet, for flys and wrist work.

Christ, the hours he had spent down here. Worth it, in the end. He never made it to the NFL but he'd stayed away from the street gangs and the punk groups, never messed with drugs or alcohol until college and then only in limited amounts, trying to impress some of the varsity guys, make buddies.

It was a basement gym in an area that had once been full of them when it had been working-class but was now trendy with the new inhabitants owning memberships in expensive health clubs and fern gyms. They worked out wearing designer sweats and three-hundred-dollar shoes, for chrissakes. Jimbo guessed you could get a hell of a sauna or steam in one of those joints.

He went to the far wall, where a seventy-pound heavy bag hung chained to the wood ceiling; a speed bag platform set up next to it. He took the padded gloves from the top of the platform, breathing normally now, feeling good, youth on his side still. He put them on his hands while he took deep breaths and blew them out. Jimbo stepped to the bags and went to work.

An hour later there was true exhaustion, but he felt like a million. Sparky had leaped around and barked at the heavy bag as he punched away, feeling the good solid sensation all the way to his shoulders when he did it just right. The knockout punch. All the way out for a solid hour.

Jimbo strolled around the basement drifting from room to room, hands on his hips, feeling good, smiling, Sparky nipping at his heels, playing around. He shadowboxed her for a while, grinning at her, saying "*Good* dog," when she'd move her head an inch and slip his punch, nip at his gloved hand. Good reflexes, the Dobie. He let her play in the yard while he showered and shaved.

He was dressed, feeling good, glowing, looking at the damn recorder. Why the hell not? He wasn't a recluse. Jimbo hit the Rewind button, then Play.

The first message was from a woman, the reporter who'd offered him money for his story. She left a number and her name, Kristina Zalinski. He hit Fast Forward upon hearing the first word of Bitsy's message. Then Kristina again, checking back. The last message made Jimbo overwhelmingly grateful that he'd checked the machine after all; Lieutenant Bobby Franchese with his deep bass told him the time (noon), the day (today), and the fact that the Major Crimes Unit had a suspect in for questioning and would he maybe like to stop by and say hello?

The suspect was GiGi Parnell.

Jimbo checked his watch, hell, 12:30; he'd called while Jimbo was in the shower.

Jimbo went to the back door and made kissing sounds, causing Sparky to come rushing toward him like a cheetah again, bounding through the door like a bullet. He opened the basement door and ordered her down; she didn't want to go, but on the second command she slunk down the steps, giving him a "What'd I do?" look. He took her a bowl of food and filled her water dish, warned her about messing up his floors, and was gone.

Bobby Franchese was a black-Italian veteran MCU dick. He was three or four inches taller than Jimbo, with razor parted hair cropped short, the part on the right. Slender but Jimbo had worked with him, knew better than to think he was skinny. Skinny like Michael Jordan is skinny. Or Ali when he won the title the first time.

Bobby sat at the command desk in the MCU office, which was twice the size of Jimbo's office, for a five-person squad. He was drinking coffee with his feet on the desk, Bobby eyeing Jimbo coolly, enjoying this.

"Big balls, this kid," Bobby said, meaning GiGi.

"Tell me about it. Christ, ten years in the joint, first night out shooting up Mikey Barboza's house for practice."

Bobby smiled. Jimbo wondering when he'd make his point but being patient, not pushing it because Bobby had been good enough to call him, bring him into it.

Bobby said, "Got a call late last night, Homicide checks in, got an unusual death occurrence qualifies for us, over on Van Buren, way west. My team gets the call, goes over to check it out, Morris and Simpco. Find a guy shot to hell, his chest blasted out, his old lady shot through the pussy, bullet came out her right tit. Crime-scene boys tell them there's a puppy in the john, Simpco hears it whining in there, begging to be let out. ME says, go ahead, let it out, Morris says nah, wait for the Animal Control unit. Simpco calls him a sissy, goes to the door and opens it, out comes this goddamn English sheepdog, hundred and fifty pounder, comes charging out of there snarling and ready to kick ass."

Jimbo was smiling, enjoying the story, wondering where GiGi Parnell fit into it. He said, "Your guys shoot it?"

"Hell, yes. All of a sudden you got guys running around, after the gunshots, the uniforms out in the street, the rest of the crew searching the house, all of them with their pieces out, screaming and shouting, wonder nobody got snuffed."

Bobby was in no hurry. He said, "Small-time drug dealer, gun seller, named Brian Solt. Old lady named

Elaine. Legally married. We figure hell, the guy sells dope, it's narco's problem, not ours; there're maybe a million guys, shoot this stiff for the stuff he had laying around the house. We're ready to give it up, call in the narco squad, let them get together with Homicide, then we find something a little peculiar." He waited then, his bait dangling. He was smiling coolly.

Jimbo bit the line but played it cool, too. He went to the Mr. Coffee machine and poured himself another cup. He came back and sat down across from Bobby, acting bored. He said, without enthusiasm, "What'd you find?"

"In the closet, up on the shelf, this Solt stiff had an arsenal. Maybe fifty pieces, on a double shelf in a walk-in, nothing exotic, stuff easy to move and pick up, you know how. Guy's compulsive, got the guns laid out in order, by firepower. First .22s then a couple .25s, up to .32s, you know? Thing was, there were a couple empty spots, between the .32s and the .45s."

"Somebody either bought or stole a couple .38s."

"That's right."

Jimbo was thinking, So what? But did not say it.

"Still, it's no big thing, except Simpco, he's trying to make up for letting the big-ass dog out of the shitter, there, and he's doing everything like a madman now, possessed, hearing everybody giggling at his back when he walks by. Simpco's paranoid—like you.

"Anyway, he stops the meat wagon guys from taking the stiff away, the male stiff, thinking he's seen something that didn't register right away. He unzips the bag, takes a good look at the guy." Bobby was drawing it out now and Jimbo was getting impatient, watching Bobby sip his coffee then excusing himself to use the washroom. Bobby came back and settled in his chair, looked at Jimbo as if he'd never seen him before, put an "Ah, yes" look on his face. He said, "You want some more coffee?"

Jimbo said, "Goddamnit, Bobby."

Bobby grinned broadly. "Finally. Got to you, huh?" He didn't wait for an answer.

Bobby said, "Brian Solt's got a tattoo on his right bicep, another one on his right forearm. Both of them jailhouse tattoos, blue ink. The first one a swastika, the second one capital letters WAB."

"White Aryan Brotherhood."

"Still, nobody put two and two together yet, you special-teams guys being notoriously closedmouthed about what you're doing. So nobody knows about Mikey Barboza or his house getting shot up, the middle of the night Monday. Tuesday morning.

"But Simpco, he gets something in his head, he wears at it like a dog on a bone, shit, comes back here, does a computer check. Brian Solt served seven years for murder, second, up in Joliet." He smiled broadly, looking at Jimbo. "And guess who his cellmate was?"

Jimbo was smiling himself now, to beat the band. He said, "GiGi Parnell?"

"Give that man a cigar."

Then Bobby told Jimbo about another coincidence. Cops in general and Bobby Franchese in particular hated and did not trust coincidences. Bobby's mind had changed somewhat on that score once when the biggest case of his career had been cracked by blind luck, coincidence, being in the right place at the right time.

This time a young girl had been talked into coming in and looking through some mug books, a punk in a bar had been hitting on her, when she'd shot him down the punk had mashed a cigarette out on her face, nearly blinding her.

She'd told the First Precinct dicks the guy had been bragging about having his first drink in ten years, telling her he'd been in the joint, so it was easy for them to comp check GiGi out of the stack of psychos, but they still covered their asses, showing her a picture of him mixed in with pictures of a dozen other cons, and she'd picked him out right away, demanded that the cops go pick the guy up, put him in jail. The cops told her she'd have to swear out a complaint, and she freaked. That was their job, not hers. Sorry lady, no complaint, no warrant. Now, about witnesses? And she'd split, afraid, leaving the dicks shaking their heads, civilians making them crazy again.

Bobby said, "He's in the interrogation room. I talked to him earlier. He started the racial superiority nonsense, trying to rattle me. Johnson's with him now. Having fun, I'll bet. Black, *and* a woman. But GiGi's having a real ball. Playing with us. Simpco waited at the house all night for him; the guy shows up, he calls Simpco a nigger. Simpco tells me later he almost shot him on the spot. Anyway, you want a shot at him? He sees you, maybe he'll do something stupid. Jandra knows you're coming. But let me tell you, Jimbo, you don't start anything, and that's an order. You're here to observe only, you get me?"

Did Jimbo want a shot at GiGi? Ha! He said, "I get you."

He went into a small room with pink walls. GiGi was sitting in there with his head back against the wall, the chair he was in tilted back, casual. A small table was in front of him with a pack of Camels and an ashtray and a water glass on top of it. Black policewoman Jandra Johnson was sitting in the second chair, talking to GiGi.

Jandra looked up but kept talking. She nodded at Jimbo.

"So you claim you don't know any Brian Solt?"

GiGi silent, staring at Jimbo, a soft smile on his lips, his eyes hard and dead.

Jimbo said, "Parnell. Back from bumping dickheads for ten years with your big black weight-lifting daddy." Jandra looked at him funny, probably shocked, wondering what the hell was going on. GiGi stared at him hard, his chin down on his chest, giving Jimbo some kind of prison yard badass look.

GiGi said, "How's it going, Officer Marino?" grinning widely now, knowing secrets. Jimbo turned to Jandra.

"Giving you a hard time?" Jimbo keeping it light, conversational, the principal talking about a problem student he liked some. Jandra just looked at him, like he was insane. Jimbo perched on the edge of the table and looked at GiGi, but spoke to Jandra.

"I popped him ten years ago, in Miami. Jesus, skinny little momma's boy, crying and whining, hadda kick his ass for him some. My God, I thought he was going to roll over and show me his ass right on the spot." Speaking to GiGi directly, he said, "Had a good time in the pen, huh, GiGi? Sucking guys off to stay alive?" Jandra got up quickly and left the room. GiGi turned red-faced, slowly tipping the chair back down, putting his hands around the water glass, his eyes never leaving Jimbo's face.

GiGi said, "Get me a lawyer."

Jimbo said, surprised, "For what? We just want to ask you some questions. About a couple of dead people named Solt, and maybe about Mikey Barboza." And there it was again, GiGi no longer mad and glaring, giving Jimbo the look that told him he knew something Jimbo didn't.

GiGi said, "This room bugged?" Then said, "It don't matter." He was deciding something, maybe about to give Jimbo a hint of what the big secret was all about, then surprised Jimbo, telling him the whole thing. GiGi said, "You're dead, Marino. And I don't care who knows it. You are fucking dead, walking around not even knowing it." The door opened and Bobby Franchese came into the room, a worried look on his face. Jimbo looked at Bobby, then back to GiGi. He got off the table and sat down in the chair Jandra had vacated, feeling her warmth there beneath him; human warmth being a strange feeling in a room with GiGi Parnell.

"I saw you at the cemetery the other day." Jimbo said it conversationally, telling GiGi he had an eye on him.

"You should have come on over, instead of waiting until we're here, all your buddies around us in a pink room. What's the matter, you didn't have the balls?"

Jimbo leaned forward, crossing his arms on the table, staring at GiGi, who stared right back. GiGi glared hatefully. Jimbo looking into him, trying to see through him. Bobby silent behind Jimbo, a spectator.

Three minutes. Four. GiGi's hand around the glass going white-knuckled. Finally the glass shattered, sending slivers into his hand. Still, he stared. Jimbo grunted. He turned to Bobby.

Jimbo said, "He found out." Then smiled when GiGi said sarcastically, "Found out what?" Still not looking at GiGi, grinning at Bobby, rising slowly from the chair, setting his weight just right, Jimbo said to Bobby's puzzled face, "That I fucked his mother. . . ," turning when he heard the chair scrape the floor and hit the wall, spinning on his heels, timing it perfectly. As GiGi leaped across the table, hands reaching for Jimbo's throat, his face an insane mask of hatred, Jimbo threw the right hand, everything behind it, landing it right in the middle of GiGi's face, feeling teeth and GiGi's nose shattering. GiGi fell back across the table, against the wall, and slid slowly to the floor.

* * *

Out in the office again—Jandra was at her desk eyeing him strangely—Bobby Franchese said to him, "He files, I'll back you up, but don't you ever think you'll see another suspect in my unit again." Mad. Holding back, though. Stopping short of putting him up on departmental charges.

"I don't think he'll file, Bobby."

"Oh, yeah? Guy gets out of the hospital, what *you* think he's gonna do, killer? Send you a thank-you card?"

Jimbo smiled. He said, "What he'll do, straightaway, is come a-hunting."

Bobby looked at him for the longest time. "You set him up?"

Jimbo said, "Well . . ." Very softly.

Bobby said, disgusted, "Like a couple of little kids, staring each other down." For Jandra's benefit, then: "I gotta file a report on this, hell, you know we'll get sued, if you're wrong." Jandra got up and grabbed her purse from the desktop, sweeping it off with an angry gesture, staring knives at Jimbo. She sashayed angrily from the room, giving them a real show.

Jimbo said, "She always walk so nice, shaking it like that?"

Bobby gave him an icy look. "You just alienated one of my best officers."

Jimbo needed Franchese on his side. "What you gotta do now, Bobby, you got to get a search warrant, go through that house of his with a fine-tooth comb, find the murder weapon."

"First you come in from vacation, kick the shit out of a suspect in my interrogation room, then you start telling me how to run my investigation? Jesus Christ, Marino, I heard enough stories about when you were with MCU, no wonder they threw you off the squad."

"They didn't throw me off."

"No, Inspector Perry just told you, 'Get the hell out or you're off the force.'" Franchese looked up, frowning, looking out the glass top of the office door, out into the corridor. He said to Jimbo, "Just like Commander Lettierri is about to tell you."

Jimbo turned halfway around in the chair, saw Lettierri throw open the office door and stomp into the room.

It was almost an exact rerun of the last time, the name and demeanor of his boss being the only things different. Vic Perry had been calm, cold and angry. Lettierri was steaming, hot and angry.

"I told Bobby to let you sit *in*, goddamnit, not abuse suspects."

"Come *on*, Commander, Jesus, it was GiGi Parnell."

Lettierri was pacing the office, shouting when he spoke. He turned on Jimbo now. "I don't give a *fuck* about Parnell, you dumb shit! I don't care if you fucking *kill* him! Just not in the goddamn headquarters building!"

Lettierri stopped pacing now and stomped over to the chair, stood towering over Jimbo. "We spent six months working this one, and we *blew* it! The punks we caught are out on bail, not one of them would talk to us. Barboza's probably in Buenos Aires by now, Portugal or someplace. We find him, extradite him, get him back here, you know what our entire *case* rests on?"

"Sure I do—"

"*Shut the fuck up!*" Lettierri stood there staring down at Jimbo, who was sitting in the chair rubbing his swollen, hurting right hand. Watching as, by degrees, Lettierri forced himself to calm down, taking deep breaths through his mouth.

"The case rests, Jimbo, on your testimony. On tapes

142

made by *you*, with bugs planted by *you*. Now picture this in your mind, if you got one, Jimbo: You're in court, see, half the Mafia on trial, the star witness being you. Defense guy goes through all the blah-blah-blah garbage, making his client sound like some innocent businessman you've spent three months of your life harassing. Jury thinking you're a stool pigeon, maybe sympathizing a little bit with the bad guys, but we'll astound them with such overwhelming evidence they'd be ashamed not to convict. Now the defense lawyer, getting maybe half a million dollars to defend these guys, he says to you, 'Officer Marino, did you indeed entrap a suspect while working for MCU three years ago—'"

"The guy killed his wife and kids, for chrissakes—"

"—and you have to say, 'Yes sir,' because it's all on record, your suspension, then your 'transfer' out of MCU. Now he turns to you and says, 'And Officer Marino, on September fourth, did you in fact beat a man unconscious, a man not even under *arrest*, mind you, in an interrogation room at police headquarters?' making us look like Hitler, for God's sake. The jury will walk out trying to put *you* in jail, they get the right lawyer on defense."

"Not if it's in Chris Haney's court."

"And a wiseass, too. Well let me tell you, *one more goddamn remark* out of your mouth, even a smirk on your hot dog *face*, Marino, and you're suspended. You hear me?"

Jimbo said nothing.

"You've been a hot dog since the day you joined the force. You come into the task force, you won't work with a partner; okay, you're effective alone. Always grabbing the headlines, always managing to be there when the camera crews arrive, that's all well and good. But let me tell you something, when you start corrupting the integrity of my task force—"

"Corrupting the integrity—"

"You heard me, when you go that far, throw six months of work down the tubes just because some stiff sends your wife dirty letters from the pen, then I think maybe it's time for you to find another line of work."

Jimbo got out of the chair, rising slowly, holding onto the arms until he was standing straight, the same way he'd done in the interrogation room.

"The fuck you think you're going? Sit down, I'm not through with you yet."

"My father-in-law, he always said I was a crook, from birth."

"Sit *down,* Marino." There was an implied threat in the voice. Jimbo waited for the "Or else," or the "Or you'll be *sorry,* thinking of schoolteachers. Of his father-in-law. He stared at Lettierri, himself younger, stronger, having just spent three months undercover and getting this for his thanks.

"Why don't you kiss my ass?" Jimbo said, and turned and walked from the room.

Francis Mahon watched him, Jimbo swaggering, eyes ablaze, looking for Val Klenck to open his mouth and say one fucking word to him. Mahon caught his eye and gave a nod of his head toward the street. Jimbo nodded back and did not break stride, right out the task force door; slamming it behind him. Klenck looked up from his desk.

To the room in general he said, "I always knew he wouldn't last. Guys like him, they never do." The other five men in the room looked at him, two nodding assent.

Francis Mahon said, "Val, you're a real asshole, you know it?" He left his desk and walked past Klenck, who was staring at him, dumbstruck.

They sat in the bar on Division, the only two cops in the place. Jimbo hated cop bars. He didn't socialize with other cops, or enjoy sitting around getting drunk and feeling sorry for yourself, telling everyone about your latest divorce or about how much you hated your job. He had told a cop once, in a bar, "If you hate it so much, why the hell don't you quit?" And the cop had looked at him as if he was insane. Jimbo blamed it on too much Joseph Wambaugh. These guys read too much, then tried to act like the cops in books.

Francis Mahon had said something he missed. Jimbo said, "What?"

"Did they tell you they found the murder weapon at the scene?"

Jimbo looked up, angry and surprised. "They never said a word."

"Guy got cute. Wiped the thing down, put it in Solt's hand, like he shot his old lady through the snatch, then committed suicide, shooting himself through the heart, twice."

"Goddamn Johnson; I said, when I was in MCU, that I would never want a female partner, and she waits three years, then goes running to Lettierri first time she sees me fuck up. It'd been just me and Bobby, I'd have gotten away clean."

"Jimbo."

"Yeah, Francis?"

"Why'd you do it."

"Whack Parnell?"

"Why?"

Jimbo thought about the letters GiGi had sent to Bitsy from the pen. And about how he'd been charged with a thirty-three page indictment, then had pleaded that down to almost nothing, considering. Out of a possible seven lifetimes in prison he'd copped and only had to serve ten. He thought too about fighting like animals in the alley that day in Miami, giving it all he had and it not being enough. And about the terror he had felt Monday when Lettierri had told him that GiGi was out. That had to be part of it, proving something.

"I guess I just want it to end, one way or the other. Shit, I know all about being detached. In control, hiding your buttons from the suspect and never letting him know he got under your skin. But I'll be goddamned if I'm gonna spend the rest of my life looking over my shoulder, waiting for somebody like GiGi Parnell to come along and blow my head off."

"You missed my point."

"Did I?"

"What I meant was, why are you forcing it, putting it in his hands? I mean, why are you waiting for *him* to come to *you*?" Francis Mahon's face all squinched up, curious, and Jimbo decided Francis was a much heavier individual than he'd ever shown himself to be.

Jimbo drove home thinking about it. What Francis had said. They'd had only two beers. They'd each bought one round, then Francis had gone back to work and Jimbo had headed home. He had to cut down on the beer.

A woman was sitting on the stone stairs leading to his porch. There was something familiar about her, but Jimbo wasn't able to put his finger on it. Like seeing someone he'd never seen in person before, only in pictures. The opposite of what he'd felt in the girl's room while he was a deep-cover operative; staring at posters of Vanna White, never having seen Vanna standing still before. That kind of feeling. He decided not to put the car in the garage yet, not until he figured out if he'd need it to transport this girl downtown. Hell, maybe she was GiGi Parnell's girlfriend, come to set him up.

The woman bounced up to him, rising as soon as she spotted the car. Walking quickly, aggressive, her hand going out as she reached him and then he got it.

Jimbo left his hand at his side, said, "You're the girl from the press conference yesterday, the one who pinned Drumwald down, got him to give my name on television." He watched as her smile died, puzzlement in her eyes.

He said, "How in the fuck did you get my address?"

She said it hadn't been easy, smiling, trying to be friendly, trying to make up the ground she'd somehow lost. "God, we go to the precinct house—the press, right?—and your friends in the squad, they give your home phone number out! Not too well liked there, eh, Jimbo?" She smiled at him, the two of them pals now. Knowing about jealousy. "But for your address, I had to bribe a guy at the electric company."

Jimbo wasn't surprised. He could just see Klenck gleefully giving his phone number away. But he was worried about how easily his address could be learned. He'd have to get Gizmo working right away on the alarms. He stepped past and said, "Excuse me."

She stepped right in front of him again and said, "No." Jimbo was about to shove past her when she said, "Let's talk business," and that stopped him. He was expecting some typical reporter garbage about the public's need to know versus other, less important things. Like his life.

He said, "You're the one called offering money, aren't you?" She nodded.

"Christine, something, Zalewski?"

"Close. Kristina Zalinski." She put her hand out again, sizing him up, seeing if he was a worthy adversary.

Jimbo shook her hand and invited her in.

He heard Sparky start to howl as they entered the house. Jimbo opened the back door and then the basement door, and Sparky raced up the steps, jumping all over him, slob-bering all over his face. He bent to her and rubbed her behind the ears, her tight little doggie ass shaking; Jesus, he could swear she was grinning. He waved a hand and the dog ran out the back door. Jimbo turned to Kristina Zalinski and nodded at the kitchen table, then closed the back door and made sure it was locked. "Here, or in the living room if you'd like. Excuse me for a minute though, okay?" He went down into the basement and checked for dog droppings. Nothing. Good old Sparky.

He found Kristina in the living room, sitting on the sofa, looking at his collection of old movies, squinting. She was a pretty woman, taller than she looked on TV. Brown hair down to the shoulders, cut in a no-nonsense style; she could probably just run her fingers through it in the morning and be ready to go. He couldn't see any makeup, but he wasn't an expert at spotting that. Small firm breasts, but they could be faked. Her eyes couldn't though. Deep brown eyes like stone pools, Paul Newman eyes in brown. Gigantic eyes. Mesmerizing.

He offered her a beer and was surprised when she accepted. He went to the kitchen and got it and a glass, took one out for himself, then looked at it, changed his mind and got out the carton of orange juice. He decided it would be bad in front of a reporter to drink out of the carton, so he poured himself a big glass and took it all into the living room.

She was standing now in front of the movies, bending down to read the lower titles. He cleared his throat and she straightened up slowly, in no hurry, now wearing big over-sized glasses with black frames. She removed them and sat back down on the sofa, crossed her legs and smoothed the skirt over them. Jimbo checked the curve of her calves, the turn of her ankles. Kissable.

148

He said, "So, how much money are we talking about?"

This got a smile. "Direct, aren't you?" Not coy though; just making a statement.

"I didn't get that amount?"

"I'm freelance, you know."

"No shit."

Kristina said, "I've written three books, two marginal, one a best-seller. All about politics and politicians. I've always wanted to write a book about police work; gritty, realistic, the problem being that most cops interesting enough to write books about are arrogant, superior idiots, who won't waste their time with a woman writer. You know what I mean. Guys like you."

Jimbo admired her timing, setting him up and laying it on him, then coolly taking a long swig from her glass of beer, looking at him over the rim. Who else had he ever known who could look sexy drinking beer out of a tap glass?

He couldn't help himself; he smiled. Not much, but some. "How much did you say?"

She put the glass down. "I'll split all profits with you, down the middle. But it has to be *my* book, none of this business with your name on the jacket, then in small print, "as told to." I don't do ghostwriting."

"Why would I want my name on a book?"

"You really don't know?" Jimbo shook his head. Kristina said, "God."

She had another beer, and told him that there were two ways to write a book about somebody. With their help or without it. As a matter of fact, she'd already done some preliminary research, had talked to some of his fellow officers and she was getting a pretty good profile on him without ever having spoken to him.

Jimbo asked, "Did anyone tell you anything good?" She

laughed a little then, enjoying herself. Jimbo noticed the line about the different kind of books, like she was threatening him.

She said, "Usually, people come out a lot better when they cooperate. Writers get mad when they have to search and dig, like with Kitty Kelly, do you think she'd have written all that stuff if Sinatra had cooperated?"

Jimbo said, "What about the guy wrote the book on Bobby Knight? He had full cooperation, constant access, and he did a pretty good job on Knight."

"God, did you ever *meet* Bobby Knight?"

"No. Did you ever meet Sinatra?"

He could tell she was figuring out that she was losing him, and before she could start the hard sell he told her he'd think about it. She looked surprised but recovered nicely, though, her heart most likely not broken, and thanked him for the beer and his time.

She said, "Do you have any questions you'd like to ask me?" A professional, being open, friendly to the dumb hick cop who probably hadn't read a book since high school.

Jimbo said, "Do you fool around?" Deadpan, not trying to smile or be cute about it. Hell, she'd asked. She gave him a critical eye, sizing him up again, her lips curled but not smiling.

She said, "I heard you were a lecherous wiseass."

Jimbo said, "Who told you that?"

You got used to being alone, after a while. You even got to enjoy it after enough time passed. Especially if you liked your own company and the person you had been married to was insufferable to begin with. And it was better if you liked old movies. Jimbo was eating a pizza, swigging an RC Cola, watching *They Made Me a Criminal* with John Garfield and Ann Sheridan. He'd turned the phone off again, ignored all the messages on the machine. He wanted to be alone tonight. Enjoying himself with Sparky lying at his feet, in his old leather chair that was wrinkled and cracked to hell, broke in real good.

The doorbell rang.

He debated whether to just let it go, ignore it like he was ignoring all the urgent messages on the recorder, wondering why all of a sudden he was so damn popular. But what if it was Gizmo? Worried because Jimbo wasn't answering his phone? What if it was someone else—GiGi Parnell— Jesus, enough what-if.

Jimbo got up and lifted his 9mm Beretta off the end table in front of the couch and held it loosely in his hand, behind his back. He walked to the big security door with the peephole, looked through.

There was a great big giant of a woman, oh man, all hair and teeth, standing out there looking ma-ad. Jimbo opened the door and the woman opened her mouth, about to speak, then she spotted him and shut her mouth so fast Jimbo heard her teeth click together. She recovered fast, though, and beamed at him.

She said, "Hi!" Sounding like a door-to-door Bible saleslady, her eyes giving him a quick up and down, a fast but thorough sizing up. "I'm Mandi, your neighbor?"

Jimbo said, "Come on in, neighbor." Grinning right back, thinking, goddamn, Gizmo.

10

Before he had even gotten out of the squad room, GiGi had spoken to the men from the Office of Professional Standards. He'd ranted and raved and said that he wanted charges brought; here he was fresh out of the joint minding his own business and they roust him and send in the same guy to beat him up who'd busted him ten years ago. They promised him an investigation, but he knew how that stuff went. A cop could murder an ex-con while interrogating him and OPS and the rest of them would sweep it under the rug. A white ex-con, that is. Lay one hand on a jig and the city would make him a millionaire.

GiGi decided that maybe it had been a mistake, telling Tombstone Paterro that he'd hand him Marino's head as a favor. That put him under the gun. GiGi had been beating the system his entire life and never yet had seen a time when he'd gotten into trouble until the cops had cold, hard evidence. He'd met guys in the joint who'd claimed they'd been convicted on circumstantial evidence, but he did not believe it. When you killed someone, there had to be hard evidence or you would walk. GiGi had a half-dozen kills now and had never served a day for any of them. And he didn't intend to do hard time again, ever.

What he would have to do was he'd have to outthink them. Which shouldn't be too hard.

But he'd told Paterro he would kill Marino and so now he would have to. And he wanted to more than ever, now that he had thirteen stitches in his mouth and lips, and his nose was busted so he had two black eyes. It would be a pleasure now, more than ever. The only thing he would have a problem with would be making damn certain that he left no loose ends, no evidence. Which was one of the reasons that he'd called the lawyer who'd done his mom's will and told the lawyer to get a restraining order slapped on the cops—fast—and to get some newsprint about the beating. That he had suffered irreparable damage, whatever; he'd told the lawyer to make it look good. The lawyer had said he'd get on it right away, probably thinking of the quarter million GiGi controlled now. Well, that was okay with GiGi, he could think whatever he wanted as long as he kept the heat away from him.

He was in the emergency room at Mercy Hospital, where he'd been stitched up and x-rayed and had been assured that there were no head injuries. He was in the waiting room, and they'd named it right, he was waiting all right. Waiting for two things: for a reporter to call him back on the pay phone and for Agnes to come pick him up.

The phone next to him jangled. It was the reporter.

He told her who he was and what had happened, and he put a sob in his voice as he told her how he feared for his life. She told him she would check it out and he should look for her byline in the morning's paper, and he hung up smiling. This was enjoyable work. It would prove to the world that he had a reason to be terrified of this guy Marino, who obviously had a score to settle and was misusing his badge and the power of the police department. And it would prove a theory GiGi had long held as truth: that reporters were even dumber than cops.

But he had other things to think about, now that the con

was working in his favor. Such as the fact that he would have to kill Marino quick. And find and kill Barboza.

The problem he was having now was that it would be all out in the open, but maybe he could use that in his favor, too. Maybe Paterro would give him a high position because he was the only one who knew that it was the mob who had put the hit out on Marino. The way it had been a few hours back, though, would have been better. Now he would be the chief suspect, no matter how many TROs and news columns were out. If all this hadn't happened, if he had laid low then, kept a low profile, then he could have killed the sucker and no one would have suspected him. They'd think the mob had had it done, which in a way would have been right.

What burned him the most, really frosted his balls, was the fact that he'd let it happen, allowed a shitheel of a cop to knock him out, one punch, jumping over the table like that with no plan, no defense, totally at the mercy of the cop. Forgetting everything Buck had taught him, letting the son of a bitch get his goat like that. Shit, Marino had baited him, set him up, and he'd fallen hook, line and sinker. All he'd had to do was laugh, say something smart, maybe about Marino's old lady, and then he would have been out of there. And could have paid Marino back at his leisure.

But man, he'd forgotten how strong that fucker was. All the years in the pen, working out, getting harder and stronger, becoming a man, had made him think the guy would be easy. Jesus, he'd forgotten all about the day in the Miami alley, battling for what seemed like hours, the guy seeming to only get stronger as the fight wore on. Then the uniform guys, shit, with their macho pride, not pulling their guns or anything, a matter of honor to them, being able to subdue an unarmed man. After it was over, feeling about as good as he did now, as they drove him away in the squad car, he'd remembered looking out of the car window and seeing Marino there staring at him, hands on his hips, looking like he'd maybe been out jogging or something, breathing hard but on his feet. Man.

Next time, it would be different. It would be man-to-man. One-on-one in a place of GiGi's choosing. No more frolicking around in police stations. No guns, no bullshit, no talking.

Agnes came into the emergency room, looking around, her eyes holding on him for a second then passing on—she hadn't even recognized him.

"Agnes," he said, softly, his lips on fire. She turned her head and looked at him, shocked.

"GiGi?"

"Let's go home," GiGi said.

Home being his house on the Southeast Side, Lester there looking at him, shaking his fucking head. Agnes held his arm as he staggered up the steps, feeling pretty good now, the painkillers starting to kick in. Lester was guiding them down the upstairs hall to GiGi's old bedroom when GiGi turned them into his mom's. There was a sudden stricken look on Lester's face.

It was as if he'd never been away. There was his mom's big specially made bed, a hospital type thing with buttons you could push to put it in any position you wanted. A quilted bedspread over it, pretty but unable to conceal the ugliness of the apparatus. The walls were filled with large framed pictures of waiflike little girls, all with shoulder-length stringy brown hair surrounding huge oval faces and gigantic blue or brown eyes that followed you wherever you stood.

Over the bed, a crucifix hung; on the far wall was

mounted a painting of Jesus Christ, smiling sagely, his hand held under his pierced heart; for some reason the heart on the outside of his clothing. Old dressers. No mirrors in the room.

The bathroom was unchanged. The aluminum grab-bars were mounted on the wall next to the commode and over the soap dish in the tub. The place smelled good, clean. Lester did a good job in his mom's room.

Agnes was walking around with him, following him, watching as tears formed in his eyes.

Her boyfriend said, "This is our new bedroom," and Agnes was not sure if she wanted it to be or not, but he was looking at her so strangely she was afraid to say anything right now.

She watched him go around the room, sniffling from time to time, his hands on his hips, like he was in some kind of a daze. He went over to the closet and opened it, an antic-ipatory smile on his lips, kind of a sad smile, making Agnes feel sorry for him. He opened it and recoiled, let go of the doorknob as if it were red hot, jumping back, slamming the door.

Agnes went to him, poor baby, hugged him, buried her head in his chest, thinking, my God, the cops doing this to him and then coming home for the first time and getting all upset.

Which proved how much he loved her, his only now coming home. He'd spent all his time with her, rather than coming home. She felt warm and comforted, wanting now to warm and comfort *him,* pay him back, love him.

GiGi said, "Honey, I gotta go to the can. Take that thing out of there and tell Lester to put it in the basement. I want it in the trash." He turned and walked away from her.

156

Agnes did not know what to do. Something in the closet, and he wanted her to get rid of it. What could scare a guy who'd just done ten years in prison?

Agnes went to the edge of the bed and sat down, stared at the blank screen of the twenty-six-inch Sony TV against the wall. My God, he took good care of his mother. She remembered his banging her head against the wall the first night when she'd come into the shower with him. Then thought about how the cops had beaten him for nothing, probably not doing much for his mood, although he acted gentle enough. If she didn't do what he wanted, he was liable to get mad at her, and she still had to think about the stack of hundred-dollar bills hidden in her closet. And the guns.

Agnes got up and walked to the closet door. Do or die. No guts, no glory. She reached out and grasped the knob.

The closet was empty of clothes or shoes; the only thing in it an old wheelchair. Jesus.

GiGi was lying beside her, after a hot bath together. He'd put something in the tub to make it smell sweet and musky, washed her down in the big claw-foot bathtub, his hands gentle and strong at the same time. She'd closed her eyes and felt safer than she could ever remember feeling.

He had said sweet things to her, telling her how pretty his babycakes was, how she had the prettiest titties he'd ever laid eyes on. The loveliest backside. As he washed her back, she'd leaned into him, her face in the light hairs on his chest while he reached around and scrubbed her down, nipping at her neck. He had made her feel all loved and warm and happy.

He even dried her off, wouldn't let her get up out of the tub. He'd drained the water and run over to the linen closet, got out a gigantic white towel and then got on his knees beside the tub, rubbing the fluffy towel over her softly, almost sensually.

She'd never bathed with any man before.

She'd never been washed down before. Or dried off.

She certainly had never been lifted out of a tub by a man who carried her effortlessly out of the bathroom and into the bedroom, putting her softly on the downturned bed, pulling the sheet up over her, tucking her in. Then smiled down at her; his face beat all to the dickens and his eyes swollen so badly she could barely see the color of them. A rainbow surrounded his eyes almost like glasses, all different colors.

She said, "I love you, honey," meaning it, feeling tears come into her eyes.

GiGi told her, "I love you too, hon." His voice strong, powerful. Man enough to speak of love.

Agnes wept.

Later he was talking to her, scaring her terribly, Agnes listening and not saying anything but shivering from time to time. When she did he'd look up at her and say, "You cold?" and she'd shake her head, biting her bottom lip, trying to smile.

GiGi's head was on her breast, his fingers gently caressing her belly, making little patterns around her navel, tickling a little but feeling good.

He told her a story about a guy named Brian Solt who had tried to rob him because Brian was pussy-whipped and his old lady had talked him into it. And what GiGi had done to them.

Finally he got tired of asking her if she was cold and got up and got a blanket, wrapped it around her. GiGi said, "You didn't want to tell me you were cold because you didn't want me to get up and leave you for even a minute, did you?"

Agnes nodded her head, her eyes closed, fighting tears. Thinking, oh, God, please let it be a fantasy.

He said to her, "You know, I used to do this exact thing with my mom, lay next to her and talk to her like this."

Agnes afraid to say, Like *this?!* but thinking it.

GiGi rubbed against her, and Agnes felt the stiffness down there against her thigh. At last, something she knew something about and could control. She wrapped her arms around him as he mounted her, entered her gently.

This time she didn't tell him she liked it rough.

Jimbo was back in his chair, the credits rolling on the screen, angry because he hadn't paid any attention to the end of the movie.

He'd had his chance, earlier, with Mandi, with an *i*, as she'd told him, and he'd said he could have guessed. She'd come in, mad, telling him that she'd been at the Recorder's office and there was no record of anyone named Roland Jefferson, Jr., ever having been owner of this house, as Gizmo had told her. Jimbo told her that Gizmo was a houseboy, trying not to smile, and he'd watched her eyes light up as she wondered about a man who apparently traveled a lot and could afford a houseboy.

"Jimbo, Gizmo. Funny names," Mandi said.

He told her he knew a Franko too, and a guy who wanted to join the club, be called Christo, and she'd laughed.

Not a good laugh, though. A phony goddamn laugh he'd heard a thousand times in ginmills late at night when people were getting desperate. Jimbo resented her phoniness.

He wondered why she didn't have a rich, full, happy tinkling laugh like—Jesus—like Kristina.

He cut it off quickly, told Mandi with an *i* that he had an early appointment in the morning, and she'd been obviously disappointed, then asked him if he was interested in selling the house, dropping it in conversationally, like, Hey, gee, by the way, guess what I do for a living?

She said, uncomfortably, "Did your, er, houseboy tell you anything?"

"About what?"

"Well, you see, I hope you don't mind, but he did tell me he owned the house, you see, and was interested in selling it, so I took the liberty of taking measurements . . ." She gave him a friendly grin, stood up, walked suggestively to him, Jimbo admiring the way she'd wriggled out of the question he'd asked her by coming up with the measurements story. She'd measured something, all right.

He was suddenly weary. Tired of the game. No more sexual politicking with this phony real estate salesman. Tired of his playing around trying to get laid, dangling a listing contract in front of her nose like a carrot. Mostly, he felt sorry for her.

He said, "Look, Mandi, this house has been in the family forty years, and it's going to stay in the family another forty, okay?" with a smile, trying to be polite while getting his point across, the point being, leave me the hell alone if all you want from me is a listing.

Mandi looked around as she walked to the door, turned and said to Jimbo, "Another forty? Meaning you are married? Children, someone to leave it to? With the new tax laws, a single man—"

"Good night, Mandi." Jimbo watched her smile drop as she realized she was just wasting her valuable time with him. Mandi walked to the door, opened it, and without another word, walked through it, blond hair held high, honor intact.

Jimbo watched the white noise on the screen for a while, wondering if he was growing up. Five years—hell—five *days* ago he'd have had Mandi in bed. But he was thinking of the other woman he had met that afternoon.

He got up to turn off the TV and rewind the tape when the doorbell rang again. It was after dark now, almost ten. He clipped the holster to the back of his belt and went to the door, looked through the peephole.

Kristina. Jesus, speak of the devil.

He let her in, led her to the couch, trying hard not to appear as anxious as he felt or as happy. He had to be casual, let her do the talking.

Only she wasn't doing much talking, staring at him with sad eyes that were deep brown and wet. She was looking at him as if he had just rescued her from something nasty. The look reminded him of the way Bitsy had looked at him when he'd come home from the hospital after his fistfight with Parnell.

Jimbo got her a beer and asked straight out what was wrong.

"I'm so sorry," she said, giving him the most sorrowful look he'd ever seen. He'd busted ax-murderers who hadn't looked this regretful.

Jimbo said, "For what?"

Her eyes were cast downward, as if she was ashamed to look straight at him. She took a sip of her beer.

"Here I am a journalist, my God, I'm supposed to be per-*cep*tive! I came here this afternoon to try and do a deal with you and right away you're mad, cussing me out for doing my job, then later funny in a way, you know? I figured you for a lightweight. No, don't say anything, let me finish.

"I went over and talked to the man everyone who knows you mentioned that I should see. A man named Gizmo. Everyone I've talked to so far, they tell me you two are inseparable. I guess I thought that if anyone could give me the real story about you, he could, if I could get him to open up.

"Oh, Jimbo, he's such a nice man. Invited me in, gave me a card explaining his disability." She hesitated, about to drop the bomb and not knowing how. Jimbo wondered what the hell that crazy Gizmo had told her. She looked up at him full out now, giving him the five-hundred-watt stare, eyes filled with respect and understanding.

"Oh, Jimbo, he told me all about Cummings, Georgia." Gizmo had told her about Cummings, Georgia. That was good, because Jimbo had never been to Cummings, Georgia.

"What did he tell you about Cummings?"

"About how you told him when he'd wanted to march with everybody else down there that it wouldn't mean anything if you went with fifteen hundred cops and helicopters to guard you, it had to be something else, something meaningful!"

Oh, yes. Cummings was that town where no black people lived. A while back thousands of people had marched down there, and they'd been guarded by a couple thousand cops. He remembered it now.

She said, "He told me how you waited until all the furor died down, and then you and he flew to Atlanta and marched the thirty miles, just the two of you, into Forsyth County and then into the heart of Cummings, stopped there for a beer at the local saloon and then walked back." Her voice breaking now, she leaned toward him, touching his knee with a manicured, pampered hand.

Jimbo, enjoying the touch, couldn't help himself. Although he tried. He remembered what he'd been thinking before, about Mandi, about how maybe he was finally growing up, maturing. He tried to tell her it was all patented Gizmo bullshit. Wanted to tell her, but just couldn't. Not when her hand was resting on his knee and he could tell all that he had to do was lean over and kiss her and he'd be all set.

Jimbo said, "Did he tell you how I kidded the bartender, put on a fake accent and introduced Giz as my brother-in-law? Looking for a nice quiet place to move the new little woman to?" He was striving mightily to keep a straight face, just starting to lose the battle when she leaned right into him, hugging him hard, laughing and crying at the same time.

She said, "You crazy, crazy nut," then kissed his neck, Jimbo trying to create something else to tell her. She said, "I'm so sorry, Jimbo, really I am." She pushed off and held his biceps with her hands, giving him a straight look dead in the eye.

"But, my God, what else was I supposed to expect from a man your age named *Jim*bo? Whose best friend is named *Giz*mo? I mean," she was laughing now, shaking her head, Jimbo not seeing what was so funny, "it sounds like something out of a Marx Brothers movie."

To shut her up, Jimbo kissed her.

Trying to explain later, he told her about Gizmo and Bitsy, keeping it light, not mentioning the animosity Bitsy had toward blacks in general and Gizmo in particular.

"She kept trying to fix Gizmo up with all these cute little colored chicks would come into her disco or the gym, wanting them to double date with us, like teenagers, trying to show Gizmo how liberal she was. Finally, just to get her off his back, he told her he was gay. Bitsy refused to even let him in the house after that."

"So you never were in Cummings, Georgia." She didn't seem mad, in the bed with the sweat drying on her well-tanned skin. More of a good sport than he expected her to be. Both of them smoking, the ashtray on the mattress between them.

"Never." He kept an eye on her in case she wanted to try a GiGi Parnell, maybe stick the cigarette into his eye.

"And I gave up my honor to you in a burst of liberal patriotism."

"Well, it wasn't that bad, was it?"

She gave him an elbow in the ribs, mashed her cigarette out in the ashtray and said, "I've had better . . ." and rolled away, but not fast enough; he had her, rolling and laughing together until he kissed her again, a friendly kiss, not passionate. Buddies. No hard feelings.

She said, "Shhh!" and sat up, listening.

"What?"

"What was that? I heard a clicking."

"Probably the dog."

"No, it was a clicking sound."

They listened, and she said, "There it is again."

Jimbo smiled. "That's the recorder turning on. It clicks when it turns on and off. I'm so used to it, I don't even hear it."

She gave him a rueful look. "I believe it. I've tried calling you. Don't you ever answer the phone?"

"Not if I can help it." The click came again. Jimbo said, "I'm popular tonight." He waited for it to click off.

She said, "Aren't you curious who's calling you at midnight?" and Jimbo told her not in the slightest.

He reached for her again, then heard the clicking sound. She said, "Jimbo, it has to be important, maybe it's your work."

"I'm suspended, I think."

Surprised, Kristina asked, "What happened?" Then the clicking, back once again.

"Goddamnit." Jimbo threw back the covers and grabbed a terry-cloth robe from the end of the bed, then looked at Kristina and threw it to her, went to the closet and found his ratty old bathrobe hanging on a hook. He walked down the hallway to the telephone stand.

Jimbo hit the Rewind button, let four beeps go by, then stopped the machine, hit Play. A familiar voice came over the machine, rasping, sounding a little out of breath.

"You cocksucker, you dirty son of a bitch." The voice was outraged, spewing impotent venom. "I buy you a goddamn machine so I can call you up when I need you and then it turns out you're not only a fucking cop, but a *thief* too, take the thing home with you, plug it in like it was a present from your fucking girlfriend or something—" Beep. Cut him off in mid-curse. Beep. Mikey Barboza was back for more.

"Okay, okay, you son of a bitch. Look, they're going to kill me, Campo and Paterro. I'm gonna get whacked out, I know it, I just fucking *left* them. Jesus Christ, you got to help me, Jimbo, you fucking owe me, without me you wouldn't have nothing at a—" Beep. Jimbo was smiling, lighting a smoke. Kristina sat next to him, hugging his arm. Beep. Then: "Listen, shit, I'm down to one more quarter, now *listen* goddamnit, I ain't got all night. I'm in the Holiday Inn Michigan Avenue, room 1977, you got that? I got to talk to you, Marino. It's a matter of life and death. I want to tell you about—" Beep. Jimbo laughed straight out now, seeing Mikey Barboza in a room at the Inn slamming the pay phone onto the hook in the booth in the lounge, getting half-bombed because he thought there was a hit out on him. Beep.

Mikey's recorded voice said, "I got something you want to hear, Marino," and then Mikey Barboza beat the machine. He hung up on it first.

Jimbo looked at Kristina. He said, "I think I just got my job back."

11

Mikey was sitting in the lounge, alone at a small round table, looking morosely at the three-piece band banging away under the stage lights, doing a lousy job of playing "Satisfaction." Jimbo walked over to him slowly, checking out the room, doubting he'd be set up in a lounge in a Holiday Inn but not taking any chances. He had two guns—one on his right hip and one at the rear of his jeans, both hanging off his belt. His 9mm Beretta in front, a Smith .38 with the two-inch barrel in back. He sat down.

Mikey Barboza looked at him. "Judas. You are a fucking Judas. Like a son I treat you and how do you pay me back? By turning out to be a cop." He spat the word out.

Jimbo wondered how many Scotches Mikey had in him. He said, "See you around, Mikey," not even moving to get out of the chair.

Barboza said, "Wait, just wait a goddamn minute." He called for the waitress and ordered another Chivas neat with a water back for himself, then looked at Jimbo. Jimbo told him a Miller. Mikey looked pained. "Christ, when I was buying you drinks all night, it was top shelf all the way, now it's fucking beer."

"You wanted to talk to me? Or you want me to come back in the morning, when you're sober, through beating your chest and playing the abused fucking wife with me."

"You ain't so tough."

"See you around, Mikey," meaning it this time, getting up to leave.

"Goddamnit, sit down."

"Fuck you, you bum," Jimbo said. He turned and walked out of the lounge.

He got as far as the lobby. Mikey Barboza chased after him, his drink in his left hand, Jimbo's beer in his right, in the bottle. Mikey hadn't brought the glass.

Mikey said, "Come on, Jesus, let's sit down over here." Staggering a little even standing still.

"In the lobby right here, downtown where anyone can see us?"

Mikey said, "Christ, you paranoid?"

In room 1977 now, Jimbo taking no bullshit; as soon as they entered he'd searched the place thoroughly, then taken Mikey's drink and flushed it down the toilet.

"Now talk," he said.

"Just tell me one thing. What'd you have on Vinnie Franchetti? I known him all my life and he introduces me to you, tells me what a stand-up guy you are, like his son, and you're a cop."

Jimbo just looked at him.

Mikey said, "And I checked you out. Jesus, you guys were thorough. Prison records, a number, everything. Picture and prints on file with the cops. You went to a lot of trouble to bust me, Jimbo."

Jimbo still stared at him, sitting in the only chair in the room. Mikey plopped onto the bed, kicked off his shoes and finally started to get down to business.

Mikey told Jimbo everything that had happened to him from the time he'd gotten the call from GiGi Parnell Monday night. Jimbo did not interrupt him; he'd figured GiGi's part out from the beginning, but didn't want Barboza to know it. Barboza had hid out and then heard about his boys getting busted, and then, God, the next day on the news Jimbo Perino, his trusted employee, the guy he was going to introduce to the real big shots in the mob.

After learning that Jimbo was a cop he'd spent the afternoon thinking about his options: go home and wait for GiGi Parnell to find him if the cops didn't first; or go to Tommy Campo, tell him everything, get his ass chewed for ripping off a member of his stable and probably still get beaten to death for trusting a cop, even a cop who'd been introduced to him by Vinnie Franchetti, for God's sake, who he'd known since he was a kid. . . .

About calling Tommy and having Campo hang up on him, a twenty-five-year friendship and the guy had hung up on him. Frantic then, shit, he hadn't even been home in almost two days, his old lady must have worn out two sets of rosary beads. Calling Tombstone Paterro this morning—

Jimbo interrupted him.

"With warrants out for you and an APB with the Staties, you're sitting downstairs drinking the last three days?" Barboza looked at him like he was stupid.

"There're more fugitives in Chicago than there are in fucking Russia, for God's sake."

Then he told Jimbo about the meeting that night.

"I go into Tommy Campo's house, the guy, I knew him when he was shooting niggers, busting into South Side numbers games when he was a kid, he treats me like a long-lost son, the asshole, patting my cheek, Christ, till I'm ready to puke. Tells me not to worry, he'll take care of everything, you, the federal grand jury, if there ever is one, the wiretaps, they'll find a way out. Just go home and take it easy. I say to him, 'Tommy, what about this warrant?' He says to me, 'Ain't you got a lawyer?' like it's nothing. I goes, 'What about this GiGi Parnell?' And that's when I know I'm in trouble, 'cause he shoots a quick look over at Tombstone and goes, he goes, 'Let us worry about GiGi Parnell.'" Barboza got up and went into the bathroom. Jimbo stood and moved away from the chair, drawing his 9mm and pointing it at the bathroom door.

Barboza came out and casually looked toward the chair, wiping his hands on a paper towel, then spotted Jimbo and jumped, his hands going to his chest.

His face was a mask of terror. "Jesus, I thought you were going to whack me out."

Jimbo simply reholstered the weapon and sat back down in the chair.

Mikey Barboza said, "Shit, paranoid fucker," trying to save face, then he just stood there and told the rest of it.

"I tell Tommy, I says, 'All due respect, Tommy, it ain't you he's trying to kill,' and Tommy says, 'Look, you fucked the guy in the business deal. In thirty-five years of business, I never fucked anyone, not even the yoms.' Like he's Lee Iacocca or Henry Ford or somebody. He goes, 'Let's just say, you paid him his money, so he got no right to come looking for you. The word's out, he's a dead man,' then he turns to Tombstone and he goes, 'ain't that right, Ange?' And Tombstone, he grunts, looking all sour and mad at the world, not saying anything."

Jimbo said, "Mikey, what are you afraid of? Shit, they *told* you they'd take care of you. Go turn yourself in, get out on bond, handle it." He was seeing how far he could push it, knowing he owned Barboza now.

Mikey said, "Hey, you know why they call Angelo 'Tombstone'? Not because he kills so many people, hell, he's better than Campo, it comes to that. They call him

'Tombstone' because when his mind is finally made up, when you are a dead motherfucker, baby, he gets all icy and cold and won't talk to you; his eyes turn cold and hard and look like little tombstones."

"Like he was over at Campo's house?"

"Exactly like that."

"Mikey, let me see what I can do."

If he played his cards right, then he could have it all. Any job he wanted, the hell with OCTF now that he couldn't work undercover, maybe he'd even quit, after he ran Barboza for a while. Shit, Kristina could get maybe three books out of this deal alone. Movie rights . . .

But he wasn't about to leave Mikey Barboza in room 1977 of the Holiday Inn on Michigan Avenue.

"Mikey, what did you mean when you said that Campo would take care of me?"

Barboza looked up, his face puzzled. "What?"

"You said before that Campo told you he'd take care of me, the grand jury, everything. What did he mean by that, saying he'd take care of me."

Barboza said, "Pay you off, what else?" Then it seemed to dawn on him. "You figure Tommy's nuts enough to try and whack a *cop*?"

Jimbo tried to save face. "Stranger things have happened."

"A wise guy planning to kill a cop? What do you figure, Al Capone's still running things?" Barboza apparently was getting off on Jimbo's discomfort. Jimbo was considering picking him up and holding him out the window—nineteen floors above the street—by his ankles, maybe take the edge off his sense of humor.

Instead, he pulled his pistol and held it at his side. Once

he had Barboza's attention, he smiled. He said, "Let's get you out of here."

He had asked her, "Do you fool around?" and she'd nearly said, "Yes, I do," and not just to get his reaction, but because, by God, he turned her on. Usually it took *power* to do that. But in his own way, wasn't he one of the most powerful men she'd ever wanted to write about? Here he was, young, arrogant, strong as an ox but smart too, not out playing the father figure in a blue uniform handing out tickets, but going undercover, working one-on-one with the mob, for God's sake. The power to make or break them in his hands.

And what had she said? Something dumb, that she'd heard he was a lecher and all he wanted to know was who had told her. Self-contained, not caring what anyone thought of him.

Generally, once people heard the word *press,* they fell all over themselves to be interviewed, then would call later, cussing and crying and screaming that they'd been misquoted. She couldn't picture Jimbo doing that. Maybe telling her she was stupid or something, but not caring one way or another about what she wrote or how she quoted him.

She'd done her homework, and boy, there was enough of it on this guy. Quite a career. Difficult too, when talking to officers he'd worked with, figuring out how much of what they told her was real and how much just resentful jealous garbage.

But she had fallen for the Cummings, Georgia, line from Gizmo, maybe because she was looking at him as a poor, handicapped troll instead of as a human being who just happened to be deaf. As capable of lying to you as anyone else. And old Jimbo didn't try to set her straight, either, until later, but that was okay, too. It had been worth it, even if it happened under deceitful circumstances. In a way, it was almost poetic justice. She couldn't count the times she had swept someone into the sack, trying to get what she could from them, lying, deceiving, manipulating them for her own purposes.

But men were different. Much vainer than women. A man could know straight off that you were a reporter out to get him, and God, think that he was charming you into the sack and after that you were effectively neutralized as a threat against him. Arrogant? Let me tell you.

Kristina searched the house carefully, looking for things, not for anything bad in particular, but for something that would give her some insight to this guy, some idea of his mind-set. Tons of books in the bedroom, thrillers, mostly; anything there? No, a lot of men liked thrillers. Books mostly in hardcover. Another nonshocker. She knew he had plenty of money. Clothes tasteful, some suits in the closet but mostly sports clothes, slacks, solid-color shirts. Good leather shoes.

The second floor had been a bust. Except for a computer in a bedroom up there, the rooms looked more like the ones you would find in a motel than a private home, everything in place, neat. No secrets here.

If there was to be something she could sink her teeth into, it would be in the titles of the movies next to the television. The problem was, she'd never heard of most of them. James Cagney, Edward G. Robinson, she knew who those guys were, of course. But seeing pictures of people on the front of a video-cassette box and knowing anything about the movies inside were two different things.

Most of the titles gave the impression of something macho, though. *The Hitman. Angels with Dirty Faces.* No Disney stuff, here.

Kristina sat on the couch, staring at the movie titles, deep in thought.

Then heard the key turning in the lock and she rose, smiling, but the dog went nuts, jumping off the carpet and racing for the door, not barking but snarling, lips curled back, ready. Jesus, wasn't it Jimbo? Then relieved when she saw the sportcoat over the jeans, saw Jimbo slapping at the dog's muzzle, saying goddamnit a few times. Jimbo walking in with another man—a very big man—behind him.

Still in his terry-cloth robe, which she held tight at the throat, a smile frozen on her face, still a little scared, watching Mikey Barboza slither into the room and look fearfully at the dog, Kristina began to smile and smile.

Jimbo got Sparky into the basement and made the introductions, watching Kristina smiling away at Mikey, wondering what the hell was going on. Maybe she wanted to write a book about *him* now. Jesus. Mikey looking from Kristina to Jimbo, making connections, winking at Jimbo when Kristina wasn't looking. Jimbo took him to the second floor and showed him the room he'd be sleeping in for the night, the bathroom down the hall. Back at the Holiday Inn before leaving he'd asked Barboza, "You got anything to bring along, a toothbrush or anything?" and Barboza had just looked at him.

After checking the house from top to bottom he went to bed, surprised that Kristina had still been there, but happy with the way things were going. Doubly happy when she threw off the robe and joined him in bed, snuggling.

Kristina said, "They'll make you commissioner if you bring in Mikey Barboza single-handedly."

"I'm not exactly going to be bringing him in."

"What do you mean?" Sounding intrigued. The plot thickens.

"I mean that maybe he can be put to a higher and greater use."

"Such as?"

Jimbo reached out and put his arm under her back, lifted himself atop her. He held his weight off her with his elbows, looking down into her eyes. "We'll see tomorrow." He kissed her gently. "You gonna stick around?"

Kristina said, "You couldn't get me away from this one with your pistol, mister."

And Jimbo said, "Hell, that's what I'm hoping to keep you *around* with. . . ."

Later, Jimbo was feeling on top of the world but unable to sleep. Too keyed up, happy. Excited. Barboza was upstairs asleep, trusting Jimbo now with his entire future and his very life. Jimbo didn't know if he liked having that responsibility. Slowly, so as not to awaken Kristina, he eased himself out of bed and padded to the kitchen, opened the basement door so the dog could roam around but hell, as usual, she started nuzzling him, man, starved for attention. Bitsy probably never even looked at the dog unless some guy mentioned he liked them; then she'd turn into a dog-lover.

He sat down at the kitchen table and took a painful inventory of his life. Thinking first of Bitsy. Feeling sorry for her now that she was two thousand miles away and not right there in front of him.

Bitsy would keep her cigarettes in her purse if she was

with a nonsmoker and go on and on about how she hated people who sucked those disgusting weeds. She'd met a born-again Christian once when they were at a party and suddenly she was a fundamentalist until the guy caught on, hit her up with some chapter and verse he'd made up and later Bitsy cried and cried, asking Jimbo how anyone could possibly be so mean.

A phony from the word go. He seemed to attract them and then wondered why. Birds of a feather? Christ, all he did was act, and he was a better make-believe person than he was a real flesh-and-blood person. Always a pro at undercover work but having no patience for the mundane aspects of the job; he hated paperwork with a passion and for that matter even calling in and telling people where he was and what he was doing. Results were all that mattered with him, getting the job done.

Lettierri had called him a hot dog, and he knew for a fact that Val Klenck and the rest of the crew, except for maybe Francis Mahon, hated his guts. He'd never been real good at making friends. Like today with Johnson, man, she couldn't wait to get out of the interrogation room and drop a dime on him to Franchese, and when that didn't work she went right to the top, down the hall to Lettierri, who'd called Jimbo a hot dog.

He wondered now if his enemies had reason for being such. Maybe he was a phony, worse in his own way than Bitsy. Hell, her game didn't have life-or-death consequences for anybody. Even tonight, with Kristina, letting her go on and on about Cummings, Georgia, and not stopping her; he'd even made it worse with the line about the bartender. Getting her into the bedroom, using guile and deception to have his way. Afraid that she wouldn't have gone if she knew the truth.

But it couldn't have been just his trying to get laid. If that was all it was, he'd had his chance earlier with the real estate shark who slept with people on the off chance that they might let her list their house. He wasn't that phony. At least not yet.

Maybe not phony at all. With him, what you saw was what you got. He didn't put on airs or tell lies, unless he was undercover. And then he was risking the loss of things worth lying to keep. Like his right to life. He never hurt anyone if he could help it. Sure, sometimes he responded in kind to assholes like Klenck, but he never went out of his way to misrepresent himself, ever. And he did do a lot of good. Got a lot of bad guys off the street.

He knew why he was giving himself the third degree in his kitchen, knew what it all was building up to. He had a vicious mad-dog killer on his back and a Mafia big shot upstairs in his old bedroom. He was planning on letting the mad dog take a shot at him and then killing him without a second thought, and that was wrong. Maybe it was wrong. He wasn't sure yet and wouldn't be until it was all over and then he would see how he felt about it. And if it was wrong he'd know it.

And the Mafia guy? Big bad Mikey Barboza? Things would be going a lot differently than anyone expected them to go tomorrow morning, if he could pull it off.

The question was: Was he doing it because it was the right thing to do, or because he wanted it to look good as a chapter in a goddamn book?

And did it matter as long as everything worked out?

It had been Jimbo who had busted his ass undercover, sweating bullets and eating Gelusils, swigging Pepto-Bismol by the bottle. It had also been he who had originally had the idea, when he'd gotten the word about Vinnie Franchetti having cancer. He'd set it up, thought it out, and lived the part for three whole months. And now, as Lettierri had said, it was falling apart.

All because GiGi goddamn Parnell had gotten out of the joint. Another two, three months and he would have had them all boxed and ready for delivery to the nearest federal prison, the badass mob guys getting hoarse from talking to the feds, trying to rat out their goombahs. And if he turned Barboza over to them now, it would all be over. There was no doubt about that. They'd busted an entire crew and not one of them had rolled over. And without that leverage they had nothing to make Barboza roll over. A bunch of tape recordings that might convict him, get him some time, but he'd also have about ten years to play around with the appeals and all.

Unless he was right and Campo and Paterro were indeed planning to whack him out.

Which was something Jimbo sincerely doubted. This wasn't some low-level pusher here, this was an underboss, a guy right under Tombstone Paterro, one of the heirs to the throne. He couldn't be whacked out like some soldier or numbers runner caught with his hand in the take. His death would have to be ordered from above; even Campo had to answer to somebody. The national commission had to approve all hits against guys of Barboza's rank, and over the years someone like Mikey would have made some powerful friends on the commission. So in Jimbo's opinion, all Mikey was afraid of was GiGi Parnell, and with good reason. But he didn't have to worry about Campo and Paterro. At least not yet.

But if Jimbo's plan worked out, then Mikey would have every reason to worry.

Jimbo patted the dog on her head, and she took this as a reason to celebrate, jumping up and down, running her head up under his hand, and he laughed, rubbed her behind her ears. Man, it was going to be hard giving her up when Bitsy came back home.

12

The pain in his mouth awakened GiGi and he laid there in his mom's bed for a minute, disoriented, wondering where he was and who he was with. He smiled when he figured things out. But smiling made the chipped front teeth hurt something terrible, so he shut his mouth tight.

GiGi got out of bed and found the painkillers, shit, Tylenol No. 3, maybe a little better than taking aspirin. Today would be the day, and thinking that, he smiled again. The pain this time didn't bother him; as a matter of fact, he welcomed it. It reminded him of Mr. Big Bad Jimbo Marino, who got off on beating guys senseless when he was in the company of his cop buddies. He'd get his chance today, show what he could do when there was no-body else around.

He sat in the little chair next to the bed, the chair Lester probably sat in when he washed down GiGi's mom or maybe at the end when he fed her. Another reason Marino would catch his lunch. Busting GiGi had kept him from his mom's deathbed. But he couldn't think about that too much or he'd start to freak, and he didn't want to do that in front of Agnes.

He watched her for a little while, sleeping soundly, look-ing so innocent and cute.

When the painkillers were going good, GiGi dressed and

walked out of the bedroom, silently, not wanting to wake his lady up, enjoying the way that made him feel. He went downstairs to the kitchen; shit, the fridge was almost empty. Lester had bought only old-man food, nothing that would stick to your ribs. He put a couple of eggs in a pan of water, figuring that a couple of hard-boiled eggs would hold him over. Later, after his lady got up, they'd go get steak and eggs. And some clothes, boy, did he need some clothes. GiGi cautiously walked over to the door that led to the basement, looked at it for a while, then threw caution to the winds and opened it.

Wooden steps leading down into darkness.

His worst defect, as a young man, had been his temper. Today he was in control, could think things out, make logical moves to achieve whatever goals he set. If somebody had to die, they'd get theirs in a way that would lead the cops to anyone but GiGi. His temper, he knew, was under control.

So he hadn't lost it when Agnes had stiffened in his arms when he'd mentioned to her that he used to lay there next to his mom and tell her things. He knew damn well what she'd thought. Him and his mom naked in bed, maybe after sex; oh man, she couldn't think he'd ever had sex with his *mom;* what kind of guy did she think he was? Looking at the basement steps, mesmerized, GiGi Parnell knew that sooner or later he'd have to straighten Agnes out on things. Later, though, after she'd got used to being with him, knew him a little better.

In the joint, the shrinks who had to work there because they couldn't get a decent job on the outside because they were so fucked up had once given him an alcohol-and-drug-dependency quiz. At first the thought of taking it had offended GiGi, but if you argued with these guys, they'd give you the superior stare and calmly ask you why you thought something was wrong, always acting like you were a chimpanzee in the monkey house in Lincoln Park Zoo, so it was better to just go along with things and get the hell out as soon as you could. Seventy-two questions and maybe seventeen of them had anything to do with booze or dope. And one of the questions—he couldn't remember the number anymore but he sure remembered the question—was: "Have you ever wanted to see your mother naked?" And in the little space left for an answer Gigi had written, *You fucking perverts*.

His mom, twenty years back when GiGi had been a teenager, always wore those out-of-date clothes, tight ski pants with the little cloth strap on the bottom that went around your feet. With a little round pot of a belly hanging over the elastic, the backside filled out pretty good but she didn't know how heavy she was back there; she couldn't see her own ass. Sloping little breasts that reminded GiGi of tiny loaves of Vienna bread, or of tacos. Always wearing tight sweaters or in the summer, T-shirts. With brownish-blond hair pulled back severely in a ponytail or teased into a giant beehive, always embarrassing him by being ten years behind the fashions, sitting there drinking her beer at the kitchen table, the only woman he'd ever known who'd smoked Camels, although he knew a woman once, in Florida, who'd smoked Pall Malls. GiGi a month out of the Audey home with his next fall guaranteed to send him to the juvie center at St. Charles. Sometimes his mom had men friends over and sometimes she drank with the neighbor lady, but he could rest assured that anytime after three in the afternoon when her shift ended at the G.E. Factory he could find her in her chair, smoking Camels and drinking whatever beer she could find on sale.

Tears filled his eyes as he remembered that night, and he ignored the boiling water and the eggs and stared into the gloom, as if looking for some answers down there. Why did he ever do it, lose his temper that way with his mom who'd never done anything but love him?

And then it hit him, sometimes he'd forget some parts of it and sometimes he'd remember. Now, looking at the scene, he remembered.

Mom always enjoyed bossing him around and he let her get away with it most of the time, because it made her feel like she was in charge of something. That bad night there had been a woman at the table with his mom and his mom had been giving him a really exceptionally heavy load of shit, giving him her own version of the Badeye, like he was supposed to be afraid or something, and she'd told him he wasn't going anywhere when he knew good and damn well that he was and he remembered his mom had the basement door open so she could hear when the washer stopped and he remembered his mom giving her ladyfriend a look like, Watch this! And he remembered her coming up to him and he'd thought she was coming to kiss him good-bye. But instead she smacked him, right across his face, and man, oh, man, he'd seen red.

It hadn't even hurt, just stung a little, but he'd gone a little crazy what with that lady watching and looking at him like he was a little baby being spanked, like the two ladies drinking beer were so superior to him, that he'd freaked. He'd grabbed his mom by the elbows and lifted her up just a little bit and spun her around, planning on slamming her into the wall and letting her go, but the no-good goddamn basement door had been open and he'd lost his grip and down she'd gone, backwards, a smoking Camel still in her hand, her face showing total shock and terror.

And even in the terrible pain she'd been in lying there at the foot of the stairs, her back broken, she'd managed to make the lady promise to tell the ambulance guys that it was an accident. That was how much she loved her only son. Even after he'd almost killed her.

When she finally came home, she didn't do or say anything for a long time. Years later GiGi saw guys acting the same way in the joint when they first came in, guys who just couldn't believe that some judge had really sent them away to where the criminals were caged. They'd lie on their bunks all day, wouldn't take jobs, their arms over their faces, maybe whimpering sometimes when the shines would wander into the cell and roll them over and give it to them. That's how his mom had acted.

She could use her arms just fine—the doctors had told them that—but for that long time she'd acted like a total cripple, not doing or saying anything much, just lying there in her bed staring at the ceiling. And at him.

He'd come in to feed her and she'd lay that look on him, that *we-know-who-did-this-to-me* glare, yet she never, ever mentioned that night again. He'd fed her and sponged her and gave her a weekly bath, carrying her from the damn tub to the bed, sometimes snuggling up with her when she'd start to cry. Sometimes some of the old anger would come back. Like when she'd lay there and call for him to come change the channel on the TV, when he'd paid extra for her to have a remote. Or when he'd got used to her suddenly being able to move her hands when she had to use the toilet, then forgetting again after she'd cleaned herself off and had called to him to come carry her back to bed. Or the one time, when he'd had to teach her a lesson.

Bathing her, GiGi trying not to let his eyes go down her to that gray patch, washing it by feel, shampooing her head and she'd said to him, "Don't get water in my ears," and he'd gone a little crazy. How the fuck were you supposed to wash someone's hair who wouldn't help you at all and not get any water in their ears! He'd been holding her awkwardly, with his right hand behind her neck while she floated in the full bathtub, rubbing the shampoo in with his left; and rather than argue with her he'd just let her go and watched as she'd gone under, her face a mask of terror, her arms coming out of the water and grabbing the edges of the big old tub but they didn't have enough strength to pull her up. He'd waited a minute and when bubbles started coming out of her nose he'd pulled her up, dried her off and carried her to bed, and from that time until the time he'd gone away, she never again had said anything really stupid to him.

He'd split every damn dime he'd ever stole or earned right down the middle with her, preparing her for the time when he'd go away or maybe get killed; and she gave the money to her brother Lester, who handled all the money for her, paid all the bills and everything even back then. He'd been trying to pay her back for making her what she was. A cripple. And it was all his fault.

None of them ever understood how it was. How could they? How could they know about the secret he and his mom shared? And so when they'd learned that he was sending her half of his money—and he'd been really lucky in Florida, Christ, lived like a king on the half he'd kept for himself—they'd dubbed him the White Heat Bandit after a real old James Cagney movie where Cagney played a psycho loony-tunes killer who had a fixation on his mother. How could he tell them that he really didn't but that he'd owed her? Shit, the guineas with their loyalty oaths and that other garbage, they had no idea what real loyalty was all about. The sacrifice it took to be loyal.

Did he ever want to see his mother naked? Jesus Christ, that's how he'd seen her more often than not. And not once ever did he get a hard-on. So much for the White Heat in-love-with-his-mother Bandit bullshit.

The only joy she'd had in later years was living life through GiGi's experiences, saying, "Come on," like a little kid, "tell me about it." And he'd always told her about what he did. She'd never had him busted for making her a cripple, so why shouldn't he trust her now?

Mom gone now, but the pain almost not there anymore, since meeting his lady. Since falling in love. GiGi smiled into the darkness below the steps, remembering something his mom used to say to him when he'd swear he'd never leave her alone. GiGi's mom would say, "A daughter's a daughter all her life, but a son's a son till he takes him a wife."

Maybe all along mom had been right about that, too.

Jimbo slept for a while, but not much and not deeply, just dropping off a little and then snapping awake really quick every time Kristina shifted or made any sounds or Sparky settled down at the foot of the bed. With the first gray light of morning he was up and dressed, feeling sorer than hell from his rough hard workout the day before, but a good, cleansing type of sore. Not the soreness of hangover.

Sparky padded alongside him into the kitchen, jumping up and down on him until he opened the back door and let her out. He filled her food dish and water dish and left them in the basement before he came back upstairs and put his coffee on.

After a time, sipping hot coffee, he heard Mikey Barboza groaning upstairs, loudly, and he smiled. Hangover would be good for him, make him humble. Allow Jimbo to call all the shots. He heard the upstairs toilet flush and then the heavy tread of Barboza's footsteps on the stairs.

Mikey Barboza looked like death, and Jimbo had to fight to keep from smiling. He asked him if he wanted anything to eat, and Barboza had looked at him and had asked him if he was fucking nuts. He did accept coffee, though, hot and black.

"How'd I get here?" Mikey asked, and Jimbo told him to cut the game, he'd be a hell of a lot more surprised than he was acting if he hadn't remembered the night just past. That had made Mikey glare at him, but Jimbo spotted respect in his eyes.

Jimbo said, "Before anything else, I gotta ask you a question." Mikey looked up, expectantly. Wet eyes, with little red lines running through the whites, staring at Jimbo. Barboza didn't look anything at all like the number three or four guy in the Chicago Mafia. He looked more like a skid row bum.

"How did you get my phone number?" Jimbo said, and Mikey sighed.

"Shit," Mikey said, sounding relieved, "I thought you was gonna ask me something hard." He tried to smile but it obviously set bells to ringing and he stopped trying quickly. "I got a guy, I mean, we got a guy, works for the phone company. Hell, we got guys, the electric company, the gas company, the water company, guys on the Streets and Sanitation, guards in the joint, everywhere man, we're *every*where." No pride there in his voice now, though; it sounded to Jimbo more like anguish.

"Which is why there ain't no way in hell you're turning me over to the feds, Jimbo. I know of two guys, personally, got whacked after they got their new ID and set up in another state. It's all on computers these days. We got guys, eat computers for breakfast. Get into anything at all for the right price. Witness Protection Program? Fuck you. Guys go in there are safe as long as they're on a whole floor of the MCC all alone, nobody can get to 'em, but once they get relocated, they're dead meat."

"I never had any intention of turning you over to the feds, Mikey."

"Then what?"

"You got any idea, Mikey?"

"Some thoughts have entered my mind."

"What'd you figure out, Mikey?"

"You want to run me."

"That's right, Mikey."

"Jesus Christ, will you quit calling my name out, for chrissakes. I know who I am."

"Sorry, Mikey."

"It ain't the name, Jimbo, it's the way you say it, like you got me by the balls and I'm on your string, in your goddamn stable or something."

"That's right, Mikey."

Barboza pushed himself away from the table, spilling his coffee. He said, "The fuck it is, Perino, or Marino, or whatever the fuck your real name is. Nobody runs me, hotshot, you hear me? Not you, not the feds, not no-fuck-ing-body."

He stared at Jimbo hard and Jimbo brought the 9mm pistol out of the belt holster, pointed it directly at Barboza's chest.

"Let's do it this way, Mikey. Either you agree to let me run you, or I bust you now, make a call, tell your goombahs Campo and Paterro you're rolling over, which they may or may not believe, then another call to GiGi Parnell, tell him you're at Twenty-sixth and California and will be getting bond soon. Then you'll have a choice. Jump into the Witness Protection Program, where you already know you'll be living on borrowed time, or else walk out, take your chances with the mob and with Parnell."

Slowly, Barboza lowered his bulk into the kitchen chair, his eyes never leaving Jimbo's. "Tommy and Tombstone, they won't waste me, they'll wait for Parnell to do it for them."

"You figured that out, eh, Mikey?"

"Then they can take over, throw up their hands, tell the other guys I'm in tight with, 'What are you gonna do? Some psycho Mikey beat out of twenty grand whacks him, hell, what are you gonna do?' I seen the act before. Hell, I been *in* the act before." Dejected now, defeated.

Then Barboza said, "I was drunk last night, you know."

"No shit, I never would have figured that one."

"You know, Marino, for a cop, you're more of a crook than you are a good guy."

Jimbo sighed. "Everyone keeps telling me that."

Barboza hung his head in his hands, knuckling his eyeballs.

Jimbo said, "Mikey?" and waited for Barboza to look at him. "You figured out yet what we're going to do?"

"We're gonna run a game on everybody, ain't we."

"That's right, Mikey, and here comes the good news. Afterward, after you put Campo and Paterro in the penitentiary for a hundred years each, guess what?" Barboza looked at him with grateful eyes, hopefully, finally seeing a way out. He said, "What?" not even remembering making Jimbo jump through hoops and give answers less than a week ago in the car, or if he did remember, not letting it bother him that the roles were now reversed.

Jimbo said, "You'll get, as your present from me, all of the Chicago mob action. I'll put you in Campo's place. Mikey, I'll put the world at your feet if you just do as I tell you."

Mikey Barboza looked through Jimbo for several seconds. "And you, Jimbo, you run the whole show, eh, is that it? I don't talk to the feds, to the State Attorney's guys, nobody but you, is that the way it is?"

"That's the way it is, Mikey."

"You run the whole show from top to bottom; they don't even know who I am, right?"

"Just one guy will know, and he's good."

"It will be just you, is that what you're telling me? Then what about the warrants? And maybe the federal grand jury indictments?"

Jimbo said, "Mikey, you let me worry about that."

Jimbo went to the phone and dialed Gizmo's number, told the computer that he needed Gizmo, either this morning or on his lunch hour, to get over to the house and get those alarms in—*now*—things were starting to heat up.

Jimbo felt a moment's fear as he hung up the phone. He was wondering if things might just be getting a little too hot for him to handle. He fought it off, telling himself he'd been in tougher spots. Later, maybe, when he had time, he might even be able to think of one.

13 Jimbo called Chris Haneys' home and learned from the Haneys' nine-year-old daughter that her dad was in the bathroom, but that her mom was available if he needed to speak with her. Talking to a nine-year-old with more poise and composure and telephone manners than most adults, Jimbo thanked her and politely asked to speak to her mom.

Jean Haney was one of the most beautiful women Jimbo had ever seen; on more than one occasion he'd asked Chris what in God's name she'd ever seen in him, and Chris had always ducked it with a wise remark, both men knowing that without Jean, Chris would dry up and blow away. Tall, regal, with warm laughing eyes—just talking to Jean could always cheer Jimbo up.

But not today. Jimbo asked her to tell Chris that he had to speak to him immediately and that he would be at the Crown Restaurant on Lincoln Avenue at eight o'clock. Jean asked about Gizmo, and Jimbo assured her that the little deaf genius was doing just fine, tempted to tell her about Gizmo's scam on the real estate woman Mandi, or the game Gizmo had run on Kristina; it was the kind of stuff Jean would enjoy, but his mind was racing this morning and he had to get off the phone, organize his thoughts. Make his plans.

To Barboza he said, "Stay here," seeing Kristina out of

191

the corner of his eye as she entered the kitchen. "You want to stick around, keep an eye on things?" he said to her and she nodded, sleepily. He noticed the excitement in her eyes, though.

Barboza said, "I ain't staying here, I'll tell you that, waiting around for Parnell to look you up. The first time he called me, Monday, he said he didn't want to go to work until he cleared things up with the cop who'd busted him. Which is you, Marino. He comes wandering in here with that big goddamn forty-four, maybe he figured out how to shoot it by now."

Jimbo couldn't fault his logic, but he was still angry. "The dog will look out for you."

"You saying dogs can't be killed, some guy shoots it with a forty-four?"

Jimbo said, "I got a friend, you can spend a couple hours at his house, until I straighten this whole thing out."

"Marino, I got businesses to run, you hear me? If we're gonna work together, you and me, I got to go take care of my businesses, make things right with the guys I didn't bail out the other night, explain things to them, pay back Paterro for covering their action for me. I get home, I'm safe. Parnell comes within a block of the house, I'll blow him into the middle of next week."

"You weren't so bold last night."

"I didn't know I had a friend, the police department, last night. It makes a difference, knowing you're gonna—" Barboza was about to say, take over the top spot, but looked at Kristina and said, instead, "be taken care of." Jimbo understood.

"Wait until I get back."

"My car's parked in the Grant Street underground lot." Barboza looked at Kristina. "You drop me off there?" Kristina looked at Jimbo, who guessed this was not the time to exert his influence over Barboza. When he had to, when it was important that he do so, he would. But it was a point not worth arguing about now. GiGi Parnell could not be crazy enough to try for him in his house during the daylight hours.

He looked at the reporter and nodded, and she said, "Sure," perking right up, enjoying the feeling of being in the middle of things, one of the crew. A freelance reporter who'd written three books doing cop work.

Jimbo said, "I gotta go," found the extra house keys for Kristina, extracted a promise from Barboza that he would be careful, and left the house.

Chris loved to tell Jimbo stories about the things that went on in his court, and most of the time Jimbo loved to hear them, throwing in some of his own humorous comments or stories from time to time. Even with all the things on his mind this morning, and with time running out on him before Chris had to drive the three blocks to the courtroom, he found himself mesmerized by the tale Chris was telling.

"Lawyer files a motion to suppress evidence; I hear the case yesterday. The defendant, a rich yuppie, works at the Board of Trade. This sucker, he was married to a girl twenty-three years old; they've been together three years, he buys her BMWs and all the other toys, and he figures they've done it all sexually, the last three years. What happened, he was paying guys to come into their town house and screw the little woman, tie her up, abuse her, that kind of stuff, must have done wonders for the girl's self-esteem; shows you how far someone will go for a nice new car.

"He lined her up with a black guy from down at the docks; big beefy sucker comes in, ties the girl up, puts it to her. Now get this; this freak, the trader, he's got a Sony minicam on a tripod, one of the self-focusing automatic babies, over by the bed, getting it all down in living color, recording every act and word. The black guy, he's banging away, the trader, he's yelling in the background, 'Fuck her, goddamn your nigger ass, fuck her!' jerking off while the stud abuses his wife.

"Well, the stud, he was playing the game a little too seriously, took his role to heart, and accidentally chokes the girl while he's coming." Chris paused to order some pancakes from the waitress; more coffee, and Jimbo patiently sat and waited, ordering his own coffee, too keyed up to eat.

Chris said, "So now, the trader, he's shooting his wad on the black stud's back, all time screaming curses at the stud and his wife, just a little normal afternoon's action, break up the day a little bit. He sees his wife's dead, sees the black guy staring with horror at the little girl dead there on the big round water bed, and the trader, he didn't get where he's at being a dummy, so he runs to the closet and gets out this beautiful silver inlaid shotgun, points it at the stud, who's still staring at the dead girl, starting to scream some now, and he blows the guy in two from maybe a yard away." Chris thanked the waitress for the food, began to dig in, talking between bites.

"The lady next door, the next town house, she calls the law, and the squad rolls up in front about the same time the trader is through getting himself dressed, he's on the phone when they ring the bell, calling 911, emergency, telling them hysterically about catching this big black monster raping his dead wife and how he killed the guy, all the time the guy sounding like his poor little heart's broken in two. He lets the cops in, they go up the stairs to the bedroom, see the bodies laying there and suddenly the trader, he gets all excited and nervous and he runs over to the video camera, which had somehow slipped his mind all this time, what with all the excitement, trying to come up with an alibi and all, and he's hitting switches, doing things.

"The cop says, 'What are you doing?' And the guy tells him nothing, just nothing, not quick enough to come up with a fast answer, get the law off his back, which at this time would be an easy thing to do, it looks open and shut. The cop's partner, a female on the force six months, still a rookie, goes over to the guy and says, 'May I see that please?' The guy goes crazy, tells her it's none of her fucking business, blah, blah, it's his house, his tape, and he doesn't have to show her shit, and she politely points her piece at this guy and takes the tape away from him, her partner all this time telling her, 'Leave him alone, huh?' shit like that, trying to call Homicide and get the hell out, turn it over and go eat lunch. The woman, she takes the tape to the recorder across the bedroom and turns on the set, plays the tape, sees the whole damn thing right there being acted out, second-degree murder, when the stud choked the woman in bed, then Homicide, murder one, when the trader kills him. She sees the guy jerking off on the stud's back, everything, hears all the shouting and screaming as the trader yelled at the stud to beat her, mark her up, all that good stuff, and she shuts off the machine, turns off the recorder and goes over to the guy, kicks his balls up into his throat and tells him he's under arrest, reads him his rights." Chris mopped up the last of his maple syrup with a piece of toast, popped it in his mouth, and said around it, "Now what do you think the trader's lawyer was arguing?"

"Violation of the guy's civil rights, when the rookie officer kicked him in the nuts."

Chris gave him a disapproving glance. "Come on, Jimbo,

think. Rights violations are federal, not state. I already told you it was a motion to suppress. You get it now?"

"The guy wanted you to rule that the tape was confiscated illegally?" He couldn't hide the wonder in his voice.

Chris said, "That's right." Smiling, waiting for Jimbo to ask him how he'd ruled.

It didn't take long. Jimbo was thinking, wondering if perhaps it was indeed an illegal seizure; nothing surprised him anymore when it came to fine points of law. His eyes widened involuntarily as all the implications hit him. "Without the tape, if you ruled it couldn't be admitted as evidence, the state has no case, right? It looks to a jury exactly as the guy tried to make it look, before the rookie saw the camera. He comes home, sees some guy raping his wife, blows him away from behind, and he walks, with the jury's sympathy." He was astounded, afraid, hoping to God that his friend hadn't ruled in the defendant's favor. He watched as Chris nodded his head, his face grave, telling Jimbo that everything he said was true. Jimbo couldn't wait any longer. As casually as he could he asked, "So how'd you rule?"

"Illinois Supreme Court ruling in *State* vs. *Collusima*, 1972. That was the precedent I used in turning him down. Once he invited the law into his house and they were investigating a felony, they had the right to use anything they find that might help them solve their case. With or without the homeowner's permission."

"Thank Christ. What about the civil rights beef?"

"That's not my problem. But I'd bet that she and her partner can argue that she acted in her own safety. I haven't seen the reports on it yet, but you can bet they wrote down that the trader made some sudden move toward the shotgun, something like that. Make her look like a saint for not shooting the son of a bitch."

"She *is* a saint for not shooting the son of a bitch."

"Let's remember, the son of a bitch is innocent until proven guilty, shall we?" Chris smiled as he spoke, then seemed to remember that Jimbo had told Jean that it was important that they meet for breakfast.

Chris said, "Jean's mad at you for saying you wouldn't come over to the house to eat and talk with me." Opening the door.

Jimbo said, "You'll thank me for not coming by when you hear what's going on," then proceeded to tell Chris what had happened last night, what he'd thought about throughout the morning hours, and part of what he was planning to do. When Jimbo finished, Chris checked his watch.

Chris Haney said, "If I call now, I can get a sub to my courtroom by ten."

Jimbo said, "What about the nine o'clock cases?"

Chris said, "You might be one of them, in a couple of weeks, if I'm not with you when you lay this out to Lettierri." Then he called impatiently for the check.

GiGi rolled off his lady Agnes and lay for a while breathless, smiling, though. In all the time in prison, through all the years, with all the fantasies and daydreams and wet dreams he'd had about being in the world and free, he'd never come close to guessing how good it really would be.

Close to tears just thinking about it, he said to Agnes, "I love you," and she hesitated, waited a second before telling him she loved him. Maybe he'd given her too much at one time, trying to show her how much he loved her. And trusted her. He'd have to slow down some, get her back to where she was after their bath last night, when she'd fallen all over him telling him how much she worshiped him. He knew just the way, too.

He said, "Love-bug, let's go shopping," and that got her attention, because she'd been staring off at the ceiling and that was getting to GiGi quite a bit because it was the thing his mother used to do for hours on end right there in that very bed.

Agnes rolled out of the bed, anticipating. "We'll get you some clothes, honey; I'll pick them out for you, show you all the new styles, get you a good wardrobe." Starting to laugh now, nearly breaking GiGi's heart because she was so goddamn unselfish; he'd meant go shopping for stuff for her, and she'd gotten all high and happy thinking she could do something for him. Lord.

And by doing so Agnes moved up on her pedestal a long way, surpassing Buck but still staying below his mom.

GiGi said, "You go to the house and get the money, and one of the pieces, drop me off downtown first. Then I'll meet you say, over at Marshall Field's? But we'll buy you some things first, okay?" And there it was, she looked shocked, the poor baby; she probably never had anyone treat her this well in her entire life. Man, she ain't seen nothing yet. He'd lay the whole fucking world at her feet if she'd let him. And everything in it.

She dropped him off without comment at the Chicago Department of Water and he was loving her more every minute. Most babes, they'd be asking all kinds of questions, what you going to do here, honey, or, how come you won't come with me? GiGi figured that he sure knew how to pick them. He told Agnes, "Be sure and check your mail now; I'm expecting a letter there," and she was gone, driving down the street in her little car slowly, waving good-bye to him before she turned the corner. GiGi was saddened at her departure. Surprised at the feeling of loss. Well, after today, they'd never have to be apart again. He entered the building and walked to the counter.

A skinny black dude was sitting at a desk, talking on the phone, eyeing the young white babe at the next desk. They were the only people in sight. The babe looked up and said, "Can I help you?" probably expecting him to cry about his water bill, but his ruined face and splinted nose surprised her. He told her he'd wait for his buddy there on the phone, causing the black guy to raise his eyes to GiGi and look at him, puzzled. GiGi hated the way the jig was looking at him, like he was some kind of badass and GiGi was crazy, but he knew in his heart that all niggers were crooks where they lived and would do anything for a buck. The city had probably hired the guy to fill some quota and he sat around all day talking to his girlfriends on the phone or trying to score some dope and treating the paying customers like shit. While on the other hand, the young white babe might well be the daughter of some big shot in the company, which made sense, or else some jig broad would have her job.

The guy sure took his time, talking low into the phone, murmuring things, and GiGi stood there pleasantly, wanting to kick the guy's teeth down his throat but having to be cool. At last the jig hung up and turned to GiGi and said, "What can I do for you, my man?" looking worried. He probably thought GiGi was a process server or a cop.

GiGi said, "Broham, this is your lucky day," and showed him just the edge of the twenty-dollar bill he held in the palm of his hand. GiGi looked meaningfully at the young white babe, then gave a short shake of his head, telling the guy he'd talk to him where they couldn't be overheard.

It took another fifty dollars, but within a half-hour GiGi had Jimbo Marino's address and telephone number, and he knew the average amounts of gallons of water Jimbo used each month. He left the office without thanking the man; wiseass jive-time spade had the nerve to hold him up for seventy bucks for the information and a guarantee that he'd keep his mouth shut. GiGi wished that he had one of the .38s with him, he'd have just let the jig catch a glance of it and it would have been the best assurance of the guy's silence that he could ever get.

Smiling, walking jauntily, king of the hill, GiGi Parnell left the building and began walking toward Marshall Field's on State Street, making plans.

Agnes said, "God, try and find a *parking* space down here?" Holding GiGi's arm, her reticence of that morning was gone. She was going to be happy, carefree and young and beautiful and all his. His love-bug. She'd let him think it, though she was having doubts. Being called love-bug by a guy who killed people and told her about it was not what she was planning on doing for the rest of her life.

But she had 213,000 reasons to act happy, not counting the wad of hundreds in her purse.

When she'd opened the envelope—it had her name on it; how was she supposed to know it was for him—and seen the check—which had been endorsed over to her, for God's sake—her first reaction was, run. Take it, put it in a bank account somewhere in the Bahamas where they guaranteed privacy. Where she could be a number, but a number worth, counting the hundreds, a quarter of a million dollars. But then she had been brought back down to earth by the reality of what GiGi had told her the night before. How he'd brutally murdered two people who had ripped him off for a couple of thousand dollars; remembering the amazement in his voice at the way he'd been wronged. How he thought he was justified in doing what he'd done. Take the money and run? Not until there was some place on earth she could hide without having to live in terror. Because he would indeed find her.

But she had his number now, that was one thing she was certain of. She had put it together after he'd left the room this morning, early, before the sun even came up. His lying in bed with his mother; screwing her in his mother's bedroom; the wheelchair in the closet; the special hospital bed. His mother had been a cripple. Agnes had lied to him about one thing only: her age. Agnes was thirty-six years old, and as a child on a soft warm June night she and her father and mother had lain on the shag carpeting in their living room and watched *White Heat* with James Cagney. So Agnes knew all about the fixation GiGi had tried to explain away the other night. Now she knew that the mother was a crip, and that his mother had up and died on him while he'd been in prison, and guess who he decided to fixate on now? Why none other that little Agnes Smycz, who now figured that God gave some people shit on their platters all their lives and then when He did indeed give them a break, He went all the way.

Little plain Jane Agnes. She'd been fat and pimply as a teenager, and she still looked in the mirror and saw a fat girl, even though she knew damn well she was skinny as hell everywhere but in the chest and the ass. Little Agnes, who'd given her virginity to a football player when she was a freshman and the senior defenseman had not only never called her up again but had tried to sell her to one of his buddies at a school dance a month later. Agnes, who had worked for her father for eighteen goddamn years—half of her entire life—for peanuts.

Well, all she had to do was keep him happy. If he wanted to do it with his mother, then by God, she'd be the best motherfuck the guy would ever want. And what would a mother want for her baby? Everything, that's what. So when he'd said to her, let's go shopping, she'd thought fast, knowing that a mother would want to go shopping for her baby first instead of herself, so she'd told him that she'd wanted to pick out his clothes, never mentioning herself.

Agnes figured that she had GiGi Parnell wrapped. As long as she played the game by his rules, she had the inside edge.

All she had to do now was figure a way to get the money into an account in her name instead of his. Tell him maybe that if he had a heart attack or a stroke all the money would go to his uncle, who GiGi quite obviously hated, and he'd think about it, but not about having any heart attack; uh-uh, he'd think about getting shot in the street and leaving his poor old mother-lover Agnes all alone in the world with nothing.

She'd given him the line after doing some shopping at Marshall Field's, and he'd gone for it like a rat for cheese. And they'd gone to the bank and dropped the check in there all nice and neat, opening a savings account in both their names. In Illinois, that put her a heartbeat away from being a rich young common-law widow.

Agnes was so elated that she was willing to go right now to a hotel here downtown and suck GiGi dry, but that was not the sort of thing his mother would do, so she kept quiet, thanking him, playing to him. And when he gave her five thousand dollars and told her to do some shopping for herself and then take a cab home, she hadn't blinked an eye, as she hadn't when he'd had her drop him off at the water department that morning. Let him be the man. Never, never nag. Get everything you wanted, and when he finally got his, everything would belong to her.

She kissed him tenderly, asking him to hurry home to her, she didn't want to be alone too long with Lester, knowing right then from the look in his eye that old Lester would be out before nightfall. She started thinking about how to go about getting him to put her name on the deed to the house.

As he drove away, waving and honking the horn, as she waved and waved, holding her left hand to her breast and smiling bravely, as if he was a sailor going off to sea, a strange, terrifying thought hit Agnes.

What if, when they came to kill him, he was with her?

Agnes looked around for a cab and as she stepped to the street a dark green Plymouth pulled to the curb, a skinny black guy driving and a stunningly beautiful black woman in the passenger's seat who waved a badge at her and said, "Honey, why don't you take a ride with us? Come have a little talk before you step into something smells bad and drags you down."

Agnes had never been inside a police station, but she'd read about them many times in books. So she never expected a setup like this.

The interrogation room was painted pink, for heaven's sake. And the building they'd come into had been clean and new. She'd expected an old brown brick building with globe lights outside the doors and the precinct number written on the glass.

The tall woman, who had identified herself as Jandra Johnson, was friendly enough, but the skinny guy, he was something else again. Needling her, all the time treating her like a hooker instead of as a working, tax-paying citizen. He'd told her his name was Bobby Franchese and she'd smiled, wondering what a black guy was doing with a dago name but afraid to ask.

Bobby said to her now, "You don't know what you're getting into, girl, playing with a psycho like GiGi Parnell."

"Shouldn't I have a lawyer or something?"

"For what?" Bobby said to her. "You aren't under arrest. We're just trying to figure out where you stand here; how a nice girl like you figures in with a killer."

"He is not a killer."

"Guy named Solt and his old lady, they were here, they'd disagree with you."

"You're just bringing me in to harass GiGi, because there's a restraining order on you and you can't go near him without getting in trouble." There. She'd told them.

Jandra said to her, "Honey, we brought you in to try and save you a whole world of grief when GiGi decides he maybe said a little bit too much to you."

"Why did you go to the bank this morning?" Bobby again, badgering her. She decided that there was nothing illegal about his inheritance, and so she told them. Bobby rolled his eyes and stared at Jandra, making Agnes feel like all of a sudden she *was* a hooker. She felt the need to defend herself.

"There's nothing wrong with having a joint savings account. Two people planning on getting married. They're supposed to trust each other."

Bobby said, "Girl, you can put on the dumb innocent act all you want, but you better hope all you did was go to the bank with him." He leaned forward, his fists on the desktop, and he moved way over until he was almost eye to eye with her. It was the closest she'd ever been to a black man and she felt intimidated, a little frightened and—she had to admit—a little turned on.

Bobby said to Agnes, "We're working on him and we're watching you. We can't bring him in for questioning because some dumb son of a bitch used to be a good cop got a little excited with him, and that slowed us up a little. But believe me when I tell you, Agnes, I'm gonna nail his ass to the wall for killing Solt and his old lady." He stepped back and took a breath.

"Solt, he was a piece of garbage, would have got it sooner or later anyway and we'd have lost no sleep over him. But did your future husband, Agnes, did he tell you how he did the wife? He put a gun in her private parts, Agnes, and shot it off. I'll show you the pictures, you like."

Agnes was remembering what GiGi had told her the night before and suddenly knew it was not a fantasy. GiGi had been telling the truth. She wondered if the guy here might be right, if GiGi would think he'd said too much to her and had to kill her. She told herself that as long as she played the good mother part she'd be able to handle him, but it was different lying in bed hearing it from GiGi and another thing altogether sitting in the pink room hearing it from the cops.

Bobby said, "If we come up with one shred of evidence linking you to anything, girl, any little crime at all, I'll make sure you go to Dwight Womens' for the rest of your natural life."

Jandra took over now, touching Agnes's arm, comforting her because Agnes had started to snivel and shake from the threats she was hearing.

"There anything you want to tell us, honey?"

Agnes pulled herself together and said, "Yes, If I'm not under arrest, I'd like to leave now."

And Bobby Franchese said, "Shit. There's sure some nasty things in this world people will do for money."

Agnes tried to ignore him. "Am I free to go?"

Bobby said, "Get the hell out of here. Next time I see you, we be walkin' instead of talkin'."

*   *   *

Jandra Johnson took Agnes aside before she left the office and gave her one of her cards, with her home number written on the back, and a little unsolicited advice. "Agnes, you call me anytime it gets too heavy. I can protect you."

Agnes just looked at her appraisingly and shoved the card into her purse.

Jandra said, "You sure there isn't something you might want to tell us, help clear this mess up?"

Agnes still did not respond.

"Agnes?" Waiting until the girl looked up, the green eyes shining, tear-rimmed. "That man is evil, Agnes. More than one girl like you thought she could handle evil. I see it all the time. You watch your ass, girl, and if he starts acting crazy on you, you call me. All right?"

Nodding, Agnes left the room. Jandra and Bobby watched her until she was out of sight, heading for the elevators.

Bobby said, "Follow him, watch him go around town paying more bills, like he did at the water department, or maybe scare the girl, get something out of her. We can go back to the house now, sit on it until he gets back. Let him see us this time. Maybe shake him up. Sooner or later, guy like Parnell, he'll try to give us the slip and go after Jimbo. Not during the day, though. He may be nuts, but he isn't dumb."

Jandra said, "She's one cool piece of business, isn't she?"

Bobby said, "They all are, till they wind up on a slab."

14

Kristina said to Barboza, "Anywhere around here okay?" as they drove down Michigan Avenue, in the S. 300 block. The Grant Street underground was less than a block away.

Barboza had tried hitting on her at the house, and again in the car, to no avail. He did not know who she was; thought she was simply a piece of tail the goddamn cop Marino kept around for laughs. He said, "Right here's fine, baby." Giving her the eye again, too prideful to try anything now that she'd rejected him twice but not too proud to look. When she pulled to the curb in front of the Encyclopedia Building he got out, winked at her, said, "Be seeing you," and crossed to the underground ramp that would lead him to the parking garage.

Mikey Barboza had spent most of his life gambling, the way any crook who never picked up a pair of dice or a deck of cards, who had never been out to Arlington or Sportsman's or Balmoral racetracks, spent his life gambling. First, he gambled that he wouldn't be caught, wouldn't wind up doing fifteen hard-time years in a federal joint under the RICO act, corrupt influences, operating a continuing criminal enterprise. And he gambled again each and every day, betting that he wouldn't wear out his use fulness to the mob. Once you lost that bet, all the chips were called in, all the markers had to be paid. For nearly three days Mikey Barboza had thought that he'd finally rolled craps.

He had good reason to think this, because, right on top, he had that psychopath mama's boy GiGi chasing after him, going to his house, shooting at him with an elephant gun. Then there was the fact that the very next day, drunk in a room at the Holiday Inn on Michigan Avenue, he'd seen his number-one boy on television and had learned that he was a cop. If that wasn't bad enough, the guys he'd sent out to work Monday night had been busted. And the icing on the cake was his old buddy Tommy Campo had hung up the phone on him.

Talking to Tombstone Paterro had never been one of the things Mikey enjoyed doing most with his time, but as Campo had grown older it was something he'd been forced to do almost daily. Mikey could tell something was wrong with one of his associates by the way the guy looked, by the way he held his coffee cup. And he could tell, straight away, that something had been wrong with Tombstone. Before meeting with him, while talking to him on the phone, Mikey had his first inkling that something very wrong was occurring. All he'd wanted, from the beginning, was a chance to explain, tell Campo why he'd had a cop on the payroll. And so he should have been glad when Paterro had set up the time for him to argue his case before the man himself. But talking to Paterro, the old gambling instincts had kicked in; he'd felt the loser's urge to throw it all away on one roll of the dice and he'd had to stop himself from doing it; from begging Campo for mercy, admitting guilt. He'd been calm, forceful, as befitted his status in the organization. And Campo had given him an act, Christ, patting his face. Campo should have ranted and raved. Campo should have called him a *strunz*. An asshole, anything, and maybe then Mikey would have believed that everything was okay, under the circumstances. But Campo had been cool, in control, shooting little knowing glances at Paterro, and that had been the tipoff. That was when Mikey had known that it was all over for him; that the least of his worries was a mole in his stable or a federal indictment. Campo, without opening his mouth, without saying a single word out of place, he had told Mikey that he was going to die. And Paterro, who had this freelancer in mind to do the job off the books, had backed the boss up by his silence.

Calling Marino had been a desperate measure: all right, a *drunken* desperate measure. He had no one else to turn to, he knew damn well how the feds operated once you wore out your usefulness to them. And besides, in the last three months, he'd gotten to like Jimbo. He kept thinking of him not as a cop, but as one of his own people, one who had just messed up. Calling him had been a drunken mistake, something that could have really cost him if he hadn't gotten lucky. But look how things had turned out.

Jimbo could pull it off, too. Hell, he'd pulled the wool over Mikey's eyes for ninety days, and Mikey had been fooled rarely in his life. He could set things up, get Parnell taken care of, and that would effectively neutralize Campo and Paterro as a threat against him, because the national commission was not about to vote him dead, not when his wife Clarice was the daughter of Don Laccavvia of Manhattan, maybe the single most powerful boss in the country. Jimbo would wire him up and he would give enough to the law so that Paterro and Campo would go away for the rest of their natural lives, and for his efforts he would be rewarded with the city of Chicago. *Madronne.*

Mikey Barboza was feeling better, for the first time in days. He had to make some calls, get some dough to the guys who'd been busted the other night, straighten things out with them, solidify his base. Marino had taken a small .32 away from him at the Holiday Inn the night before, but that was no problem. He had an arsenal in his house. All he had to do was get there.

All in all, everything, as far as Mikey Barboza was concerned, was working out for the best.

GiGi Parnell was tired and impatient, running low on Tylenol No. 3. His mouth hurt something terrible. He was beginning to have a little trouble with his eyesight too; the bright sunshine was starting to bother him. Fucking Marino. He drove back to the South Side and parked the car a couple of blocks from Barboza's house, through playing around now, ready to get it done this time. Go right in and get Mikey's location from the old lady if he wasn't home, or wait for him if he was expected back. GiGi couldn't waste any more time with fun and games. He had to get on with his life.

He walked casually to the large hedges and turned left, straight up the driveway and up to the front door, his hand on the .38 inside his waistband, ready to shoot whoever might be guarding the house. No one around, at least not outside; no cars, either. Which didn't mean much; there was a gigantic garage out back, might be filled with Cadillacs and Lincolns.

GiGi opened the screen door and pushed the washer on the hydraulic doorstop all the way to the cylinder, stepped back, and kicked the wooden door right under the lock, as hard as he could. The door splintered at the hasp, but held. He reared back and gave it another shot, a little higher this time. The door flew open and he was inside, gun out, scanning the room.

Nothing. No one.

Holding the gun in both hands now, pointing straight ahead of him, he began to search the house.

He found the little old fat dago broad on the phone in Barboza's den, screaming hysterically into the mouthpiece in Italian. Shit, no time to fool around with her, she might be talking to someone other than the cops, who would have to search around, find an interpreter before they could talk to her. GiGi fired from the doorway, the bullet taking off most of Mrs. Barboza's left arm, and before the arm hit the ground he was over by the desk, hanging up the phone, grabbing her by her hair, screaming at her.

"Who the fuck were you calling!" shouted into a blank-eyed, dead face. Jesus, the shock had killed her. Too bad. He didn't have anything against her. But he wasn't the one told her, go ahead, marry Mikey. Sometimes you had to pay for your mistakes. He let her go and she dropped hard to the carpet, making a dull final sound. R.I.P., honeybunch.

GiGi looked through the drawers in Mikey's desk; felt around the carpet and the walls for a safe. Nothing. A couple of grand in the drawers, which he added to his wad. But no big money. He went to the steel gunrack and checked the lock. It would take too long to bust the damn thing.

GiGi wondered who Mrs. Barboza had called. Whoever it was had heard the gunshot, there was no doubt about that. If it was the cops, the address and phone number she was calling from would be looking the emergency operator right in the face from his computer terminal, and they'd be here any second.

GiGi noticed a Rolodex open on the desk, and walked over to it, looked at the name the thing had been flipped to. Angelo Paterro. Jesus Christ, she'd been calling Tombstone. GiGi was safe.

He walked back to the front door and inspected it, trying to figure a way to rig it so it would look okay to Mikey when he came home. Impossible. The wood was cracked and splintered. He hadn't been using his head. He should have gone around back, where the damage would have been less noticeable.

Two things happened within the next minute that made GiGi smile. He heard the car revving down before it turned into the driveway and he pulled the door wide open, hoping Barboza would think that his Mrs. was moving something or having something delivered, what with the screen door still held wide open by the washer. He heard the car pull into the paved circular turnaround in front of the house; heard the engine die. He smiled. GiGi heard the car door slam and stepped into the doorway, gun out and pointed. If it was the cops, then Agnes was a rich woman. If it was Mikey Barboza, then GiGi had it made.

It was Mikey Barboza. Standing in front of the house with a suspicious, shit-scared look on his face, wondering if he should come on in or run away. GiGi made up his mind for him.

He said, "Say there, Mikey, how's it going, buddy?" Smiling, enjoying himself. He said, "Why don't you come on in, we can have a little meet over to your den." He watched Mikey walk with his head down, dejected, knowing damn well what was about to happen to him. He mounted the steps slowly. GiGi stepped back as Mikey passed him, no use looking for trouble. The guy had nothing to lose; he might think it worth the trouble, try to jump him, get the gun away.

GiGi closed the door as best he could and said, "In the den, there, Mikey, that's right. Uh-huh, there's someone there I want you to see."

* * *

When Mikey Barboza saw Clarice lying in a crumpled heap on the floor in a pool of her own blood, he didn't think of her as fat little Claire the Holy Roller bitch; nor did he think of her as the daughter of Don Laccavvia of Manhattan, either. He thought of her as Clarice Laccavvia, young, slender and vibrant, the girl he had married twenty-seven years ago this month on a warm September morning at St. Patrick's Cathedral in New York. He'd been eighteen and she'd been seventeen, and—and he spun and gave an outraged howl and leaped at GiGi Parnell who sidestepped like a ballerina and hit him hard alongside his head with the pistol. Mikey fell to the floor, hard, whacking his nose on the carpeting, his eyes open, seeing the blood seeping from his nose onto his rug. He whimpered, and GiGi smiled again.

GiGi said, "How much you make a week, Mikey?"

Mikey Barboza looked up, uncomprehending, and said, "What?"

"I asked you, how much you figure you make a week? Just a ball-park figure."

GiGi smiled as Barboza looked at him; he could tell Barboza's mind was racing, as it had been on Monday night back at the office, trying to figure a way out. He said, "GiGi, most weeks, I guess, ah, maybe five, six grand." Smiling as he finished, maybe thinking that GiGi was going to let him off the hook for a year's wages.

GiGi said, "And now you're gonna die for a month's pay, you stupid fuck." He pointed the gun at Barboza's head, smiling, starting to giggle as Barboza began to beg for his life. GiGi walked directly to him, put the muzzle of the pistol right in his face, between his eyes. Barboza shut his eyes tight, begging, crying now, pleading, telling GiGi he'd do anything if only—

The telephone on the desk rang.

Angelo Paterro had been eating his lunch, doing his business, when his wife beeped him on his pager. Two people alive had that number; his wife and Tommy Campo, and neither had ever called him on it before. When he had gotten it he had explained patiently to her not to be bothering him with calls to bring home a loaf of bread, whatever, and from that day to this, it had been understood: If it isn't life or death, don't dare call. He left the table immediately and went to the phone booth over by the coatrack, dialed his home number, unafraid that there might be a tap on the line. The restaurants he frequented were checked every week for bugs, as was his home phone.

His wife told him that Clarice Barboza had called and had been screaming for him in Italian when she had heard a terribly loud noise that could be nothing but a gunshot, and Paterro hung up the phone without comment and went into the men's room. He dashed his face with water, then locked himself in the stall and sat there, his head in his hands, trying to figure it all out.

Christ, using amateurs to do your work for you. Sometimes you had no choice, but it seemed to him that every time he did use anyone that he hadn't handpicked, they fucked up.

Clarice screaming in Italian, then a gunshot. It could only mean that the young psycho ex-con had overlooked one of the most cherished rules in the underworld; never hit a man in his home, and never, ever, under any circumstances kill a member of the man's family.

What made this case special was that the dead woman's father was maybe the most powerful man in the world when it came to Angelo's line of work; a man who would not sit back in his wing-back chair with the little tassels on the bottom, accepting excuses about Barboza owing Parnell money. He'd see through that in a second. If just Barboza had been killed, then the don would take it, accept the fact that his daughter was now a well-to-do widow before her time. But now that was all out the window. The don would want Parnell, alive, to play with for a while, and the wife and children and grandchildren of everyone even remotely connected to the murder of his daughter.

That stupid son of a bitch of a cowboy.

But there was one thing he could not do, and that was warn Parnell that he was in danger. He had to make sure that the punk thought he had Paterro's blessings all along, that he had done the right thing and would be rewarded for it.

But what if—unlikely, yeah—but what if maybe just the goddamn TV had blown up or something? He was sitting here thinking about killing Parnell this day, offering the corpse to the don of Manhattan, without even checking.

Angelo rose from the commode and dug into his pocket for another quarter. He went out to the pay phone and dialed Barboza's home number.

He heard Barboza say, "He-hello?" with tears in his voice. Terrified. And Angelo knew he'd been right the first time. That cowboy had murdered Clarice and was now playing with Mikey.

He said, "Mikey, listen to me without interruption. Is GiGi Parnell there with you?" Barboza began to babble, begging for his life so loudly, calling Angelo by name, making Angelo so angry that he nearly hung up the phone, but if he'd done that, then Barboza would be dead by the time he calmed down and called back.

Angelo said, "Mikey, shut up!"

GiGi Parnell came onto the line and Angelo told him to wait a minute, put Barboza back on. A second later Mikey was asking him if he could live again, probably decided already, asshole that he was, that Angelo had told Parnell to leave him alone. There was hope in his voice, although he was still making a woman of himself, begging. Angelo said, "Mikey, now this is extremely important; did you have your phone checked this week like I told you?" Remembering back when he'd ordered Barboza to do so and thinking then that the man was too cheap to have it done every week.

But Mikey seemed to be telling the truth, maybe he thought Paterro was having him killed for being cheap, saying over and over again, "Yes, yes, the line's clear, I have it done every week!"

Angelo quietly ordered him to give the phone back to Parnell.

GiGi was in his glory, what with Barboza on his knees next to the desk begging for his life, too scared to even try to move on him, and Angelo Paterro, the number-two man in the entire mob, on the phone, shooting the breeze with him. He said, "Mr. Paterro, you want, I'll wait awhile, till you get here, before I shoot this piece of shit." Tough, on the muscle, one badass to another.

Angelo obviously didn't have a sense of humor though, because he ignored the remark and said to GiGi, "Did you whack the woman, too?"

"Well, she was here."

"You did good, kid, you did real good. Now kill that fucking whiner Barboza before he shits himself and then you've earned your forty grand, understand?"

Shocked, GiGi said, "What about Marino? I'm gonna get him too, Mr. Paterro, I told you I wanted him too."

"Kid, I don't give a fuck what you want, you kill that Portuguese bastard and meet me at the same restaurant we met in yesterday, you hear me?"

GiGi was beginning to think that maybe he was in a little trouble with Paterro, so he said, "One more thing, Mr. Paterro," and when Angelo barked "What?" GiGi pointed the gun at Barboza's head and pulled the trigger three times. When the sound stopped bouncing around the room, he put the phone back to his ear and said, "You hear that?" Grinning into the phone, but Angelo didn't say anything. GiGi heard him breathing for a couple of seconds, then the line went dead.

To the bodies of Mikey and Clarice Barboza, GiGi said, "Some people, got no fucking sense of humor." Then he wiped his prints from the phone, searched Barboza's body and added the roll of bills he found on Barboza to his ever-growing wad—shit, he'd have to call his new lawyer, look into tax shelters if his sources of income kept growing.

GiGi grabbed the Rolodex from the desk, and carried it with him openly as he left the house and walked back to his car.

15

Kristina was elated. She had a super-cop and a certifiable best-seller on her hands. And she had access to his house when he wasn't there.

The problem with most people, in her experience, was that they wanted you to write only good things about them, and nobody is all good. Everybody has warts. She wasn't planning to do a hatchet job on him; as a matter of fact, the opposite was true. She was really starting to like the guy. But she knew damn well that if she was going to find the warts, she'd have to search on her own because all he would show her was the makeup covering them.

She drove back to Jimbo's house after dropping Barboza off—wow, what a character *he* was—and spending a couple of hours at her apartment calling around, trying to get something going on the new book idea. She parked at the curb and let herself into the house. She went floor to floor, looking for evidence of the warts; finding little. She heard the dog in the basement; Sparky had barked when Kristina had first come in, and then settled down, maybe smelling her scent. What about that? A fearless undercover cop who kept a Doberman pinscher for protection. Protection from what, though? From the Outfit? Not likely.

No, the dog was maybe a blemish and she was looking for warts. Well, she'd just have to talk to him, worm it out of him; the dark side of his character. If she was crafty enough, subtle enough, she'd find it.

She kept going back to the odd movies on the bookshelf. Some of the answers would be in them, if she could figure them out in the proper manner; there was more here than met the eye. She couldn't put her finger on it yet, but some of the answers would be here, in the movies.

She heard a key in the front-door lock and turned, surprised; Jimbo shouldn't be coming home already—it was only eleven-thirty—but it wasn't Jimbo, it was the kindly looking little elf friend of Jimbo's, the other half of the Marx brother duo she was dealing with. The guy who could lie through his teeth while looking you dead in the eye, going for your sympathy.

She smiled, broadly, one con man to another, and said, "Hello, Gizmo." Hearing the dog going insane downstairs.

Gizmo appeared shocked to see her. He said, "I'm here to install some alarms." Then looked around. "Is Jimbo home?"

She had to rub it in a little, let him know that she was here and with Jimbo's blessing. She said, "No, but he gave me a key, and I came here after I—after I did something else this morning. . . ."

Gizmo smiled back at her, making her feel foolish, petty. He said, "Did you get him straightened out, about Cummings, Georgia?"

"Gizmo," she put just the right amount of condescension in her tone, "did you actually expect me to believe that fairy tale?" She was waiting for his answer when the door-bell rang, and she had to tell him that it had; he couldn't hear it.

Lettierri was really on the rag now, ranting and raving, and it got worse the longer he carried on. For starters, warming up, he'd told Jimbo there was a restraining order on the department and they were being sued for a couple of million dollars.

"I'll call the fucking U.S. Attorney right now, get him in here, have him tell you that Barboza's going away for ten years, you stupid shit!" Giving Chris a look that said a lot about his revised opinion of anyone who would go along with this ridiculous plan Jimbo had cooked up. "You don't need to play any grandstand fucking games, Marino." Leveling a killer look at Jimbo, who sat there, not about to flinch.

Jimbo said, "Goddamnit, Commander, if you'd just calm down and think about it—"

"I told you not to say—"

"Uh-uh," Jimbo said. "I'm telling *you*, boss, you take it or leave it, because that's all there is left. Now just shut the hell up and listen, or we do it on our own."

"You want to run Mikey Barboza? Bust the fucking mob and put him in charge and then bust *him*? Jesus Christ . . ."

Jimbo said, "You through?"

Lettierri said, "Go ahead, you dumb shit, I'm listening."

Jimbo smiled, giving Chris a "Thanks a lot" look; Chris hadn't said word one since they'd entered the office.

"You said it yourself, Commander, the case is blown. None of the guys rolled over on him even when he didn't throw their bond. I got called in too early, before we had all the evidence against the higher-ups, Paterro and Campo. We got enough to maybe put Barboza away, sure, but we'd never touch the top dogs. Parnell threw the monkey wrench into my plans. Now we use him.

"We pick him up, I don't care for what, a weapons charge, driving without a license, whatever, we talk to him, tell him, leave Barboza alone for six months. Shake him up real good."

"Goddamnit, Marino, that won't work, Parnell's already tried to kill Barboza twice, you think he's gonna change his mind about Barboza because we *tell* him to?"

"All right, okay, granted, it's still cold; I don't have it all worked out, but just roll with me a minute. So now Barboza puts Paterro and Campo in the joint, we put him right in the top spot; then let GiGi loose on him." Jimbo sat back and smiled, looking and feeling good.

Lettierri just stared at him. Jimbo looked at Chris, noticed he was doing the same thing. Suddenly, his mouth began to hurt from trying to keep the smile on his face.

Chris finally broke his self-imposed silence. "Are you one of us or one of them?" Softly said, but firmly.

Jimbo let the smile drop.

Lettierri said, just as quietly, "Let me get this straight, Marino," looking at Jimbo in a way Jimbo had never seen him look at him before, as if he was a suspect in a child molestation. "You want us to put Barboza in the top chair, then have him *assassinated*?" Jesus, the guy sounded like Gizmo, his voice rising three octaves on the question.

Lettierri's face was all lines and shadows, scrunched up, disbelieving. Chris just looked extremely sad. Jimbo stuck to his guns.

"It's that," he said, "or I tell the U.S. Attorney that we used duress to get Vinnie Franchetti to introduce me to Barboza; that we dropped charges against the kid in trade for the intro."

Lettierri said quietly, "I ought to suspend you for conduct contrary to acceptable police procedure. We're still the good guys, Marino, and don't you forget it. We don't kill people or set them up to be killed because they've broken the law. You've spent too much time with them; you're burning out. Take two weeks, relax. Get your mind back." And that was that.

Where he'd messed up was, he'd given it all to them too quickly, hadn't given them enough time to think things over. They were in the quiet bar on Division, Jimbo drinking a tap Michelob, Chris with a martini in front of him, slowly stirring it, watching the lemon peel turn in the clear liquid.

Chris said, "I called the chief judge for my district, lined up a floater to sub for me, took a precious day off that I could have saved, done something with my family . . ." He let it trail off. Jimbo knew what he was saying.

Jimbo said, "Instead of going with me, hearing me set up a guy who deserves to die?"

"Maybe he does, Jimbo, but it's not our job to execute him." He turned his head away to light a Camel. Jimbo beginning to worry now, he'd never seen Chris this quiet, this distressed.

Chris said, "Look, you took the whole thing to heart, Jimbo. I can understand your being upset. Really pissed, wanting to get even. But we have to get these guys the right way or else we're no better than they are."

"I disagree."

"I know. And that's what breaks my goddamn heart." Chris threw a ten-dollar bill on the bar, told the bartender to give Jimbo another beer and keep the change. He got up off the stool and looked sadly at Jimbo, his eyes wet. He looked three inches shorter than he had that morning.

"Do me a favor, okay, Jimbo? Don't call me at the house for a while." Chris Haney turned and walked out of the bar.

He should have told Chris the whole thing that morning, instead of just part of it. Should have run it by him, see what he thought, instead of just giving him the meat of it and leaving the potatoes for Lettierri's office. Maybe if he had, they'd still be friends.

He sipped his beer and thought of Chris. On a camping trip with the entire Haney clan the summer before last, the girls sitting around the campfire listening to Jimbo and Chris tell ghost stories late at night. Chris getting out of bed at three in the morning and making wiseguy remarks but signing every tap order and warrant that Jimbo had ever brought him. Even this morning, taking the day off to go with him to see Lettierri. Christ, friends like that were rare. And now Chris tells him not to call him at the house anymore, as if speaking to him would contaminate the Haney women. Two little girls who called him Uncle Jimbo and a wife who was like a sister. Gone from his life just like that.

All right. Maybe Chris was right. Maybe he *had* taken being called in too seriously, but, goddamnit, it wasn't Chris or Lettierri out there three months, with their asses on the line, then getting called in because some half-wit had been released from the joint. And it wasn't Jean or Lettierri's old lady getting letters from the joint telling them in graphic detail how they were going to be raped and executed because their husbands had done their jobs and gotten a piece of garbage like GiGi Parnell off the street.

He thought about calling Richard (call me Richie) Corneale, the State Attorney, to see what he thought of his scheme, but just as quickly as he had the idea, he rejected it.

Tuesday, during the debriefing, he'd thought he'd gotten

his cop attitude adjusted; had it back in place. But now he knew he didn't have it back yet. They weren't talking about a simple entrapment here, putting a guy away who they knew was guilty but just couldn't *prove* was guilty. They were talking murder.

Chris had backed him up back then on the entrapment. Lettierri had told him, once, that he thought it was a good piece of work and it was too bad he'd gotten caught. Now Lettierri had thrown him out of the office and had nearly suspended him and Chris had told him not to call him at his home anymore.

Jesus Christ.

"Why so glum, buddy? You got the clap or what?"

Jimbo turned to see Francis Mahon perch his behind on the next stool and order a beer for both of them from the bartender. Old Francis Mahon smiling, his white head of hair unkempt; blown around out there in the Chicago hawk wind. Turning to Jimbo and telling him, "Jesus, three months of work down the tubes, somebody comes along and pops Barboza in his own house like he was just another Joe on the street. Sometimes, justice is served."

Jimbo said, "What?"

Gizmo read the woman as she told him the bell was ringing and he laughed. He walked to the door, said aloud, "Mandi . . ." with amused exasperation, shaking his head back and forth.

With nothing to fear on a beautiful warm September morning except the killer dog downstairs, he threw the door wide, smiling, trying to think of a suitably wiseass remark to lay on Mandi—

Suddenly he was pushed back into the house and he was looking right into the barrel of a goddamn gun, and there was the guy he'd heard about a million times but until now had never laid eyes on, but he didn't have the time to think about it because GiGi was lifting the pistol, slamming it down on the top of his head, and he was going down, down, into the darkness.

GiGi raced into the house and slammed the door behind him, laid the little dude out and turned the pistol on the bitch sitting there looking amazed. "Where the fuck is he?" he shouted, nervous, about to finally be done with it, knowing that the only way Marino could beat him was to get the drop on him.

The babe said, "He's not here." Obviously she knew him, knew what he was here to do, shit, Marino had most likely been crying to her about GiGi since he'd learned he was released.

Admiring the woman, though, her cool. As if this wasn't happening to her, the cold bitch.

He noticed the jig on the floor stirring and he said, "Nice and easy, come on, get on your feet." The guy ignored him, so GiGi went over to him and put his foot in his ass, and said, "Get the fuck up, what are you, deaf?"

And the woman said, "Yes, he is."

He turned to her, the pistol inches from the jig's head, and said, "He is what?" Getting it then, what she'd said. "The nigger's deaf?" Smiling, enjoying it. A nigger who couldn't hear you talking about him and who couldn't talk back. Man, heaven.

He grabbed the jig by the back of his dirty-looking shirt and dragged him to his feet and the little fool did a really dumb thing—he lunged for the gun. GiGi could have blocked him quite easily, the guy was old, slow, but he let him get nearly to the pistol before he made his move. Knowing the jig would expect GiGi to pull back, be ready for it, GiGi went forward, fast, driving the gun hard into

225

the nigger's soft flabby little belly. He heard the whoosh of breath explode from the guy's mouth, saw him double over.

GiGi smiled at the babe, said to her, "Now watch real close, here, love-bug, cause this could be you, you try anything stupid." And he laid the butt of the pistol against the back of the jig's neck as hard as he could, hearing the bones crush in there, feeling the things turn to powder under his hand.

That got her attention. Before the jig hit the ground dead GiGi was running to her; he saw her eyes widen with terror and saw her mouth open to scream, and he hit her one, a good one with his free hand, knocked her right to the ground. He helped her up, sat her down back on the couch, shushed her a few times. Slapped her when she tried to pull away from him, the babe crying, almost hysterical, her arms waving around her face and the tears flying down her little red cheeks like a waterfall.

"Calm down now, woman," GiGi Parnell said, then slapped her again when she didn't listen to him. Man, you hit them and they only got worse. Dumb.

GiGi went to the nearest lamp and ripped the cord from the base, threw the babe down on the couch and tied her hands behind her back. There was enough cord left over to tie her feet behind her too; the cord attached to both her ankles and her wrists, from behind. She'd be out of the way. He put his handkerchief into her mouth, stuffed it in there deep and told her if she spit it out, he'd fucking kill her.

He listened to her calm down slowly and soon she was just sobbing quietly. Good. He had some thinking to do.

Paterro's suddenly changing his mind worried GiGi. Why would he want to do that, suddenly not wanting the cop killed, out of a clear blue sky telling him to meet him at the

Greek restaurant? Something was up. In the wind. And it smelled to GiGi like his shit.

Okay, his shit was in the wind. Now what was he going to do about it? Was Paterro setting him up?

He walked around the living room, hearing some kind of wild animal going nuts in some other room, sounded like the basement. He wanted to make sure but couldn't afford to leave the living room, let the front door out of his sight. He couldn't let Marino surprise him or get the drop on him. He also couldn't waste a bullet on a dog. He'd shot Barboza's fat old lady once; Barboza three times. He'd had the hammer on an empty chamber, so that left one bullet. And that one bullet was reserved for Jimbo Marino.

He had the Rolodex with Campo's address and private phone number. And Paterro's, too. Remembering that death was a two-way street made GiGi smile. If he had to, if push came to shove, he'd kill them both, too.

But one thing at a time.

First, he had to take care of Marino. Then he'd see about the other guys.

GiGi sat down in the old cracked-leather chair, then got up and positioned it so he could see both the front and back doors, the kitchen doorway just giving him enough of a line of vision to make out the second door in the house.

He wished the goddamn dog would shut up. The way it was barking, it would have a stroke if it didn't.

Jimbo drove home slowly, feeling dejected, lonely. Lonelier than he could ever remember feeling. Three people in the entire world he trusted, and two of them had rejected him; were no longer friends.

Barboza dead, too, that didn't do much for him.

If he'd just kept his big mouth shut, none of it would have happened; Barboza would be dead and he could shake his head and say, like Mahon had, "Three months down the drain," maybe pound his fist into his palm for effect, and he'd still have Lettierri and Chris for friends.

But he hadn't and he didn't, so there was no use thinking about it.

Chris hurt most of all. A lot of years as friends down the tubes, there, flushed, gone forever. Not able to think about what he could do to get that valuable friendship back, he tried to force what had happened out of his mind.

Maybe they'd all been right all along. From his father-in-law on down to last night, Barboza saying he was more of a bad guy than a good guy. No, crook, Barboza had said crook. As if it made a difference what some stumble-bum drunk of a mobster thought of him.

And maybe it did make a difference at that. Jimbo this morning in his kitchen telling Barboza, "Let me take care of that," acting like a tough guy. Trying to impress a bum.

He flashed to James Cagney in *Public Enemy*. Near the end, after he'd been shot all to hell and he was falling into the gutter, he's on his knees and he looks at the camera and says, "I ain't so tough." Jimbo knew now precisely how Cagney felt.

"I ain't so tough," he said aloud in his LTD Crown Victoria, turning onto Orleans street, heading for home.

Sadly smiling because man's best friend Sparky was at home. Sparky still loved him. He brightened up when he saw two familiar cars at the curb—Kristina's and Gizmo's. And a Mustang parked down the street that he didn't recognize.

Gizmo could easily set up enough alarms in the house to protect him from anything. From three GiGi Parnells.

He wondered how many had been installed already and if he would be safe just walking in without setting something off.

Walking to his door, Jimbo was feeling very sad but knew things could be worse; Gizmo could have abandoned him, too. And Kristina. Jesus, the Marx brothers, Gizmo, Jimbo and Franko. Now Chris had his own name-partner in Kristina. He put his key in the lock and opened the door, thinking, Harpo, Groucho, Chris, Kristina, closing the door behind him and turning to face the living room.

And GiGi Parnell was right there, standing behind the chair that had been moved so Jimbo could not spot him if he was to look up as he entered. GiGi was holding a pistol on him.

Jimbo saw Gizmo on the floor in an unnatural position, that gentle head perched at a terrible angle on the shoulders. He took two deep breaths in and out, through his mouth, trying to get his mind together; it was happening too fast for him.

GiGi Parnell said, "You want to say something about my mom now, you cocksucker? Huh? Or tell your little bitch here about how you spanked me in a fucking alley?"

But Jimbo barely heard him. He was looking at Gizmo's glazed eyes, the truth sinking in. He said, "Goddamn, Gizmo."

Parnell was coming at him now, raising the gun, and Jimbo wasn't thinking, didn't even try to dodge the blow that glanced off his forehead and made him stumble. He stayed on his feet and looked at GiGi.

GiGi held the gun in his belly and reached in, took out Jimbo's 9mm. Then stepped back.

Parnell standing in front of him but a few feet back, ready, expecting him to make a move. The gun in both hands but steady. Like a rock. Jimbo stared at him. If he had to die, he could at least do that right.

Out of the corner of his eye he saw Kristina tied up on

the couch, Christ, if she was forty years older and in a wheelchair, Parnell could push her down a flight of stairs, giggling.

Somewhere far off, it seemed to him, Sparky was going insane.

A feeling of reality gone, of illogic, came over him. Of unbalance. Christ, in his own house with the madman; Gizmo dead.

He said, "*Fuck* you, Parnell." And the White Heat Bandit smiled at him.

"How's it feel, huh? It feel good? How about it, buddy, with the shoe on the other foot for a change. You like it? No cops around to protect you, no squad full of Miami cops, no niggers to impress like yesterday. Just you and me."

GiGi backed off, all the way to the stairway leading to the second floor. Without taking his eyes off Jimbo, he threw Jimbo's piece upstairs, then opened his gun and removed the bullet; placed the bullet on the first step and the gun on the second.

"Just the two of us, you and me, Marino. Whoever gets to the piece first wins."

He was smiling broadly, cool, unaffected, while Jimbo was sweating and shaking.

"This time it won't take fifteen minutes, will it?"

Jimbo backed away as GiGi advanced, his hands in front of him in the classic boxer's pose, fists ready, loose, not tight fists; he'd tighten them as he swung. Twist the punch as it landed. Hands up under his chin, breathing heavily through his nose while GiGi was moving with fluidity; Jimbo almost had to admit to himself that the guy was poetry in motion but couldn't. If he did, he'd give up.

GiGi dancing around like Baryshnikov, doing a complete turn and his foot came up and *wham*, right on the side of

Jimbo's face. The force of the blow staggered him back and GiGi kicked Jimbo as he backed up, in the gut, a good solid one. Jimbo felt the air forced out of his lungs and almost panicked; the guy was too fucking good for him, no doubt about it. His back hit the wall next to the kitchen doorway and he moved just in time as GiGi threw a punch from his hip, not a boxing punch, some kind of karate punch; the fist came straight out at an angle, no looping or hooking. It broke through the dry wall and—thank Christ—the bastard had hit a stud; he was howling in pain, trying to pull his hand out of the large hole in the wall, for the moment vulnerable. Jimbo hit him hard in the kidneys; GiGi freed his hand and turned and Jimbo hit him as good a right cross as he'd ever thrown, right on the bridge of the broken nose and GiGi screamed in pain, giving Jimbo confidence. He pummeled GiGi's gut with wild, looping lefts and rights, driving him back into the kitchen, up against the sink, his head bent back. If Jimbo could get him up a couple inches, he'd drive GiGi's head right through the window; maybe cut GiGi's jugular vein.

GiGi was using the sink for leverage while Jimbo continued to hit his midsection. He leaned back, got his balance, breathing through his mouth, trying to work through the pain; ignore it until the job was done, for the first time feeling fear, thinking maybe he could lose. He got his right foot free and kicked out just as Buck had taught him, feeling something give in Jimbo's left leg, and the fucker was moving back a little, stumbling, the weight off GiGi now and he slashed with the side of his right hand, across the neck, hitting solidly, seeing Marino buckle, ready to go. Marino staggered across the floor, running away, the cowardly piece of—no, no, trying to hide out in the basement—

Goddamn, the dog was in the basement.

*   *   *

Jimbo had been holding his own, driving into the guy for all he was worth, until GiGi kicked him in the knee and he'd felt the joint bend backward. He stumbled away and he'd caught one on the neck that had made him see blackness; staggered back, felt the basement door and heard the barking as he threw the door open and yelled *"Pasha!"* and there she came, Sparky the cheetah racing up with her teeth bared, lips curled back, making a beeline for GiGi and she had him between her jaws and he was screaming and shouting, forgetting all the jailhouse kung fu stuff, trying to survive with the dog's teeth sunk in his neck. Jimbo hobbled to the living room and reached the steps, grabbed the pistol and the bullet and with shaking hands managed to put the bullet in the cylinder on the run, heading back for the kitchen, his heart pounding, his lungs on fire. He knew his knee was badly bruised but managed to limp quickly into the kitchen and grab Parnell's head and put the pistol barrel under GiGi's goddamn murderous chin, saw the look of stark terror in GiGi's eyes as Jimbo screamed at him, *"Die, fucker,"* and pulled the trigger.

The sound of the pistol in the small kitchen made the dog jump back, the limp dead body of GiGi Parnell sliding down the sink as she moved, to the floor. Jimbo had to fight the urge to kick it. His hand dropped to his side and he let the pistol go, not even hearing the metal death machine hit the tile.

Sparky was leaping at him, tongue out; Christ, she was pissing all over the kitchen floor. He stooped to pet her and she shrank back, afraid he was going to beat her for peeing on the floor, and suddenly he had the strongest urge to cry.

The tears almost came, as Jimbo looked at the noble animal cowering as its beloved master bent, afraid she was going to be beaten after just having saved his life.

He sat on the floor and fought the urge for a while, and Sparky came to him cautiously and sniffed his face; licked him.

Jimbo got to his feet and went to the kitchen drawer, got a butcher knife and walked into the living room, turning his head as he passed the body of his last true friend. He cut the cords binding Kristina and got the gag out of her mouth. She reached for him, screaming that she thought she was going to be killed, thought that animal was going to kill her, and Jimbo couldn't help it, he just had to get away from her. With him beat all to hell, and Gizmo dead on the floor, all she could think about was herself.

He went to the front door and threw it open, his heart in his throat, dropped the knife on the carpet and stepped out into the warm September sunshine. He breathed in deeply, again and again, trying to get some warmth within. It wasn't working.

He dropped to the stoop, sitting there thinking that now he was truly a cold-blooded killer, sniffling as Sparky came up whining terribly, and he said, "But he *deserved* to die." She looked him right in the eye, wagging her behind at him, tongue out lapping around there and he said, "I ain't so tough."

Sparky licked him.

Jimbo said, "James Cagney. *Public Enemy.*"

Sparky wagged her behind and licked him some more.

Jimbo reached into his back pocket and got out his wallet. Christ, he had no choice but to kill the guy but it still felt wrong. He stood carefully, feeling the pain in his knee something awful now.

Jimbo Marino removed the badge from the little piece of folded leather and threw it as far as he could. He looked down at the dog, starting to get himself under control. He said, "Clint Eastwood. *Dirty Harry*."

Kristina came out onto the stoop now, looking afraid and humble. Shaking. Jimbo breathed deeply once again, no longer in danger of crying. Under control. He'd be okay now.

In a little girl voice Kristina said, "Who was he?"

Jimbo was amazed that she did not know. But of course she wouldn't. She'd been a kid when the White Heat Bandit case had hit the front pages. A kid, like he'd been.

He didn't feel like a kid anymore.

James Cagney again, this time dead on the stairs of a church in a different movie, *The Roaring Twenties*. Gladys George, the devoted but often jilted girlfriend, chasing after him, seeing him there dead with the big beefy Irish cop racing up, saying the same thing Kristina had just said. So he answered her the way Gladys George had answered the cop.

He turned to her and said, "His name's GiGi Parnell. He used to be a big shot."

Kristina looked at him strangely but kept her mouth shut.

Jimbo figured he could face the sight of Gizmo now but first he knelt down and threw his arms around the dog, squeezed her tightly, and she went apeshit on him, wagging her behind so hard she nearly knocked them both down the steps.

"*Good* girl," he said. "Sparky's a *good* girl." And damnit all to hell, there they were again, just behind his eyes. Those damn tears. . . .

16 Lettierri told him to hang his badge on his shirt so the bluesuits could tell he was one of them and Jimbo didn't know what to say. He'd called Lettierri right away, without a moment's thought, instead of the 911 emergency number. Old habits and all that . . .

But it was more than that. He was sitting on his carpeted stairs, on the bottom step, poor old Sparky locked in the basement again, but hell, if he let her loose, one of these gung-ho kids might blast her and then he'd have to shoot one of his fraternal brothers and he couldn't have any of that; not when he'd decided, just a few minutes ago, that throwing his badge away had been a mistake.

Lettierri was just covering Jimbo's back now, hanging around making sure that the Homicide dicks didn't give him too much of a hard time; being jealous because Jimbo was a minor cop celebrity. And minor was all it was.

He was putting things in perspective as he listened to Kristina give her statement, telling the cops how terrified she was, every other goddamn word out of her mouth being me, me, me.

After what seemed like hours they took Gizmo away, and Jimbo felt his throat constrict as they zipped the heavy black rubber bag up over the weathered face. He wished GiGi Parnell had ten lives he could take from him, and even then it wouldn't be enough to make up for Gizmo. Not even close.

He noticed Lettierri standing over him and moved his eyes from the chalked outline that had been Gizmo's last stand and looked up, raising his eyebrows, not wanting to talk too much. Suddenly he and Lettierri were buddies again.

Lettierri said, "They found almost forty grand in his pockets." Jimbo didn't move a muscle, but his mind was racing. He was thinking, *forty grand?*

"That goes a long way toward putting us back where we were, Jimbo." Lettierri spoke softly, for Jimbo's ears only. "I mean, the way you were getting, what I was seeing, I thought maybe we'd find the body stripped of *jewelry*, for chrissakes."

Jimbo just stared up at him, still thinking of GiGi Parnell lying dead on his kitchen floor with forty thousand dollars on his body and he hadn't even thought to check his pockets.

Wondering what he would have done if he had.

Kristina came and stood beside Lettierri, calling Jimbo's name softly, like a considerate lover trying to wake a heavy sleeper. He looked over at her.

"They're through with me," Kristina said, and Jimbo had to stop himself from saying, So am I. He just looked at her. She said, "You want me to stay?" Almost pleading. Her bottom lip was trembling slightly and her right eye was twitching. Hell, she wasn't a cop; hadn't been trained at all, had never had to face death before in her life. . . .

It wasn't her fault. He said, "Yes." Softly, grateful as soon as the word passed his lips because she lost a lot of her tension, seemed almost ready to cry. He knew how she felt. It seemed he was empathizing with everybody all of a sudden.

She said, "Thank you," just as softly, and wandered away, back to the couch.

She sat there and stared off into space, every so often reaching her hand up and touching her face, making sure she was real and still there. Jimbo turned back to Lettierri.

"It's all over, eh, boss?"

Lettierri giving him the smile then, reminding him almost uncannily of Chris Haney, about to drop a bomb, holding back until the timing would be perfect. He said, "Well, there *is* just one more thing. . . .

Five minutes later, Jimbo cornered a couple of the blue-suits hanging around drinking his coffee and asked them to go across the street, give it a search for his tin.

Agnes had cabbed to the house GiGi Parnell had inherited from his mom and watched the afternoon soap operas, Uncle Lester joining her, sucking around, the old fart, trying to make friends. Probably knowing who held all the cards now.

Between shows there was a bulletin stating that a just-released ex-convict, Gigliamo Parnell, had been killed while trying to murder a Chicago police detective, details at five. . . .

Agnes smiling at the news, looking over and seeing that old bastard sitting there on the couch with tears in his eyes. Stunned as Lester slowly lowered his head into his hands and shook for a while real quietly. Thinking, Christ, you'd think he'd be happy, now he gets to stay. . . .

She got up and walked to the front door, opened it and walked out, her purse with the savings account book at the bottom snug against her breasts. She'd call a cab from the gas station down the street. Smiling, Agnes closed the door behind her, picturing the look on her father's face when she told him she quit. She smiled sweetly at the unmarked squad car at the curb.

Friday morning, fewer than five full days since being pulled off the undercover operation, Jimbo Marino entered the Embers Restaurant and looked at the two goons standing by the door. He said, "Don't even *think* about stopping me," his badge held in his left hand, his right hand inside his sport coat, resting on the butt of his 9mm. They looked away, and he walked into the dining room, found Angelo Paterro in a booth eating something that smelled terrible and looked even worse, across from some fat slob who was talking fast, pleading. The guy shut up when he noticed Angelo staring up at Jimbo, looked at him, and Angelo Paterro told him to get lost. The guy nearly ran from the booth, giving Jimbo plenty of room.

Jimbo slid into the booth across from Paterro, in the seat the fat guy had just slithered out of, and handed Paterro a piece of paper.

Paterro said, "What the fuck is this?"

Jimbo said, "That, Angelo, is a warrant for your arrest. Conspiracy to commit homicide, twice. Also, the feds want to talk to you, something about operating a continuing criminal enterprise."

"I want my lawyer," Paterro said, looking around, probably wondering where the rest of the boys were. You didn't come to arrest Angelo Paterro all by yourself.

"That's fine, that's your legal right, you see, Angelo, I got no problem with that, I want you to be happy." Spreading his hands out, showing Paterro how agreeable he was, thinking how much Gizmo would have loved to see this performance. He dropped his hands and said, smiling, "Course, your lawyer comes around, then Campo has to find out all about this, and we already know how he treats his people when they get in a little bind. Guys like Roland DiNardo last year and Barboza yesterday."

Paterro looked confused, his thin high forehead getting all lined. He said, "He'll find out anyway, once you arrest me."

Jimbo grinned. He said, "Look at the date on the warrant, Angie."

"It's blank."

"That's right."

"So what the fuck is going on?"

"The way I see it, Angie, you can tell those two goons out front that I was just in here making threats, acting the fool. I don't care. That way you're covered with Campo."

"Bullshit, I see where you're going, and I ain't playing the fucking game. I never ratted on nobody in my entire fucking life and I ain't about to start."

Jimbo smiled at the way the cool, urbane, sophisticated crook fell into the speaking patterns of his childhood when he got rattled. It made him feel good to know that Paterro was sweating.

It was time to play the trump card.

He took another folded sheet of paper out of his inside jacket pocket and said to Paterro, "Search warrant." And dropped it on the table. "Before Barboza died he told me and my commander that you kept hot diamonds hidden in your house."

"Bullshit!"

Jimbo leaned over and almost whispered, "*I* know it's bullshit, and *you* know it's bullshit, but the judge who signed this warrant and the jury who'll convict you, give you life up in Joliet, *they* don't know it's bullshit." He lightly punched Paterro's arm and said, "You know why I made it diamonds? 'Cause they're small. That gives me the right to look anywhere the diamonds might be. In a wall safe, inside your mattress, under carpets . . .

"As a matter of fact, I can tear your entire fucking house down and there isn't a damn thing you can do about it."

"You cocksucker."

Jimbo said, smiling, "Not me, you're gonna be the one sucking cocks, for the rest of your life, married to some great big sucker who will do anything he wants to do to you. Hell, the black guys on the inside, they laugh at you goombahs, take turns with you—"

"How come the warrants ain't dated?" Meaning to Jimbo, what do you want me to do?

"Well, Angie, there's the good part. See, I was thinking, me and my boss, you give us enough to get Campo, I mean get him *good,* we turn you over to the feds, get you into the Witness Protection Program, you serve maybe ten years safe and sound on some army base somewhere with the marshals guarding you so no one can get next to you, then they give you a new ID, new face, everything, and you live out the rest of your years in peace and serenity."

"I gotta think about it."

"Sorry, Angie. Now or never. I leave here with you in cuffs or I leave here alone, waiting outside for you to dump the bodyguards, we go to your house and you tell me all about it. Hell, a smart guy like you, I wouldn't be surprised to find out you've got some real nice stuff, evidence-wise, in the house. The only question being: Do you give it to me and I testify in your behalf, or do I find it myself and still send Campo away forever, but with you for company?" He sat back and folded his arms across his chest, eyeing Paterro, knowing damn well that the mobster had no choice. The only thing he needed Angelo for was to make it easier for him and Lettierri; they'd get Campo either way, if, and here was a big if, Paterro did indeed have incriminating evidence in his house.

He found out all about his "if" when Paterro grabbed the warrants and handed them back to him, sweating heavily now, no longer looking dapper, cool, Fred Astaire about to dance on a ceiling somewhere.

Paterro said, "I give you Campo, good and solid, I do ten, right?"

"That's the deal."

"You authorized to make it?"

"You got the word of not only myself but of United States Attorney John R. Drumwald."

Paterro said, "Meet me in front of my house in twenty minutes."

"Angelo, if you play around with me, let me tell you something, you'll think GiGi Parnell was your old lady."

It was after midnight before he got home, weary, exhausted, but happy.

Paterro was already gone, whisked away with his wife to a safe house somewhere, not even Jimbo knew where. He'd been allowed to go on the Campo bust, and it had gone a long way toward making him feel better about Gizmo's murder, but it still hurt, tore at his heart something terrible. God, how he'd loved the look on Campo's face when Lettierri had told him he was under arrest and Campo saying, "For what?" The poor little innocent bastard, amazed that anyone would dare bust him. Lettierri had done himself proud though, telling Campo, murder, eight, ten times. Bribery, extortion, then saying, "Hell, just let me read you your rights; we'll be here all night otherwise."

Jesus Christ, they really had them. Both of them, Campo

and Paterro, the last of the old-time mobsters. The battle would begin tomorrow, the young turks fighting for position, knocking each other off for what they thought was theirs.

Jimbo couldn't wait.

The best part of the whole thing, though, was that at the bottom of the warrants, where the judge's signature belonged, was scrawled the name of the one friend he hadn't let down.

His machine was only blinking twice. Jesus, out of the public eye a couple of days and they forget all about you.

He went to the basement door, opened it and let Sparky out, the big lover dog jumping all over him all the way to the back door. He left the back door open so she could get in when she was done, and walked over to the stand and checked his messages.

He winced at the sound of Bitsy's voice, but it was soft, surprisingly soft, and happy-sounding.

"James? Oh, I've got the most *wonderful* news. Daddy and Elena are getting di*vor*ced (giggle)! Oh, that's not the *great* news! The news is Daddy and I have decided to become *born* again; we've found the most *won*derful preacher! What I was wondering, we'll be sending someone down to close the shop, but could you take care of Sparky for me, sort of a gift to—" *Beep*.

Jimbo smiled. Sure thing, Bitsy.

The second message was from Kristina. She was selling the copyrighted story to a wire service; there was interest in a movie deal, and of course they were dying for the book.

Jimbo shut the machine off and went over to the couch, sat down. Sparky came in and he got up and shut the back door, went back to the couch, sat there and rubbed her behind the ears for a time, absently.

"Good girl," he said.

He rubbed the dog's ears and thought of a little black troll who couldn't hear but who still never missed a trick.

Already the memories were fond, and he could see a time when they would also be painless.

He looked down at the dog and she seemed to smile up at him.

Jesus, Dobies were supposed to be *mean*.

He said, "Sparky, this looks like the beginning of a wonderful relationship."

Sparky wagged her nubby tail, her head going to the side as the doorbell rang.

He put her in the downstairs bedroom, closed the door, then went to the front door and looked through the peephole. He shook his head and smiled, opened the door and let Chris Haney in.

Jimbo said, "The first thing Paterro says, he looks at Drumwald as the agents are handing Drumwald the little minicassettes full of evidence, and he says, all pissed off, he goes, 'I should have known that fucking Barboza was too cheap to have the house phones swept,' and Drumwald, he's grinning from ear to ear, he says to Angie, 'Tell me about it, Mr. Paterro.'

"You want a beer?"

Chris walked into the house smiling, going directly to the couch and sitting down. He said, "I'd love a beer."

Jimbo walked to the kitchen feeling good, like a million bucks, knowing there was nothing like a cold beer to get the conversation flowing; help patch the rifts. He thought of GiGi Parnell, the White Heat Bandit. If GiGi was supposed to be the White Heat Bandit, Jimbo wondered, then why was it that he himself was the one who felt on top of the world?

He put the thought out of his mind, wondering how long it would take to fix things between them, so that he could then let Sparky out of the bedroom; give Chris a good scare.

Then thinking about how good it felt to be one of the good guys again.

About the Author

Eugene Izzi was born and raised in Chicago and, except for the two years he spent in the army, has lived in the Chicago area all his life. He took jobs as a steelworker and a construction worker prior to devoting himself to writing full-time. His short stories have appeared in several magazines. He now lives in a suburb of Chicago with his wife and two children. His first novel, *The Take*, was published last year by St. Martin's Press, and he is currently completing his latest novel.

THE MEASURE OF A MAN
IS HOW WELL HE SURVIVES LIFE'S

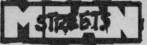

BOLD NEW CRIME NOVELS BY
TODAY'S HOTTEST TALENTS